D0053498

NSA

WITHDRAWN FROM COLLECTION
OF SACRAMENTO PUBLIC LIBRARY

3/99

AUG 27 1999

APR 0 2001

JUN 23 1995
NOV 2-6 1996
JUN 26 1998

FEB - - 1994

DANGEROUS
TO KNOW

DANGEROUS TO KNOW

MARGARET YORKE

THE MYSTERIOUS PRESS

Published by Warner Books

A Time Warner Company

Publisher's Note: This novel is a work of fiction. Names, characters, places, and incidents either are the product of the author's imagination or are used fictitiously, and any resemblance to actual persons, living or dead, events, or locales is entirely coincidental.

This book was first published in 1993 by Hutchinson, London.

Copyright © 1993 by Margaret Yorke
All rights reserved.

Mysterious Press books are published by Warner Books, Inc., 1271 Avenue of the Americas, New York, NY 10020.

A Time Warner Company

The Mysterious Press name and logo are registered trademarks of Warner Books, Inc.

Printed in the United States of America
First U.S. printing: February 1994

10 9 8 7 6 5 4 3 2 1

Library of Congress Cataloging-in-Publication Data

Yorke, Margaret.
    Dangerous to know / Margaret Yorke.
        p.   cm.
    ISBN 0-89296-500-2
    1. Women—England—Crimes against—Fiction. 2. Family violence—England—Fiction. 3. Marriage—England—Fiction. I. Title.
PR6075.O7D3 1993
823'.914—dc20
                                      92-51042
                                          CIP

Walter Brown sat in the train and unfolded his evening paper. His neighbour across the aisle was a woman reading a book. He saw trim black-stockinged legs with neat ankles and small feet. He liked small feet. Walter caught a glimpse of long dark hair drawn back into a knot at the nape of the woman's neck. He wished he could see her face, but it could have been a disappointment: she might be old and ugly; Hermione, after all, had small feet, and though not yet old, was very plain. She had once had long hair, too, but recently had cut it off.

He sighed, and turned to the financial pages. Shares he had bought in a property company were falling; the recession had hit all such firms hard. Still, things might be picking up; there had been more people about in the West End tonight than when he last went there a few weeks ago. He had sensed bustle and interest in the air; or perhaps it was simply his own sense of anticipation that made him optimistic.

A male voice spoke from the seat beyond the one opposite him. He heard, uttered loudly, a crude comment on the female legs and ankles only a few feet from him and which he had already admired. A second voice, also male, speculated on what lay beneath the black skirt covering the woman's knees, and the first voice hazarded various possibilities. Walter noticed the black legs twitch slightly, then one shin was twined round the other and immediately further obscene comments came from the unseen taunters.

Not a soul in the coach stirred or spoke as anatomical probabilities were discussed, and a third man, who sat facing the other two, leaned round the back of the seat opposite Walter to leer at the woman before joining in the debate.

Listening, Walter stirred uncomfortably. No woman should have to put up with these insulting observations, and, contemplating intervention, he tried to catch the eye of a man sitting opposite the victim, but he studiously held his paper up before his face, intently reading. A woman next to him had closed her eyes, probably in self-defence lest she become the next target, although the high back of the seat concealed her from the three foul-mouthed passengers.

Solo action might be hazardous, Walter judged, but briefly he considered pulling the communication cord and complaining to the guard. That could mean giving his name. There might be consequences, visits from note-taking officialdom, even a statement required, any of which would be most unwelcome. Meanwhile, the woman herself was showing no distress, no longer twitching, reading on as if she could not hear what was being said.

Perhaps she couldn't. Perhaps she was deaf.

This was a comforting theory and it explained her calm, but she had, at the outset, shown some reaction. She could always move, he thought, for there were spare seats further down the carriage, but if she did this the men might follow her, aware that they had scored. She was probably wise to remain where she was, with himself and the other male passenger at hand.

Walter should have been on an earlier train, though Hermione never knew what time he would be home; he liked to keep her alert, but he was rarely as late as this. His evening's activities had given him an appetite, and instead of going to the tube he had wandered down various streets until he came to a restaurant whose dim interior attracted him: there were candles on the tables, red plush hangings. He had gone in and had lingered over an excellent steak served with a wine sauce, and half a bottle of good claret. He had enjoyed his meal and felt soothed, almost benign, his day well rounded off as he boarded the train. Now this unpleasant display by three inebriated oafs threatened his mood.

While he still pondered on what action to take, he was spared further indecision—an emotion rare for him—because the train was stopping and the targeted woman was getting out. This was Stappenford, and Walter noted that she walked along the platform towards the footbridge; she was not merely escaping to another coach.

The men went on talking about her after she had gone, but the game had lost its appeal and after a while their remarks became general rather than particular.

Walter was reprieved.

He had not seen the woman's face, nor she his.

Hermione heard him come in.

When he was not home by ten o'clock, she had turned off the oven in which his dinner was keeping hot on a plate placed over a shallow dish of water—a method which delayed the drying-up process—but she did not throw it away. He might demand it at midnight or whenever he chose to arrive. He would not hesitate to wake her and order her to prepare something fresh for him if he deemed it by now inedible; this had happened before, though rarely.

They had no microwave oven. He would not permit it, declaring they were an extravagance of whose safety he was not convinced. It was her duty, he added, to prepare food at times to suit him, not her.

Dinner was supposed to be at half-past seven, earlier when he had a village meeting, which was frequently, as he was on almost every committee. When the girls were at home he had been more punctual, but since they left things had become increasingly difficult and his movements less predictable. Then, Hermione had a reason to keep to a time-table and their presence in the house provided a buffer of sorts between their father and herself; now that was gone, and Hermione welcomed every meeting, every late return from town; anything that kept them apart was a boon to her.

There had been a time, while the girls were young, when she had taken him to the station in the morning and met him again at night. In those years she had needed the car to take the girls to school and their other activities, and Walter kept regular hours or telephoned if he missed his usual train. Now, though, he said that she had no use for it and he took it each day to Freston station where it sat awaiting his return. Hermione was restricted to places she could reach on Sarah's old bicycle and, once a week or so, a shopping trip by bus.

Her days were spent rigorously cleaning the house so thoroughly that it was always ready for an inspection by Walter, who would become incandescent with rage if he found a smear of grease or a speck of dust anywhere. She also helped deliver meals on wheels in the village, cleaned the church, and carried out other voluntary duties, but never in more than a subservient role.

"Hermione will do that," people said, and when she was asked, she did.

Because they had grown up with it, Hermione's daughters, Jane and Sarah, took her servitude for granted. By the time they began to see what a prisoner she had become, they were planning their own escape, and after they left, taking away the limited protection their presence had given her, Hermione's few pleasures and compensations vanished too. She was now very lonely, and Walter's persecution, hitherto often veiled, grew more overt. She began to wonder if there was a way out for her, or some means by which she could improve her life, but she had no money of her own and had never trained for a career. She was the daughter of a schoolmaster and her mother had died when she was only ten. Housekeepers had looked after them both at first, and Hermione planned to take care of her father when she had finished her own education, but he died suddenly just after her A-level examinations.

Alone, bereft and frightened, she had been staying with a school friend when she met Walter at the friend's local tennis club. In her vulnerable state, it was easy for him to cast himself in the role of knight on a white charger and carry her off in triumph to his castle, at that time a flat in Coventry. His conquest assuaged Walter's wounded pride because an older girl—one of a series—had recently turned him down. It also, by means of Hermione's inheritance from her father, soon enabled him to live without a mortgage in a comfortable house bought with money from the sale of what had been her home.

Hermione thought about this as she lay in the darkness wondering when Walter would return. She had lost everything that had been rightfully hers, for the succession of houses into and out of which they had moved had all been bought with the proceeds from that first Victorian semi-detached villa in the Midlands. She had let him deflect her from the university where she had been promised a place if her A-level grades were good enough, which they were, not listening to her aunt's suggestion that she wait and marry after she had her degree. At that early stage in her life she had taken a wrong turning and she would never cease to pay for her mistake.

So many years lay ahead. Walter was only fifty-one. How could she endure another twenty, maybe more, like the past? And things were getting worse. He had not hit her until the girls left home; since then, it had happened several times.

What could she do to change things? Wondering, devising and discarding impossible schemes, at last she drifted off to sleep and when he came home, though he made a lot of noise, switching on the bedroom light and moving heavily about the room, both of them maintained the fiction that he had not disturbed her.

He woke her in the small hours, asserting his rights. He had taught her what they were on their honeymoon in Torquay, and he punished her whenever she failed in obedience. Before they married, he had seemed so loving and protective; where had all that feeling gone? Hermione was convinced that its loss was her fault. Because of her inexperience, she had failed him in every aspect of their life together from the intimate to the domestic, and so he had ceased to love her. She strove to improve, to gain housewifely skills, and did so, but he never acknowledged any accomplishment, always looking for and finding something to criticise.

For a long time she blamed herself for failing to provide him with a son; after the two girls were born in the first two years of their marriage she managed only several miscarriages before a necessary hysterectomy.

It was Hermione's daughter Sarah who told her that the sex of an embryo was determined by its father. Hermione was not sure that she believed this comforting theory. She sometimes thought about it while she endured Walter's embrace, if it could be called that. Tonight she smelled some sort of scent on him, a musky odour. Turning her head away, biting her lip until it was over, she decided it must be her imagination.

2

Mrs. Fisher looked about for a vacant table and could not see one. Primmy's, the large department store on the outskirts of Creddington, was popular for many reasons, not least its modernised cafeteria which was comfortable and served delicious, low-priced meals. Because it was so pleasant, many shoppers timed their visits to include lunch or tea there. When her daughter had suggested a day's shopping to buy Christmas presents, Mrs. Fisher had been pleased. It would be an outing, a small escape from routine. The store was on the edge of town and meant a short drive; there were varied faces around to watch, and the merchandise was of high quality and well displayed. Mrs. Fisher planned to buy Wendy a rose-coloured cashmere sweater for Christmas; as a child, Wendy had looked well in deep pinks and reds, and they would become her now. Even as she formed the intention, she knew that her daughter would exchange a rose sweater for something in grey or beige; still, the attempt would have been made and a sweater bought.

Mrs. Fisher knew that she was lucky to live with her daughter and not in some retirement home, but she stifled feelings of envy when she received letters from her few surviving contemporary friends who still lived in their own houses and maintained their independence and freedom. Wendy allowed her little of either, and she would be angry if Mrs. Fisher failed to find a well-placed table for them now. Having chosen a baked potato with cheese, Mrs. Fisher had left her daughter waiting in line to pay for their food. There were a lot of people ahead of her and the delay would be considerable. Looking around, Mrs. Fisher saw a table for four where just one woman sat; she might finish by the time Wendy arrived.

Mrs. Fisher walked towards her. The woman was half-way through a bowl of sustaining soup; she seemed unalarming, even agreeable, but then Mrs. Fisher liked most of the human race. She asked the woman if she might join her.

Hermione Brown looked up and saw a pretty old woman with pink cheeks and fluffy white hair, well dressed in a navy wool jacket and a pleated tweed skirt. A red silk scarf was tied around her thin neck. Blue eyes smiled down at Hermione, who agreed that the other seats were free.

"My daughter and I have been doing our Christmas shopping. We like to begin in good time," said Mrs. Fisher. "Let me show you what we've found."

She extracted from her carrier bag, marked with Primmy's name printed in green on a yellow ground, a figured silk purse, a child's colouring book, bath lotion, and other small packages; the recipients would be people with whom Wendy, a remedial teacher, worked. Hermione admired everything and asked whereabouts in the store each could be found; she would have to buy presents for the few people Walter thought should receive gifts, though he begrudged spending money on his colleagues at work. Last year he had bought nothing for them, but had been given a box of peppermint creams, a tiny pot of exotic mustard, and, by the director, a half-bottle of Chivas Regal whisky, which Walter knew had been bought at the duty-free shop on a fund-raising trip to Geneva.

"My daughter helps care for children," Mrs. Fisher said. "But she has Wednesdays free so she brought me shopping today. Such fun, isn't it? I love coming here." Her bright eyes looked into Hermione's and she seemed to be sharing a secret. "My daughter's very good at picking out the best things to buy."

It seemed to be true. Hermione recognised the trophies of a skilful shopper. How nice for the mother and daughter to have a day out together, she thought; you often saw such pairs, easily recognisable, and she used to bring the girls here when there was any money to spare. From time to time she sold one or more of her father's old books to raise enough to finance some treat or even an essential expense. Walter was not interested in books and never noticed if any vanished from the study shelves.

The two were still eagerly chatting, Hermione's soup cooling as she made enthusiastic responses to her companion, when a figure loomed above them. A very large woman set a tray down on the table. Hermione was ready to smile at her new friend's daughter, but when she looked up she saw one of the ugliest women she had ever beheld in her life. Towering above them, Mrs. Fisher's daughter looked almost older than her mother. She had iron-grey hair arranged in a sausagelike roll around her head. She was sallow, with froglike pouches beneath her small brown eyes, and she had several pendulous chins. Her large, undivided bust, revealed when she removed her fawn raincoat and draped it over the spare chair, was shrouded in bile-green acrylic. Hermione did not look further down as she tried to mask her surprise, glancing across at the old lady whose demeanour had entirely changed as she helped unload the tray. The daughter did not speak, and Hermione returned her own gaze to her plate after one swift look at those blue eyes which no longer looked bright and full of laughter. How could such a hideous woman be that pretty old lady's daughter? How could nature play such a trick? Or was she adopted?

Thoughts of this kind ran through Hermione's head as, in silence, she swiftly finished her own meal. The newcomer was now complaining about having to wait so long in the queue. People couldn't make up their minds, she said, and the service was slow. The mother said nothing, concentrating on her potato, eating it with very small mouthfuls. When Hermione rose to go, pausing to put on her coat, which she had pushed over the back of her chair, she smiled at the old woman and silently mouthed "Goodbye" before leaving.

She could not get them out of her mind as she went to the hardware department to buy a new washing-up bowl and a few other things which Walter had agreed might be replaced at the lowest possible price for quality goods. There was no hardware store in Freston, their nearest town; it was Primmy's or nothing, she had told him, though not in such positive terms.

That ugly woman had once been a baby, Hermione reminded herself, and must have been pretty then, or at least a warm, appealing bundle. You had no control over the genes you passed on to your children, though you tended to blame yourself for their shortcomings, or she did; Walter added that her poor upbringing of their daughters had rendered them both disappointments to him.

They were not to Hermione, however; she loved them fiercely, had tried to shelter them from their father's angry, strict rule, and was glad they had managed to get away. Now they each stood a chance of being happy.

She carefully preserved the invoices relating to her purchases; they were entered on the charge card. She had the use of very little cash, and she had to account for every penny she spent.

Sometimes she wondered what she would do when she had sold all her father's books. Luckily some of them were rare, sought-after editions and she had found an antiquarian bookseller in Creddington who was interested in anything she took for his inspection.

Walter's severity was, Hermione felt, due to his own upbringing. His father was an army sergeant who gained his commission, and he had expected Walter to follow a military career, but he had not secured a commission. After doing his

National Service—Walter was just old enough to be conscripted—and gaining his corporal's stripes, he joined the Territorials and did well there, enjoying the activities they engaged in, the camps and manoeuvres and the regular meetings; most of all, he liked wearing the uniform. Happy with army rules, he applied similar regimentation to life at home, and Hermione and the girls had no choice but to obey his decrees. During the years, Walter had changed his job several times. When he married he was with a firm making electrical goods, but it had been bought out and during the subsequent reorganisation his job went. He had sold cars—he was a skilled mechanic, thanks partly to his father and partly his army years—and had worked for an insurance company until again he was made redundant. Now he worked for a small charity which at the moment was based in a building destined for eventual demolition under a redevelopment plan; the rent was low because of the uncertainty of the lease. Funds were raised for research into a rare disease. Walter was efficient at accounting and coordination; he had scant interest in the actual cause. He and the director were paid; the rest of the staff were volunteers.

They had moved house whenever Walter's work dictated; this had meant changes of school for the girls and the ending of Hermione's fragile friendships with the mothers of some of their fellow pupils. The Browns had lived in Merbury for five years, in a square modern house on a small estate inserted into the original village. The furniture, most of it originating from Hermione's father's house, had followed them round, with the sale of a few antique pieces to finance the purchase of new carpets and, occasionally, where the old ones would not adapt, new curtains.

Walter, during his childhood, was accustomed to frequent moves dictated by his father's army career; it was a pattern he had subsequently followed, although he said he intended to stay in Merbury. He had plans to become important there, now that he was too old for the Territorials. He never spent an evening at home if he could find a reason to be elsewhere.

As the two girls grew older, and heard him often proclaim that he believed in serving others, they sometimes asked why he did little to help at home.

"After all, charity begins there," said Jane, who had become rebellious in her teens, even dying her hair blonde, but Walter confined her to barracks until she agreed to dye it back to its original mud brown.

Jane had hated the last move, which tore her away from established friends and a school where she was doing well, and she failed to get into university—a blow to Walter but not to Jane, who wanted speedy independence. At eighteen, when she was officially of age, she left home and went to work in a shop in Reading, sharing a flat with two other girls; some weeks later she moved in with Felix, a man she had met at a party. They separated after less than a year and now she was living in a squat with a group of young people who were mostly unemployed.

Sarah was in Italy, working as a nanny near Florence. She often wrote to Hermione and urged her to come out for a visit, but how could she? People thought all women had achieved equality with men now, but it was still a question of money; if you were married without an income of your own, you were as surely chained as your mother or your grandmother had been, unless you were prepared to break away and take your chance.

Hermione had not found the courage for that. Besides, if she did escape, what would Walter do? He might hunt her down and force her to return. He would want to punish her for the disgrace she would inflict on him if she left him.

But some money would make life more tolerable. She had no qualifications for work as a secretary or for any other sort of career, and even if she found someone to employ her as an untrained worker, Walter would discover what she was doing because she would have to pay tax. She knew women were taxed separately now, but he would be sure to find out and he would make a scene at her place of employment, if she managed to find one, and get her dismissed.

There must be an answer, though, some means of working without him finding out. It would be a beginning.

On the way home, she thought about the possibilities, in between wondering about the pretty old lady and her hideous daughter.

3

Walter saw the woman on the train again a week after she had been subjected to the lewd barracking of the drunken men. He recognised the neat ankles, the small black low-heeled shoes. This time the skirt which showed beneath her coat was patterned with tiny flowers. Perhaps she travelled up every day, a commuter like himself. He had not noticed her before, and he often looked at the legs of women in trains. Their faces, and the rest of them, he found unsettling. Like Hermione an only child, he was adrift when his daughters were born. A boy he could have managed, taught to hold a straight bat, play football, use a gun, all the masculine skills he admired, but girls were different. He hid his fascination with their soft prettiness when they began toddling about. Hermione had known better than to expect his help with their rearing; modern men changing nappies and pushing prams around were out of line, in Walter's view: let them see to the home—mend fuses, paint the place, change tap washers, dig the garden; the rest was for women. With all this sharing advocated now, neither partner knew who had responsibility for what. He'd made sure that things were properly organised; Hermione knew her duties and he was master in his own house. He was re-spected in the village—not yet a churchwarden, true, but a sidesman now, dressed each Sunday in his dark suit, and crisply shaved. Hermione took her turn at arranging the flowers and cleaning the brasses as well as other parish duties for which he readily volunteered her services.

Now, sitting opposite the woman who had been the butt of those louts' insults, Walter could see her face. She had a pale complexion, a full mouth, and her long, dark hair was softly drawn back past her ears, in which she wore gold studs. Walter, using his evening paper as a screen, surveyed her discreetly and felt an almost overwhelming urge to unpin that hair, spread it out, run his fingers through it, smell it.

He thought about speaking to her, apologising for failing to protect her on that earlier occasion. But probably she had not recognised him, would not connect him with that experience; better not let her know that he had been a witness who had done nothing to halt her persecution.

Even so, when she got out of the train at Stappenford, he followed her.

Mrs. Fisher had enjoyed her little chat in the dining area at Primmy's store. She often sought encounters with strangers when let off the lead Wendy so firmly held. Opportunities for conversation were not easy to contrive and people sometimes failed to respond when she spoke to them; perhaps they thought her intrusive when she meant only to be friendly. Of course, she was old, and maybe they thought that she had lost her wits; often the old were ignored or patronised, and sometimes bullied.

Today there had been the clever shopping to display and discuss; Wendy had an eye for bargains. She took her mother shopping most weeks, but trips to Primmy's were rare treats; usually they went to the supermarket, where Mrs. Fisher was left on a chair near the door—a few chairs were supplied for the fragile—while Wendy made her well-planned assault on the shelves, pushing her trolley round without ever having to backtrack as she selected what was needed from her neatly written list. Sometimes, just for the fun of outwitting her daughter, Mrs. Fisher would dart from her chair—or at least would move as rapidly as she could manage—and venture down the busy aisles in search of some small luxury for herself—scented soap instead of the serviceable Lux, pleasant enough of course, which Wendy bought for them both, or a bar of milk chocolate. She still had control of her own money, though she paid much of it over by banker's order to cover her keep. She had to be wary, on these forays among the shelves, to ensure that she returned to her seat before Wendy finished her own shopping. Once, there had been an embarrassing experience when she had been called for on the store Tannoy. She always paid at the quick check-out, since she never had more than two or three items, and she would buy presents for Wendy on these excursions—Turkish Delight, if available, or peppermint creams, or hand lotion. These were things Wendy liked but thought frivolous and never bought for herself. She always seemed angry when her mother gave her such gifts but her plain, bleak face would change expression, the nearest she ever came to a smile. Mrs. Fisher knew that Wendy had never forgiven her for being so pretty herself and failing to hand on her looks.

While she was a child, there had been hope of improvement; Wendy had not been overweight then, and it could be said that her sallow skin and bootbutton eyes were striking. Her mother had always dressed her in strong colours which complemented her appearance; pastel shades would merely have emphasised her own want of appeal. Her hair had been thick and luxuriant, with a natural wave; she had worn it long and loose, held back from her face by an Alice band, except for school when it had been plaited in two long braids. When she was twelve she had cut it off herself, with her mother's cutting-out scissors, declaring that attending to it—brushing it, the lengthy drying process when it was washed—was a waste of time which could be more usefully spent. Since then she had seemed to cultivate, almost revel in, her ugliness.

Wendy was a good pupil at school, always among the top few in her class, but she did not enjoy games or music, dancing or drama, the more relaxing side of the curriculum. She went to a teacher training college, and thereafter taught in schools overseas, where she married a fellow teacher with missionary aspirations. They spent some years in South America, where Wendy's husband was killed in a road accident; there were no children. Mrs. Fisher had thought her son-in-law a nice man, though dull; she had seen little of him since they had been spreading enlightenment and the word so far from home, but she felt sorry for Wendy, who soon after she was widowed picked up a severe infection and was ill for some months. After that she decided to return to England and she became, in due time, headmistress of a suburban primary school where her old-fashioned methods enabled the children to do well, since they were taught to read and write and even to add and spell, but eventually she clashed with younger colleagues who believed in free expression. She retired early and began working voluntarily with handicapped children. Mrs. Fisher believed that here Wendy had found her true *metier*; the work required great patience and in this area Wendy had it in abundance; the children loved her, and her great experience was of immense value. She was, however, no longer young, and was often tired and therefore irritable when she came home; Mrs. Fisher, in her turn, strove to be patient and understanding.

During the day, while Wendy was out, she had some freedom and she had made friends simply by going about the place on her own, visiting the library, and Brenda's, the café where she sometimes had morning coffee. Well, perhaps they were not exactly friends, since she had never dared invite anyone home after the time she asked Mr. Potter to tea. They had met in the chemist's where he was buying corn plasters, and Mrs. Fisher had recommended a chiropodist Wendy had found for her. Mr. Potter had knocked over his teacup and had not only drenched the carpet but broken the cup, which had rolled against the fender. Mrs. Fisher had mopped up the spill and had tried unsuccessfully to pretend she had smashed the cup, but Wendy had met Mr. Potter departing as she came back from school. There were remarks stating that of course you are free to have your friends in, but just who are these friends? Where did you meet Mr. Potter? Not at church, I'm sure. And I can't permit people who can't behave to enter my house.

But it had once been Mrs. Fisher's house, and the china was originally hers, too. The late Mr. Fisher, however, seeking to avoid death duties and at the same time aid the daughter he admired but found hard to love, and confident that by so doing he would ensure his widow's security, had left the house to Wendy with her mother entitled to life tenancy.

Wendy, then living in a flat near her school, had moved in at once. The house was hers, after all. Her father's insurance arrangements paid off the outstanding mortgage and a lump sum was left which Wendy used to convert part of the large house into two flats. She and her mother lived on the two lower floors; a separate entrance led to the tenants' flats above, and since they were at work all day, Mrs. Fisher never saw them except occasionally at weekends when they were permitted to use the front garden. She and Wendy retained the use of a tiny rear plot. Wendy had sold the rest to a developer and three bungalows now stood where the Fishers had grown vegetables and where there had been a long lawn with a cedar tree giving shade. It had been a profitable transaction. Mrs. Fisher sometimes wondered what Wendy had spent the profits on; she still dressed drably. Perhaps she had given all the money to the handicapped children.

The area around the house had changed so much in recent years. Mrs. Fisher had once known all her neighbours, but other houses had changed hands and some, like hers, had been converted into flats, even knocked down and replaced by small boxes on the original site. There were none of her old friends left.

"I hope you weren't talking to that woman at our table, Mother," Wendy had said, after Hermione Brown had left them in Primmy's.

"I asked her if the seats were free," Mrs. Fisher truthfully answered.

"It doesn't do to go talking to strangers," Wendy said. "It's a waste of time and uses up energy."

What a lot you miss, my dear, thought her mother, wondering if it would be fine tomorrow so that she could walk up to the shops or the library and find someone with whom she could chat.

Walter followed the woman from the train along the platform, up the steps and over the footbridge. She crossed through the booking hall and went into the street beyond. It was raining, and the road and pavement glistened in the light from the street lamps. Several cars waiting near the station entrance swiftly swallowed the passengers their drivers had come to collect; other travellers hurried into the car park which stretched beside the track. Walter's quarry, her umbrella up, hurried along the road towards the town, and he, moving without reason, motivated by an impulse he did not examine, set off in pursuit. He could see the coil of her long dark hair lying between her shoulder blades as he strode behind her. He had an umbrella too, and he raised it; as well as protecting him from the weather, it was a useful concealment as he kept pace with her, not overtaking.

At the top of the hill leading from the station she turned left and walked away from the shops towards the residential area of Stappenford. He followed. There were other pedestrians about, all hurrying, most with umbrellas raised. One man held a newspaper over his head. It was a fine, driving rain, the sort that does not instantly soak but penetrates by degrees.

Walter trod in a puddle but he did not notice, so intent was he on his pursuit. The woman turned a corner and he noted the name of the road as he followed her down it. Some two hundred yards along it she turned left again, then disappeared. She had entered the driveway of a house. Walter marked it; it was near a letter box. When he reached the house, she had already vanished inside. The number, 18, in neat white figures was painted on a board fixed to the gatepost.

He studied the house, a semi-detached, solid construction built probably in the 1930s, well maintained and painted. A porch light illumined the front door, which was glossy black. As he watched, the light went out. He turned away and walked back to the station to catch the next train home, where Hermione exclaimed at how wet he had managed to get walking the short distance from the platform to the car in the station yard.

She scurried round, finding him dry socks and another pair of shoes, meanwhile finishing the dinner preparations. He had a meeting that night and had cut it rather fine, with his diversion. There was no time to do more than complain to Hermione that the fish pie was dry and contained too much pepper.

She had hung his raincoat by the boiler in the lobby beyond the kitchen, but it was still wet when he left. He wore his Barbour coat instead; he liked to look the part of a country gentleman in Merbury.

After he had gone, Hermione, let off lightly that evening with only minor fault-finding, washed up and laid the table for breakfast, as she did every night. Then she took the local free paper into the sitting-room. She had retrieved it from the piles of paper kept for recycling in the garage. Walter never read it, banishing it unopened every week, but, denied the daily paper which Walter bought at the station, took to the office and never brought home, she always rescued the free one. She liked to read the local news, and there was an advice column which answered questions on family problems. The replies were always wise, whether the difficulty was sexual or about the rearing of children or the management of pets. Sometimes Hermione contemplated writing in and describing her own troubles, but she knew the counsellor would tell her to cut her losses and get out; that was the line she took in such cases.

But I can't, thought Hermione for the umpteenth time.

Tonight, after reading the advice to a troubled stepmother whose own children could not get on with their new siblings— *You must remember*, wrote the columnist, *they did not choose one another; you and their father chose each other and the children had to take their chance*—she began reading the Domestic Situations Vacant column; this was something she could do, a way of earning money for which she was equipped. Today there were advertised a cleaning job three miles away, at Prendsmere, and another in Creddington, which was about twenty-five minutes by bus.

The wise counsellor would advise positive action, Hermione knew. Before she could think better of it, and with Walter safely out of the house, she telephoned both would-be employers and made appointments to meet them the following week.

Then she went to bed. The weekend, always the most difficult part of the week, lay ahead. One thing unfailingly took place several times then. What would happen if she refused? Out of touch though she was, Hermione knew that now you could refuse, though Walter reminded her that with her marriage vows she had surrendered the use of her body to him for life. It was also true that she had promised to obey him. How archaic that sounded to modern girls like Jane and Sarah. Now you could go to law and accuse your husband of rape.

But how could you prove it? There would be only your word for it, and she was conditioned to obedience. Perhaps, if she got both, or even one of the cleaning jobs, it would give her enough courage to quote the law at him and refuse him what he said were his rights.

But did you have rights over other people? Had she none over him? Why was it one way? Surely you had duties and responsibilities? She did her best to discharge those—her domestic ones, at least, and those towards her daughters which were their due. You could have expectations: she had expected affection from her husband, a wish to see her happy, but she had been disappointed. Perhaps you had a right to such expectations, but you had no right to exploit another person for your own satisfaction.

With the girls gone, could she go too?

Her mind churning with these thoughts, Hermione found it difficult to sleep, and her pretence did not deceive Walter when he returned from his meeting.

She lied, though. When he seized her by the shoulder, turning him towards her in their bed, she told him she thought she was getting a cold and perhaps he should not come too close. It made no difference.

Walter's hands, circling her throat, clenched. He was imagining that they held great masses of dark silky hair. Once, Hermione's hair had been long enough to twine around her neck, but she had cut it off.

4

Hermione felt excited as she waited for the bus which would take her to her first interview. The single decker trundled through Freston, stopping near the market square to let off shopping passengers. Then it continued through the edge of town, passing near the station, along the country roads.

In different circumstances, in another family, she could have looked for work in one of the shops in Freston. She would not have been too proud; serving at the till in the supermarket, if she could learn to work it, would have suited her as wel! as helping sell antiques. She could not type, much less operate a word processor, so an office job would have been beyond her capabilities. But Walter would find out if she worked openly in Freston.

Theresa Cowper, Hermione's prospective employer, had taken time off from work to see her, since Hermione had said that she could not come in the evening. She was waiting as Hermione, damp and tousled because it was raining, walked from the bus stop, as directed, past some shops and into a close near the church at the top of the hill. Orchard House was separated from its neighbours by high stone walls. Wrought-iron gates opened on to a front garden with a lawn bordered by rose beds. A blue Renault stood parked outside the front door, which opened as soon as Hermione pressed the bell.

Theresa Cowper was in her late forties; she had dark curly hair which cascaded around her head, falling to her shoulders. She was well made up, with defined brows over brown eyes, and had a wide mouth covered in bright lipstick. Hermione found her alarming and was glad she would be out during her hours of employment if she got the job. Intimidated before a word was uttered, Hermione's demeanour was even humbler than was normal for her. Ms. Cowper showed her swiftly round the house, which was well furnished with modern pieces, and where curtains in abstract prints hung at the windows. There was pale carpeting almost everywhere, and a study equipped with tubular steel chairs, a glass-topped table and a huge black leather sofa. Two of the bedrooms seemed designed for teenagers, with small portable television sets in each, and bright duvet covers on the beds. In one, some stuffed animals were arranged on a window seat; in the other, poster-sized pictures of notable football players lined the walls.

"I live with Jeremy Davis," Theresa told her. "His children come most weekends and then the house turns into a bit of a tip." She smiled, saying this, and suddenly seemed less formidable. Hermione could not know that the previous evening she had stormed round sweeping and tidying so that the potential domestic saviour would not be frightened off.

She then offered Hermione more money than she would ever have dared to ask for herself.

"I've got to beat supermarket wages, haven't I?" she said. "And if I employed a cleaning firm, it would cost me an arm and a leg. Besides, I'd rather have someone I know."

But you don't know me, thought Hermione, who had said that her name was Mary Brown. Now she waited to be asked for references. She could not give them; to do so would betray her secret. Even the vicar could not be trusted with such a confidence, especially if required to collude. The Brown part was correct, of course, and it was a very ordinary name, but there were not too many Hermiones around. Ms. Cowper, however, did not mention references, and it was arranged that Hermione would come on Tuesdays at two o'clock. She had decided that she could not manage Mondays, because she always had so much to do herself after the weekend, and because she could not guarantee to arrive early on Tuesdays, it seemed best to settle for the afternoon. Hermione had expected difficulties over this, but Ms. Cowper said that as she and Jeremy were out all day, it made no difference to them. Hermione offered no explanation for her problems; "never explain," someone had once said, and in this instance certainly it seemed to be good advice.

Theresa said she would be there to let her in on her first day's work and would then give her her own key. How trusting, thought Hermione, walking away with twice as much money as her fare had cost. She had no idea that her grave manner, her obvious superiority and her suitably dowdy but respectable appearance in her baggy tweed skirt and much-washed Marks and Spencer's sweater, had so impressed Theresa that she thought herself the most fortunate of women to have secured a perfect treasure.

She was to go on thinking so for some time.

Hermione was happy as she set off down the hill towards the bus stop. She had just missed one bus and there would not be another for nearly an hour so, as she had cash in hand, she went into a café which she had seen among the row of shops. She might even have a bun with her coffee.

She entered Brenda's, saw a free table near the window and sat down. Soon a waitress in a pink flowered overall brought her a cup of coffee, and she chose a sticky Bath bun from among those on offer. She was cutting it to bits, enjoying the scrunchy sugar on the top, when through the window she saw an old lady walking along the pavement; she approached the café, came in, and peered round in the warm atmosphere. Hermione recognised her at once; she was the woman with the unfriendly daughter—Hermione tried not to think of her as hideous—whom she had met in Primmy's not long before. Moments later, Mrs. Fisher was sharing Hermione's table once again, though she had had to be reminded of their earlier meeting.

"When your daughter arrived, I'd just finished my lunch," said Hermione, with a tactful readjustment of the facts.

"Ah yes," said Emily Fisher. "Wendy doesn't like to talk when she's eating," she added, in token apology.

"Do you live near here?" asked Hermione. Primmy's, after all, was only a mile or so along the road, two stops on the bus.

Mrs. Fisher said that they did and supplied her name and address—Sycamore Lodge, in a turning half-way up the hill.

"Perhaps we'll meet again," said Hermione, and, made expansive by her unusual sense of freedom, recklessly added, "I'm starting a new job in the neighbourhood."

When Mrs. Fisher asked her what it was, she told her the truth.

"Wonderful," said Mrs. Fisher warmly. "I don't know Theresa Cowper, but you'll change her life for her, I'm sure. She's lucky." She wished Wendy would agree to employ a cleaner instead of herself turning the place upside down on Saturdays and emerging exhausted from the fray. There had been Mrs. Noakes once, now long retired and moved to Weymouth, where she lived near her son.

"It's going to change mine, too," said Hermione. "Do you come here every day?"

"No," said Mrs. Fisher. "It depends on the weather and how stiff my hip is. I've got a touch of arthritis, you see. But I try to get out most days when Wendy's at work."

She looked guilty, saying this, and both of them suddenly giggled, like schoolgirls.

"Does she go to work on Tuesdays?" asked Hermione in a casual tone, as if the answer did not really matter.

"Yes. Almost always. She has a white Peugeot car," said Mrs. Fisher. "If it's parked outside the house, then she's at home." The garage had gone, in the renovation scheme.

Hermione had had her invitation.

Each morning, now, Walter looked up when the train stopped at Stappenford, hoping that the woman with the long black hair would get in, and would be in his part of the train. He looked out for her in London, too, for if he saw her there he could follow her, sit near her on the journey home, begin a conversation. When this did not happen, he began putting his head out at Stappenford in the mornings, though she might be so far up the platform that it would be impossible for him to identify her before she boarded the train. After a few days of this he earned surprised glances from his fellow passengers, many of whom were regular travellers like himself, so he abandoned the practise and instead began moving about the train, sitting in different coaches instead of always in the fourth from the front which had been his custom hitherto.

He had not been back to the King's Cross area since he had seen her. The first time he had picked up a woman there had been on impulse, when he had come up to town by car and had driven, by chance, down a street patrolled by prostitutes. It was dark, he was on his way home, and he stopped, brusquely beckoning over a girl he had noticed who wore her hair in a long plait drawn forward over her shoulder. She was very young. He liked them young. After this, he always hunted on foot. The savagery he kept banked down most of the time sometimes surfaced, and one woman protested, but she had met other rough customers and he had done no more than bruise her. Subsequently, he had been in many cheap hotels and tawdry rooms, and he had tried out various things he had read about in magazines.

As he sat in the train going home, in his dark suit and with his raincoat on the overhead rack, no fellow traveller would have suspected what scenes were being played through Walter's mind. Many of the regular commuters slept between stations, their inner clocks warning them when to wake so that they did not miss their stops. Walter did not need to do this. He exercised for five minutes each morning before the mirror, and at weekends and on occasional evenings he jogged, in a grey track suit, and expensive shoes because it was folly to risk injury through being inadequately shod. He was physically fit and his job was not demanding enough to exhaust him, requiring only accuracy and application and, as he was fond of telling his colleagues, organisation. He allowed no emotion to enter into his relationships with them. Walter told others what to do, and he was efficient; one thing he had learned in his brief military career was how to delegate and how to accept his own role in the hierarchy. He considered the charity had been lucky to secure his services, but at his age he was the fortunate one. While there was no liking between him and Simon, the director, there was respect. Walter suppressed his fascination with blonde Belinda Arbuthnot, who smelled of lavender or roses; he caught wafts from her when he passed behind her desk on the way to his small office, a tiny cubicle partitioned from the main office by walls ending two feet from the ceiling. She and another woman, Rosemary Kent, worked irregular hours to suit themselves, but at busy times came in most days. Walter found Rosemary unattractive; she was thin and elegant, and she designed the appeal literature. All women alarmed him, but they intrigued him, too; he spent much time fantasising about close encounters with their faceless bodies. He was even afraid of Hermione, whose expression of resignation when he moved towards her had to be instantly obliterated from his vision. She, however, was his: as much his as his car, his house, the clothes he wore; his to do with as he wished, officially handed over in the marriage ceremony all those years ago in return for being housed and fed for life. That was how things had always been; all this feminist rebellion was responsible for many of today's ills. Look at his own daughters, both off doing what they called their own thing, heedless of filial duty. Why, they had wanted for nothing, not even during the worrying spell when he was made redundant, before he secured his present position. The fact that he had come into some money from a seldom-seen childless uncle had been fortuitous and had made possible the move to Merbury, which Walter had seen as socially desirable. He now had some investments, and in spite of his salary being modest, could afford the ever increasing fares to and from London.

Hermione, in a fit of courage, had suggested that he might use the legacy to set up his own business, but he told her she did not know what she was talking about and the matter was his to decide. He had made a few moderately successful deals on the stock exchange, but was not venturesome, and he paid into a pension fund for himself.

Fortunately Hermione had never been extravagant. When he met her, he recognised an unformed malleable girl. He gave her fair but minimal housekeeping money and required her to render a strict account of how it was spent. If she needed clothes or chemist's goods, she had only to justify the cost and the money was provided. Never mentioned now was the fact of the small capital sum she had inherited from her father which, with the proceeds from the sale of his house, had been put into the purchase of theirs. When Walter's uncle died, Hermione had asked if she might have it back—it was three thousand pounds—but Walter had pointed out that she had received this many times over in benefits accruing from her life with him.

Walter had not forgotten his own first hard months as a private soldier. Like dogs and horses, people had to be broken before they would come to heel. This process had almost disappeared from contemporary life and hence there was now no discipline. Take those louts on the train that night, for instance, with their insulting comments to the woman with the long dark hair: some square-bashing would soon knock them into shape; so would a good thrashing. He had been beaten often enough as a child and it had not harmed him.

Walter's failure to intervene, to rescue the victim, still made him smart. A man of his experience should have been able to sort out the drunks almost with a glance. Next time, he would not be found wanting.

A few nights after he had followed the woman when she left the train, Walter again got off at Stappenford and went to the house she had entered. A light burned in the downstairs window, and he walked up to the front door and rang the bell. He would pretend to be selling something, he planned, and when she came to the door he would show surprise at recognising her, refer to the incident and make his apology.

But no one answered the bell. The light must simply be a decoy to warn off burglars.

He went away, but he did not abandon the plan he had been forced to discard; he could always try again.

The next night he returned to the dark streets behind King's Cross, and for a time he forgot about the woman, except that he dreamed one night that Hermione had hair like hers and he was winding it round her throat to strangle her.

5

Hermione's second prospective employer could be reached by bicycle. Full of confidence after securing her first position, she pedalled up the hill and out of Merbury, turned right before she met the main road and set off past the pig farm for Prendsmere. It was a dull day, cold but dry, and a sharp wind blew in her face as she pedalled along the lane, over a small bridge spanning the river, past a timbered barn and there, a hundred yards further on, was the entrance to Downs Farm. There were no downs around; perhaps it had been named after a previous owner, thought Hermione, freewheeling over the tarmacked drive to a grey stone farmhouse with a tiled roof. A child's swing hung from the branch of an apple tree.

A tall, thin man with very straight dark hair which fell forward to collide with the frames of his spectacles, led her into a drawing-room with flowered linen covers on the chairs and sofa. Ash was piled high in the open hearth and a film of dust lay on every surface.

"I'm the househusband," he told her. "Nigel Wilson. I'm a freelance journalist and I write in between looking after the children and minding the washing-machine. The children are both at school now, in Prendsmere village which is further on down the lane, as you know, I'm sure. My wife's a dentist.

She spends the weekends putting right all the things I've failed to do. I can't manage."

"I can see that," said Hermione drily, looking round.

"We had someone who came twice a week," he told her. "She got pregnant and had to leave. We had a nanny for a while before that, but we don't need one now."

"How old are the children?" asked Hermione. She had expected to meet Mrs. Wilson and was trying to adjust her ideas. Why shouldn't the man stay at home if it was easier for his work? Maybe the wife earned more.

"Fiona is seven and James is five," said their father. "Let me show you round."

The house was very untidy, but it had a more comfortable feeling to it than Theresa Cowper's; perhaps it was just because it was older and was set in such lovely surroundings, thought Hermione, longing to get busy putting things away. It was obvious that he was going to offer her the job, and, primed now by her earlier experience, she firmly requested the same sum, saying it was what she was paid in her other position. Theresa was going to pay her bus fare too, but Hermione could cycle here—it was not on a bus route—so that did not apply.

Again, she gave her name as Mary Brown and agreed to come on Thursday mornings.

"Could you stay now?" asked Nigel, for it was Thursday. "I'll put your bike in the car and run you home."

She stayed, borrowing a plastic apron patterned with various sorts of gourds which she found on a peg in the kitchen. Like Theresa's, this was fitted with every modern aid, and was much cleaner than the rest of the house. Nigel had to show her how to operate the expensive vacuum cleaner with its built-in tools, and when it was time for her to go, he poured her a glass of white wine from a bottle that was in the fridge.

"You've transformed the place," he told her truthfully. "And I've got through a lot of work."

She had seen his word processor in his study, where there

were shelves of books, mainly works of reference, and several filing cabinets. He had explained that she would not be expected to clean his room.

"I'll do the floor," she decided, frowning at it. It looked as though it had not been swept for weeks. "I won't touch your papers or anything else."

She swept round while his printer spewed out pages of typescript. Hermione was rather intrigued but she would not allow her curiosity to show; it might annoy him and she was not here to operate anything more technological than the domestic equipment, which posed enough challenge as it was.

The bedrooms overlooked the garden where the lawn ran down behind the house to a stream, fenced off for safety with high wire mesh. There was a swimming-pool, now covered with dark green canvas for the winter, and there was a hard tennis court. There was a deep freeze the size of a small garden shed, and a pony in a field. Lucky children, thought Hermione, without envy, as she dusted Fiona's collection of small china animals and parked James's cars neatly against one wall.

Nigel bundled her bike into the back of his Volvo estate car, but she made him drop her at the top of the hill leading into Merbury.

"I can manage now. Thank you," she said.

When Nigel's wife, Laura, returned that evening and discovered that he had not obtained Mary Brown's actual address, she expressed disapproval, but Nigel, who was curious about this new employee, had already consulted the telephone book and found two families named Brown in Merbury. He had rung both while Hermione was still in the house and only one had answered; he had pretended it was the wrong number, and so it was, for Mary Brown, living at the other one—Brown, W.P., 6 Willow Close, Merbury—was at present out at work.

"Ring her up," he told Laura. "Tell her she's done a good job."

"She has," Laura admitted. It had been a relief to return

and find everything so clean and Nigel no longer feeling guilty because he had forgotten the time while working. He was wonderful with the children, picked them up punctually, and played with them, giving them their tea; that was more important than keeping the place tidy.

She dialled the number he gave her and a woman answered. "I want to speak to Mary Brown," she said.

Heart pounding, Hermione replied that she was Mary Brown. Laura asked if she was satisfied with the terms and conditions of her employment and Hermione said that she was.

"The house looks very nice," Laura acknowledged. "Thank you."

Hermione replaced the handset, her heart thumping. What if Walter had heard her side of the conversation? He was out tonight, but when he was at home, he expected her to answer the telephone and call him importantly to speak to whoever was on the line, for of course the calls were never for her.

"I think we should draw up some sort of contract for Mary Brown," Laura told her husband. "It's best for both sides. Then there can't be misunderstandings."

"There won't be," said Nigel. "We're bloody lucky to get her. I bet her husband doesn't know she's taken this job and any red tape may make her decide it's not worth the hassle. She's probably saving up for a surprise holiday for them both, or some such scam."

"Well, don't blame me if it doesn't work out," said Laura.

Nigel hoped Mary would have some other project she needed to finance once her immediate aim was achieved. If she stayed, he might have time to get on with the thriller he had started as an escape from writing about rural matters for a monthly magazine and the humorous column he wrote weekly for another publication.

Mary Brown was good news. Long may she stay, he thought, going back to his study while Laura did the ironing.

*   *   *

Why didn't I do this years ago, Hermione had thought, free-wheeling home from the top of the hill.

She felt brisk, invigorated by her morning's work, not the least bit tired. The wine had set her up, she supposed, finding bread and cheese for her lunch. She'd been lucky. Both new employers were friendly. She realised that they were anxious for her services, and things might seem less delightful as time went on, but she would be alone at Theresa Cowper's, and on future visits to Downs Farm, now that she knew how the various appliances worked, Nigel would no doubt concentrate on his word processor and leave her to it.

He seemed nice, if rather languid. Dusting the main bedroom, straightening the quilted spread on the king-size bed, she had wondered about the life he shared with his wife. Were they happy? Did he fall upon Laura physically, in the way Walter used her, as some sort of vehicle for relief?

She knew he didn't. She had watched enough television when Walter was out to have learned that an emancipated woman like Laura Wilson with a lucrative career, earning as much as her husband, if not more, would not stay in such a partnership. And why should she? Contracts were two-way; if one side failed to honour the undertakings they had given, how could the other hold things together alone? It took two to tango, as people often said. In the space of two days Hermione had met contemporaries whose lives were entirely different from her own; she could profit from this in more ways than just financially; she might learn how to change things for herself.

She had to bustle about at home to make sure that she had forgotten nothing and that Walter's meal would be ready when he came back, with no excuse for complaint on any score. When Laura Wilson telephoned, Hermione understood immediately why she was checking up, and simply gave hearty thanks that she had not had to invent a reason for the call to put Walter off the scent. It was lucky that he was at a meeting—a church one this time. She knew that the vicar thought most highly of him; Walter was the treasurer—he was good with money. But the vicar, in Walter's eyes, had done no wrong except practise a low church form of religion and introduce a number of modern gimmicks to the services, and Walter considered helping the church to be his duty. Hermione knew that he saw it as a means of social advancement; it brought him into contact with people he might never otherwise have met, such as the Mountfords who lived at the Manor. The vicar had not fallen below Walter's expectations, as she had done. Hermione had earned constant reproof and punishment because she was, in Walter's words, incompetent and worth-less, plain, dumpy, and a failure as a mother. Evidence for this was the failure of both girls to follow the programmes mapped out for them. He mentioned neither; Sarah's flight to Italy was, he had declared, particularly disgraceful. She had had a passport because she had been abroad on school trips and the family had been on holiday to Brittany several times. Walter had put Hermione on his passport, something that amazed the girls when they discovered it. To finance her flight, Sarah had worked in a supermarket on Saturday mornings while pretending that she was in the public library, studying; then, during a spell of holiday work in Walter's office—a job he had insisted on her doing as they were short-staffed and were mounting a specific appeal—she had stolen cash which she was counting. She had gone away the next day and Walter had at once suspected what had happened. He had checked the books and had made good the amount himself before anyone else could learn what she had done.

Later, she had written from Italy enclosing a first repayment, saying that she would return the full sum in time. Walter had said her name must never be mentioned in his presence again, nor did he ever wish to see her, however penitent she was.

But she did not repent, her mother knew; she had seen her chance and taken it—the wrong way, Hermione considered, but she had gambled on Walter covering up for her because to do otherwise would wound his pride. He owed her the money, too; a girl had a right to expect some financial backing from her father.

With fifteen pounds in her purse after a morning's work, Hermione felt rich. She'd be earning thirty pounds a week; before long she would have a hundred pounds. She might be able to take on another employer, if things went well and nothing suffered at home. Theresa Cowper and the Wilsons would provide references, if they were satisfied. All would depend on Walter finding no new excuses for complaint, but he did not need reasonable grounds: he would detect invisible slivers of skin left on a boiled potato or a carrot, see tiny creases in a shirt—they were cotton and had to be ironed—find hairs in his hairbrush if it were not promptly washed, scold about wrinkles in the bed sheet or fat left on a chop. His ability to find something to criticise adversely was unlimited, and so was Hermione's potential for failure.

Not for the first time, she began to contemplate moving into what had been Jane's room and fitting a bolt to the door. Even Walter would stop at breaking it down in pursuit of what he called his rights. Wouldn't he?

Walter was growing increasingly frustrated at his failure to see the woman from the train again. He had now become obsessed with the idea of apologising to her, telling himself that this was all he wanted from a meeting. The subject was so much on his mind that one day at the office, when for once everyone was having a sandwich lunch, he asked the director what he would have done if he had been on the train and witnessed the behaviour of the louts. In describing the scene, Walter did not reveal his own lack of valour, but declared that someone else present had told him what had happened.

"I hope I'd have at least sat next to the victim," said Simon, the director, a bearded man in his forties whose holiday delight was to go bird-watching in remote places. "And you can pull the communication cord. Best to do it as the train pulls into a station, I believe. There's more chance of getting help on the platform."

"Not on some," said Belinda Arbuthnot, who had been making coffee and now arrived with a tray of mugs. "My sister's is a wayside halt and after two o'clock there's no one there to sell you a ticket. There's a machine, but it's tricky to work, so my sister says."

"I think what you've told us about was a minor event compared with what can happen," said Philip Shaw, who was helping out with the new appeal while waiting to do voluntary service overseas. "The things that go on when football hooligans are travelling can be far worse. I won't describe what happens in front of you ladies," and he grinned at Belinda and Rosemary, who both spoiled him and whom he loved to tease in a mild way. "I don't think I'd be very brave if I found myself in the middle of a mob like that."

"We need to return to proper values," Walter declared. "Good manners. Consideration for others."

"Arm the police," said Belinda, and was at once opposed by Simon, who said that would lead to shoot-outs on street corners throughout the land.

"And it wouldn't help your pal on the train," said Rosemary.

Later, she told Belinda that she was sure it was Walter himself who had seen the incident.

"He's ashamed because he didn't do the right thing," she said, and began wondering if there was more to Walter than she had imagined. She had marked him down as a fusspot of exemplary rectitude and a boring individual; perhaps he was also, though he hid it well, prey to doubts.

That evening, Walter got off the train at Stappenford again, and he made the journey through the streets to the woman's house. This time he rang the bell, and after a pause a man came to the door. He was balding and stout, dressed in corduroy trousers and a maroon sweater worn over a checked shirt and a mildly floral tie. He was at least sixty years old.

Walter was ready. He had brought a small pile of printed appeal envelopes and handed one over.

"Would you care to give a donation for our valuable research now, or shall I call back later?" he said, holding one out.

Silently, scarcely glancing at Walter, the man reached in his pocket and took out a pound coin which he put in the envelope, then handed it back.

"Is there anyone else in the house who would like to contribute?" Walter asked, trying to detain the man, who had already turned away. She must be there somewhere—the man's daughter, of course; he was too old to be her husband.

"No," said the man, and he closed the door upon Walter, who walked angrily down the road.

He had been ready to show a valid collector's licence, but one had not been requested. He would put the pound in the office box tomorrow; at least the cause would benefit, though he had gained nothing. She must be working late again, perhaps to be subjected to more insults as she travelled home.

Walter waited to see if she got off the next train before he boarded it to complete his journey, but there was no sign of her. He had drawn blank today; why was he never lucky?

So many things had gone wrong for him: first the disappointment of his failed military career, then the various jobs which had folded up around him as staff were reduced and people made redundant. His had been the misfortune to be employed by organisations where reshaping of the original business structure had involved harsh pruning, and in Walter's opinion each firm which moved him on had shown lack of judgement in discarding him when there were other much weaker shoots which could be eliminated.

This garden metaphor pleased Walter. All stock had to be

tended and tied back, uprooted when of no more use, and this applied to Hermione, the most disastrous of all his pieces of bad luck. She had never even approached the targets he had set for her development. She was a weak shoot. She should be cut out, destroyed, that others might survive.

She had seemed appealing when he met her all those years ago. Hoping to acquire a social circle, he had joined a tennis club. He liked watching the women players in their short pleated skirts and white briefs. He was on the visiting team when they played a match against a club of which Hermione's school friend was a member. Hermione was helping with the teas and seemed shy and modest. Hearing about her father's recent death, Walter's protective instincts were aroused; he was drawn by her meek, pale face with the sad eyes. Here was someone he could influence and mould.

She still had a pale face and sad eyes, but she had lost any allure she ever had; now the only pleasure he got from her was seeing her cringe, wounding her verbally and using his strength to dominate and control her. Walter was the master: he had to be in charge, but he deserved better.

It wasn't too late to start again. People often did, at his age: found pretty young women who appreciated an older man. All that prevented him from finding someone young and luscious was Hermione herself.

No one would miss her, if she were to disappear. The girls had left; they did not need her now. If she were gone, the house would be entirely his. Alive, she might have some legal claim to part of it if they separated, but not in death. She'd made no will. There was nothing for her to leave the girls except a few bits of jewellery that had been her mother's.

What if she were to have an accident? One that had been carefully arranged?

6

Hermione was astonished at how quickly life could change. While the girls were at home she had always been busy, but in spite of Walter's exacting standards and the various duties in the village which she carried out, lately she had had time to fill. She read a lot, borrowing historical romances from the library, all she felt able to concentrate on now, though once, under her father's guidance, she had enjoyed reading Dickens and Jane Austen. That was so long ago, in what seemed another life.

She had never done much socialising with other women in the village. Many of those her age had jobs which took them out by day; others had children who were still quite young. Pam Norton, opposite, was always friendly, but Hermione was afraid she would realise how things were if she came often to the house and had not encouraged casual visits. The Browns did little entertaining; once or twice a year a few couples came to dinner, when Walter's instructions were so elaborate, and the post-mortem after each event so detailed, that Hermione dreaded the occasions, and was so anxious about the food that she was a stiff and awkward hostess whose guests did not enjoy their evening.

Now, with her work, she did not mind giving up the escape

she had found in novels and in watching television, for she was living at first hand. She found she had speeded up; her own chores went more quickly because she was less inclined to drift off into dreams while polishing the silver or peeling potatoes. Hermione's fantasies had never been of a romantic nature; they were more nostalgic. She would think of her quiet, peaceful life with her father, her days at school where she had had a successful but undistinguished career and where she was happy. She would remember her friends and wonder what had happened to them; she had lost touch with all of them after she married. When she wanted to send them Christmas cards, Walter had said it was too expensive; now they would have mutual friends, he declared, none exclusive to one or the other. She had obeyed this direction, and by the time she was ready to rebel, her friends had long since crossed her off their lists. Few of them even knew her married name.

The wedding, happening so swiftly after her father's death, had been small, attended by only a few guests. She had worn a white dress and veil, and the friend with whom she had been staying when she met Walter was the only bridesmaid. Her aunt, her father's sister, had held a reception at a local hotel. The aunt had died a year later and now there were just some distant cousins whom she had not seen nor heard from for years.

Walter did not approve of her reading novels; she hid them from him, and never read in bed. It was best, then, not to be awake, though sleep, feigned or genuine, was no protection.

Time, however, had made a difference. Walter was sometimes impotent, a matter which he blamed her for, but it had inhibited him. He was less liable, now, to risk failure, but she could never be sure of her own safety. Sometimes, when he came back late from London, he was as vigorous and demanding as ever.

She wished he would find someone else. It would solve everything—he would leave and set up with his new wife. He would have to provide for her, she supposed, if that happened. He might be happier, though she would pity anyone he might choose as his next partner. She accepted that she had been the wrong wife for him, but he had chosen her, swept her off her feet when she was in the shock and depression of grief and scarcely aware of what was happening, and he had not had her excuse of youth and inexperience. Her friend's mother, like her aunt, had suggested waiting a while before taking so important a step, but Hermione had seen nothing else to do and had declared that she loved Walter.

What she felt was gratitude, and she was flattered. She responded to the attention Walter so briefly gave her as a dog might react to petting, and it was romantic. Walter had given her flowers, taken her to dinner and the theatre, bought her presents. All that stopped on marriage, when he bought her a cookery book and an apron and told her to get on with looking after him.

Now, however, she had a future. She was a domestic cleaner with two well-paid jobs. She returned to Theresa Cowper's house in Creddington, and after doing the tasks agreed, always had time for a quick whip round the rooms which were not on that week's programme, and she always did the ironing. Her money was left on the table with a note thanking her for what she had done the previous week. Theresa appreciated her and the result was a warm glow of satisfaction as Hermione pocketed her money. She left a note of her own. *Hope everything OK. Catch on main bedroom window faulty, have tried mending it but needs bigger screwdriver than one in kitchen drawer.*

There was no need to answer the telephone as there was a machine. When it rang, it was odd to hear Theresa's disembodied voice asking the caller to leave a message. Then the caller would talk to the machine. Hermione tried not to listen since the subject might be private. She adapted quickly to her new way of life, and she was glad she went to Creddington in the afternoon as all her own chores were done by then and she could relax in the bus. She liked being alone in a house so different from her own and wondered about the lives of Theresa and her partner Jeremy. Once, he arrived while she was vacuuming the sitting-room, letting himself in and suddenly appearing, a big man with a neat, dark beard.

"Ah—you're the treasure," he said, rushing through the room to the study beyond, where he began rummaging in a desk. "I'm not a burglar—I'm Jeremy, come to collect some papers." He reappeared to stand in the doorway, beaming at her. "We're glad to have you," he said. "Sorry the place is such a mess. My kids were here for the weekend." He glanced through a file he held in his hand, then, turning away, said, "Mary, isn't it? Nice to have met you."

Two minutes later he had gone, leaving an impression of physical exuberance and energy. Hermione felt invigorated by the brief interlude.

And he had called her a treasure.

After work, there was plenty of time to walk down the hill and catch the bus which took her home long before Walter would arrive, even if he was on time. She would already have begun dinner preparations—peeled the potatoes and prepared the vegetables, at least. He liked straightforward English food: nothing fancy or highly spiced, not even a mild curry, and he enjoyed steamed puddings and pastry pies. He never put on weight, but Hermione, who nibbled at the left-overs, was now quite plump, nearly fat. The extra exercise, however, and the cycling to Downs Farm, had their effect, and after two or three weeks Hermione's skirts began to feel loose as she shed several pounds.

By the time she went to see Emily Fisher she had lost half a stone.

This time the old lady recognised her immediately. She had been wondering if Hermione had picked up her oblique invitation and was wishing she had been more direct.

Hermione had caught an early bus so that she could call before going on to Theresa Cowper's house, because each time she had gone past after work, planning a visit, the white Peugeot had been parked outside and she realised that Mrs. Fisher's daughter had come home.

"How lovely to see you," said Mrs. Fisher, ushering her in.

"I'd have come before, but I don't finish until half-past four and that's too late," Hermione explained. "So I thought I'd come on my way in to work instead. I hope it's not an inconvenient time—were you resting?"

"No—reading the paper and wondering if there was anything worth watching on television," Mrs. Fisher said. "I enjoy horse-racing and golf—not football, I'm afraid."

Walter watched a lot of football on television, intent upon the game, oblivious to anything beyond the screen.

"I watch it too," said Hermione, who had watched much less since she began working.

"Tell me how you're getting on," Mrs. Fisher said.

Like a lover free at last to mention the name of the beloved, Hermione felt immense relief at speaking about her work. She described the two different households. Mrs. Fisher knew Theresa's house as she passed it on her way to church, where she went with Wendy almost every Sunday.

"It's got a beautiful wistaria growing over the front," she said. "And prunus by the hedge."

"I don't think they're great gardeners," Hermione told her. "It's a mess at the back—very weedy. Not tidy for the winter."

"Well, I expect the wistaria and the prunus were there before them and will continue if they move," said Mrs. Fisher.

Hermione could not stay long, and Mrs. Fisher said, "When you come again, bring your lunch and eat it here—bring sandwiches. If you'd like to, that is."

"I would," said Hermione. "Thank you."

"I'd invite you to lunch but—" Mrs. Fisher did not need to finish the sentence.

"I might be prevented from coming," said Hermione. "It's best if I'm independent."

And if the Peugeot was outside, she could walk on and eat her sandwiches when she reached Theresa's house.

On her next visit, Hermione brought Mrs. Fisher some homemade shortbread. Another time, she bought some freesias for her at the florist's in the row of shops near the bus stop.

"You mustn't spend your money on me, my dear," Mrs. Fisher said. "Your company is such a pleasure."

Very soon, both of them were looking forward to their meetings, which now took place every week, and Hermione had to keep a strict eye on the clock to make sure she wasn't late for work.

Wendy, seeing the freesias when she came home, accused her mother of needless extravagance in buying them.

"An admirer gave them to me," said Mrs. Fisher.

"Really, Mother, how can you talk so foolishly?" said Wendy, and wondered if her mother was becoming senile.

One afternoon Jeremy, Theresa Cowper's partner, was in the kitchen eating bread and cheese when Hermione arrived.

"Hi, there, Mary," he said. "How are you?"

Hermione was happy. She had enjoyed her lunch with Mrs. Fisher, who had shown her round the garden and pointed out plants she had grown from seeds brought from various countries she had visited on holidays long past; there was a chestnut tree grown from a chestnut she had picked up in Italy and an oak—still very small—which had sprung from an acorn found in France, as well as other plants.

"They remind me of my husband and my travels," Mrs. Fisher had said.

Now Hermione answered Jeremy.

"I'm well," she said. "And you?"

"Bowed down with business cares," he said, not looking in the least oppressed.

"I don't know what you do," said Hermione.

"I rob banks," said Jeremy, making a fierce face.

Hermione laughed.

"Oh yes? Then am I an accessory after the fact?" she asked.

"You should laugh more," said Jeremy, looking at her more closely. "You've got a very pretty smile."

He was amazed to see colour flood her face after this remark. She turned her head away to hide her confusion.

"I'd better get on," she said. "Shall I clear up in here now? Have you finished?"

Jeremy took her by the elbow and turned her gently round to face him.

"You're not used to people telling you you're pretty, are you?" he said. She wasn't really pretty, but being paid a compliment did a lot for a woman. He felt her arm tense beneath his hand. "Don't worry," he told her quickly. "I'm not going to leap on you and have my wicked way with you. For one thing, it's no fun if the lady isn't willing, and for another, I have to get back to work. But you should start thinking of yourself as attractive, Mary. You are, you know, even in your working gear." He scarcely meant the words, but she did have a certain timid charm. Her hair was a mess; it looked as if she'd cut it herself.

Hermione's heart was thumping under her shabby fawn sweater. Was this sexual harassment, such as you read of in the press? She didn't feel harassed or threatened in any way; rather the reverse.

"I'm not worried," she said, speaking as calmly as she could. "And I still don't know what work you do."

"I'll tell you next time," he said. "Now I must dash."

7

Walter saw the woman on his way home the next day. He was bound for his normal train and emerged from the underground to see her ahead of him, hurrying across the concourse to check the departure screen's information about the platform before boarding. He recognised her immediately and felt his pulse rate quicken; there were the small feet, the neat pumps, and the same printed skirt showed beneath her hip length jacket. She paused to buy an evening paper, and Walter did the same, standing close behind her as he waited to pay, almost near enough to touch a strand of her dark silky hair. He imagined he smelled the scent she used, a flowery fragrance. Into his mind shot images of other things about her, matters referred to by the louts on the train that first evening, and he felt excited as he followed her, getting into the same coach, able now to face her.

She did not look at him as she took her seat, holding on her knee her large black bag. Walter was ready to smile at her, and for an instant, after she had settled, her gaze swept across him but unseeingly, as if she were unaware of him or of the other passengers now joining them. Walter contemplated speaking to her but decided to wait. He had already made up his mind to leave the train when she did.

She read her paper throughout the journey, never looking up even at stops when passengers entered and left, stepping past her feet which she kept neatly tucked as far out of the way as was possible. Walter glanced at the trim ankles in sheer black tights, the small shoes.

Who was she? What did she do? He speculated, his own paper held up before him. After a while he felt calmer and was able to check the prices of his shares. Tonight all things were possible, and when the train stopped at Stappenford he was up and opening the door for her before she had risen herself.

He stood back to let her precede him off the train. She gave a curt nod and he was not sure if he heard a word of thanks, but instantly he was down on the platform behind her and he caught her up after she left the footbridge.

"Those train doors can be difficult," he said. "They're often stiff. Things will be better when we get the new turbos on this line. That should happen after Christmas, I believe."

The woman ignored him, walking on, out of the station, but Walter was not to be deflected.

"I wanted to apologise," he said. "There was a night some weeks ago now—two months, I believe—when some men on the train were rude to you and I did nothing to assist you."

She still took no notice of him, now hurrying up the hill, but Walter was persistent.

"It was disgraceful," he said. "Disgraceful of those louts, and disgraceful that I and the other passengers remained silent. We passed by on the other side," he proclaimed.

"Well, it's too late to do anything about it now," she said, and moved away from him to cross the road, dodging between cars.

Walter went after her, undaunted.

"It's not too late to apologise," he said, catching up with her on a stretch of cobbled pavement outside a pub.

"I accept your apology," said the woman, not stopping.

"You don't travel regularly on this line," Walter persevered.

She turned then and faced him. She had very level, well-marked brows above eyes whose colour he could not make out in the light from the street lamps.

"You are harassing me," she said. "I had to put up with it on the train from those three yobs. I don't now. I can go into this pub and get someone to telephone the police, and I will unless you go away immediately."

This wasn't the scene Walter had envisaged. She should have been grateful, even tearful, evinced helplessness and fragility. Instead, she was glowering at him with eyes which he now saw were rather small and deep set. She had taken a folding umbrella from her bag and held it like a weapon.

"I'm not harassing you—I'm apologising," said Walter.

"I warned you," said the woman and walked on towards the pub.

While Walter stood there, she went inside. He hesitated. Should he follow, bluff it out? Carry it off with a joke and a smile and drinks all round?

He decided not to risk it. Why had she been so rude? If she was surprised at being addressed by a stranger, surely she could tell from his appearance that he was not to be feared? She hadn't given him time to explain. She should have listened to him.

Walter was seething with anger when he returned to the station platform to wait for the next train to Freston.

The next day at the office, Rosemary and Belinda noticed that Walter was in a bad humour. He was usually scrupulously polite in a distant, austere way, thanking them formally for tasks performed though somewhat curt when directing their operations.

He spoke irritably on the telephone to a man who had given them his old typewriter when getting a word processor himself, and who had run off for them numerous leaflets at cost. Other leaflets were later than promised, hence Walter's grievance.

"Thinks just because he's doing us a favour he can be late on delivery," Walter fumed, crashing the telephone handset down on its rest and storming out of his cubby-hole office, along the passage, and down a flight of stairs to the cloakroom. There was only one, shared by the sexes, and normally, before setting off there, Walter looked round to make sure neither of the women was out of the office and so perhaps in occupation of the sanctuary. Today, in his haste, he failed to notice that Rosemary was absent from her place. He rattled the cloakroom door impatiently and then, realising it was locked, stood in the passage gazing out of the window at the roofs beyond, with the heavy grey wintry sky lowering above them. His arms were crossed and his shoulders hunched, a rare stance for him and noticed instantly by Rosemary when she emerged.

"All yours, Walter," she crooned, gliding past him, and when she returned to her desk she asked Belinda if he had a stomach upset.

Belinda had heard the angry voice on the telephone.

"He's had a row with Henry," she said. "He forgets you can hear every word that's said when he's in his sanctum."

"We can't afford to quarrel with Henry," said Rosemary. "He does us too many favours."

"Trouble at home," said Belinda.

"Or just trouble," said Rosemary, as Walter returned, still scowling.

That night he stayed late in London, taking himself off, after the day's work ended, to the streets where, as darkness fell, girls and women began to appear, parading themselves, legs bare or in patterned tights exposed beneath narrow short skirts, lips garishly painted, hair dyed and tortured into various styles.

When he came near them, Walter's pulse rate increased and energy seemed to fill his body. He forgot the reduced subscriptions to the charity and its falling balance at the bank; he forgot the perfidy of the woman with long hair and the shortcomings of his wife. Now he was stimulated, eager, on the prowl. He wasn't interested in the women with short curled hair or smooth crops; he wanted someone with long tresses which he could wind in his fingers.

The same evening, Belinda had had to collect some shoes from a repairer near the office who stayed open late. Leaving his shop, she had seen Walter ahead of her, walking off in the opposite direction to where he would catch his usual bus. It seemed odd, but then Walter was odd. When she first started working for the charity, she had assumed to him to be unmarried.

"Why do you say that?" Rosemary had asked.

"He doesn't like women," Belinda said.

"The same goes for plenty of married men," said Rosemary. "He's very efficient."

Everything Walter worked on was completed accurately; there was no need to run a single check through his figures, and annually the accountants showered him with praise. He often found mistakes made by other people.

"We're not all good at figures," he had once said, almost tolerantly, when Belinda had done a sum on a scrap of paper because she had mislaid her calculator. He, of course, could add up as fast as that machine, or so it seemed. His desk and files were orderly; papers on his desk were arranged like soldiers on parade. He would sigh when he saw piles of cheques and bank notes on Belinda's desk, wondering why she did not use methods he advocated for sorting them into neat heaps to avoid confusion.

The next day she told Rosemary that she had seen him heading off in the wrong direction after work.

"Perhaps he was going to meet his wife in town—take her to a show," said Rosemary.

"He wasn't going west," said Belinda. "More north or east, I'd say. And at quite a bat. He was in a hurry."

"He must have had a date," said Rosemary.

"I don't believe that for a minute," Belinda declared.

They discussed various possible destinations for Walter, ranging from massage parlour to strip show, and decided that each was as unlikely as the other.

"But you can't be sure," said Belinda. "People do strange things."

"Yes," said Rosemary. "I know."

Neither saw a report in the paper that a prostitute had been strangled in a back street behind King's Cross the night before. She was very young, and she had long dark hair which had been tied around her neck.

8

Things were getting worse at home, except that Walter seemed to be returning later and later; now he was rarely on his normal train and even if he came back at a reasonable hour, and had no meeting, he often went out after dinner, sometimes in the car but sometimes simply walking. Hermione had no idea where he went and she did not ask. She found his silent hostility very frightening, but she forced herself to forget about it when they were not together. She had her own diversions now, her two days a week when she was occupied and earning.

At Orchard House she was alone, though after her brief meetings with Jeremy she kept expecting him to appear and rather wished he would. After his children's visits the girl's room was chaotic, but the boy's was very tidy, as though he did not want to leave his imprint on the place. Hermione wondered how well they accepted the arrangement with Theresa. Where did their mother live? Was it all amicable and happy? It must be disconcerting to have two homes, two loyalties. Were they fond of Theresa or did they resent her as, perhaps, usurping their mother's role? There were all sorts of questions to which she would have liked the answers.

She mentioned the family to Emily Fisher, who had never seen any of them.

"I don't know what Jeremy does," said Hermione. "He came in one day when I was there, but he wouldn't tell me about his job. Perhaps it's something weird."

"He's probably an accountant or a bank manager," said Emily.

"Maybe, but I think he's more likely to be a musician or a landscape gardener," said Hermione. "Though he doesn't exactly look like either and there aren't any violins or clarinets about the place. But then not all musicians have long hair and dress untidily."

"Are you fond of music?"

"I was, but so long ago it's as if it wasn't me," said Hermione. "I played the piano at school, but not really since then. The girls never learned. Walter thought it a waste of time and money." The piano that had been in her old home was sold before their first move.

"Do you play records—listen to concerts on the wireless?" Mrs. Fisher had not learned to talk about the radio.

"No. I don't know why," said Hermione, and added, sheepishly, "Yes, I do. Classical music—orchestral music—opera—doesn't soothe me." She paused, and then confessed, "It makes me unhappy."

"It makes you long for things you scarcely know you've missed," said Emily, nodding.

"Sort of—uncomfortable, somehow," said Hermione, now embarrassed. "Silly, isn't it, when the radio's there and it's free. I listen to talks and things and watch television instead."

"During the war cheerful music and comedy programmes were relayed in factories to keep people's spirits up," said Emily. "And military bands have a purpose." She decided not to mention the lunchtime concerts of classical music in London. "I can understand why people listen to so much pop. It takes their minds off their own troubles. People don't want to be uplifted all the time, just diverted." She looked at the clock on the mantelpiece. "You must go, my dear. You'll be late."

*   *   *

"Hermione's looking very well these days," said Robert
Mountford, chairman of the parish council, before a meeting
at which fouling of the pavements by dogs, the introduction
of more street lighting, the problems of increasing acts of
vandalism such as graffiti in the bus shelter and on other walls,
and a break-in at the village hall were on the agenda. "Nice
to see her blooming," he added. He and his wife had discussed
Hermione's brighter looks, noticed by them in church.

"What? Oh, she's always very well," said Walter impatiently. "She's never ill. Now, about this business at the village
hall—I intend to propose that we should patrol the village
ourselves, since the police seem unable to do it—catch the
hooligans in the act. I often walk about myself, hoping to
apprehend them, but so far without success."

"Who'll form this vigilante force?" asked Robert Mountford
drily. "The parish council?"

"Volunteers. Two men a night should be sufficient," said
Walter.

"All night?"

"Well—till one or two at least," said Walter. "I've walked
round as late as eleven or twelve."

"But you've caught no one."

"No."

"Perhaps they've seen you coming," Robert said.

"Well, then, if it's made them desist, it's been a useful
exercise," said Walter.

"Would you patrol till two and still go up to town next
day?" asked Robert.

"Certainly," said Walter. "On a rota system."

"I'm not sure you'll find many takers on a permanent basis,"
said Robert, who, since he was retired, could foresee an obligation to be a volunteer at least once a week and did not care for
the prospect.

"We could float the idea at the meeting," said Walter.

"Toss it about a bit. See what people think. Safeguarding property is a public duty."

Robert could see that Walter was longing to command the troops thus raised. The man was full of energy, fizzing with it.

He determined to suggest, instead of Walter's scheme, an approach to the police with a request for more of a presence, particularly after the pubs closed, and this was the action eventually approved. In order to forestall Walter's evident intention to undertake dealing with the police, Robert said that he would mention it to the local inspector without delay. Walter could not be relied on to deal tactfully with such a matter.

Walking home after the meeting, irritated by the failure of his plan, Walter flashed his torch around. Piles of dead leaves caught up in the shrivelled growth of valerian and aubretia at the base of a wall beside the churchyard gave out a noxious smell: dog droppings, caught in the withered vegetation. Gone were the days when a man with a barrow patrolled such village areas keeping nuisances of this kind under control; now, occasionally, a road-sweeping vehicle came round, but nothing was done about the footpaths. People didn't care, that was the trouble. It was left to individuals like himself and Robert Mountford to deal with problems others ignored.

Walter resolved to handle this one himself, on Saturday, when people would be sure to witness his act of public service.

When he reached home Hermione was in bed, her back turned towards him. By the light of his bedside lamp he could see the hump of her body beneath the bedclothes, the top of her head just visible. He needed comforting for the failure of his plans and he reached out to turn her over, claim what it was her duty to supply.

"No," she said, loudly and firmly, when his hand, heavy and strong, caught her by the shoulder and pulled her over.

She had never said no before, though she had lain resistant, needed storming. He was much stronger than she was; he had always prevailed before.

But not this time. Somehow she writhed away from his grasp and got out of bed, standing there in her long-sleeved blue cotton nightdress, her arms crossed over her breast.

"No, Walter," she said again. She was trembling. She wanted to say, "I'm not going to let you rape me," but she could not utter the words. Instead, she made for the door, but Walter was before her.

"Get back into bed," he said, and hit her several times across the face.

Since the girls had left home, he had often hit her, but she had never before defied him like this. Usually he hit her after he had subjected her to the dreaded physical invasion, or if he had failed because of his own inadequacy. She often cried at such times and he liked to give her real cause for tears.

Tears came into her eyes now, but she stood her ground.

"You don't frighten me," she said, untruthfully. "You're nothing but a bully."

She was standing between him and the door, and although she was shaking with fear, she managed to open it and get out of the room before Walter, briefly frozen in surprise at her defiance, could prevent her. He grabbed her nightdress and it ripped as she tried to bang the door behind her, but when he, his power of movement restored, seized it in his turn, he stubbed his toe and the sudden pain made him pause again, allowing her just enough time to escape to safety. She went into Jane's room and locked the door; earlier, she had bought a good strong bolt and fitted it. She had planned this move for days but so far had lacked the courage to carry it out. Now, provoked once too often, suddenly she found it.

He banged on the door for a while, turning the handle, rattling it, cursing and threatening revenge, and she knew that ultimately there would be a heavy price to pay, but not yet. Eventually, Walter gave up and went away.

She had felt a great a sense of achievement when she managed
to fit the bolt, making holes for the screws by banging in nails
because she did not know how to use Walter's drill and was
afraid of breaking it. They had held, and she was safe, if only
for a while.

That night, neither of them slept for long.

The next morning Walter cut himself shaving, and when he
came downstairs he had a piece of tissue still attached to his
cheek. He was in a very bad temper.

Hermione had risen early, but her clothes were still in the
main bedroom. She put on some of Jane's—a pair of frayed,
patched jeans and a shapeless sweater which Jane had left
behind when she went away. The jeans were too tight but the
baggy sweater covered the gaping zip. She found a safety pin
in her sewing-box downstairs and fastened them with that.

There was a comb in the downstairs cloakroom. She tugged
it through her hair, which needed washing. Would Walter
pull all her clothes out of the cupboards and throw them
round the room? He often did this, sometimes telling her that
everything was so untidy that it must be sorted out, and
sometimes without giving her a reason. Her handbag was in
the bedroom and he might turn that out, but her savings were
not in it; she had put the money in an envelope between the
pages of a cookery book on the kitchen shelf. It was a very safe
place; Walter was not interested in cookery, but as he had
bought the books for her early in their marriage he would not
damage them. Apart from her, he never harmed things he had
paid for, though he complained about anything that did not
fulfil his expectations; he claimed that he had bought her by
housing her and feeding her through all these years.

When he came downstairs she poured boiling water into the
kettle for their tea as she had done every day for the greater
part of her life. Walter did not approve of coffee; it was bad
for the nerves, and what he had at the office was enough in

any day. He did not approve of women in trousers, either, but had had to endure the sight of his daughters in jeans, like their peers. Not Hermione, however: it would have been impossible for her to buy them since she had to account for her expenditure, and she was sure she would look dreadful in them because she was so plump.

She was ready for war to break out over breakfast. She told herself that if Walter hit her, she would pour boiling tea over him.

Walter was still too angry even to speak, and when he saw her in the shabby sweater, the faded jeans, her face white, with hollows beneath the huge eyes and round one of them dark bruising, his fury grew. He was trembling with rage as he took his place at the table in the dining-room, seeking for damaging words with which to berate her and almost afraid of his own anger, for which Hermione was entirely responsible, in his view. She was to blame for everything, even the rebuff from the woman on the train.

Hermione sat facing him in silence, and when the tea had stood for long enough, she poured him out a cup, concentrating hard because she was shaking and she did not want to spill a drop. To do so would invite further trouble, even another blow.

Walter ate his boiled eggs, his two slices of Hovis bread toasted just enough, with marmalade and low-fat spread. He was in some ways a modern food faddist but was inconsistent, with his liking for steamed pudding and rich cake. Once, Hermione had dared to point this out to him, to be sharply told that if he wanted her opinion he would ask for it.

She waited for his first remark of the day, but none came. In silence Walter ate his meal. Her senses hyper-acute with nerves, Hermione could hear the scrunching of his toast, even, she felt, the swallowing of his tea. Without speaking, he left the table.

She sat there, not daring to move until he left the house and she felt safe.

In the train, Walter recalled Robert Mountford's remark about Hermione looking well—blooming, he had said. She hadn't looked well this morning, he thought with sour satisfaction. If she hadn't been so quick getting out of the bedroom last night, he would have taught her a lesson she would not forget. How dare she defy him in that bold and brazen manner! What had got into her? Had Robert Mountford paid her a compliment direct? Surely not.

Walter had taught her many lessons throughout the years but she had failed to learn; still she denied her duty, though she had promised in church to honour and obey him. Walter conveniently forgot that he had made reciprocal promises about cherishing her.

The bruise was an unfortunate result of last night's incident, however. He hoped she'd put some concealing stuff on it before she left the house. She was going to a coffee morning today in aid of church funds. He had remembered it without being reminded, and before leaving the house had placed two pounds on the card advertising the event, which he put before her as she sat at the table nursing a cup of tea. This would take care of her entry and a modest purchase. Walter had no need to say a word; she understood the purpose of his action.

Tonight, when he came home, he would apply the next instalment of the new lessons she must be taught, but he must not leave marks where they would show. There were other places where she could be struck, spots where bruises would be hidden.

Hermione had no intention of going to the coffee morning. She had already said she could not help that day, for it was Thursday and she was off to Downs Farm. She put the two pounds in her purse; she had earned them.

She was astounded at herself for harbouring this thought, then even more astonished that she had not thought like that before. Why had she not stood up to him years ago? She had told him he was a bully. Didn't bullies crumple when outfaced? Not always.

After he had gone, she made herself a cup of strong coffee; they had to have it in the house for visitors; even Walter accepted that. It might help to pull her round; she felt dreadful, and knew she looked a wreck.

She had found it difficult to swallow, not just because Walter's blows had hurt her jaw, which they had, though her teeth were unaffected. She had cried for what seemed hours last night, stifling her sobs so that he could not hear them; as a result her throat still ached. She soaked some toast in the coffee and nibbled it. All through breakfast she had been conscious of the fast beating of her heart, and she knew that Walter was as full of scarcely contained fire as a smouldering volcano. At any moment she expected him to explode. She had put a big knife under the cushion of her chair, where she could reach it quickly if he attacked her again.

I wouldn't use it, she had told herself, putting it away after he had gone, I couldn't. You hear about such things, but they don't happen to people like us.

But all this is happening to me, she thought bleakly, and it's always been the same. She wondered about Jane and Felix. Had he behaved like this and was that why they parted? Of course not: she was answered in a second. Felix was a gentle, weak man, with whom Jane would not have stayed unless he treated her properly. Perhaps he was too weak, she thought, with sudden perception. Jane needed to lean on someone. It would be nice to go and see her; she had enough money for her fare but she couldn't go today, and anyway would not want Jane to see the bruising round her eye. Some tale of banging into a door would satisfy Nigel Wilson, if he noticed it, but not Jane; she would want the details.

Sarah's departure had coincided with Walter's intermittent impotence. Hermione had read advice columns about this problem, which in many ways she welcomed since it reprieved her, but Walter's anger was now expressed not mainly in sarcastic taunts or destructive criticism but in open rage. Frustration, she supposed, feeling guilty because she was the cause of it.

From novels and magazine articles that she had read, Hermione knew that there had to be another side to sex than her experience of it, but there were frigid women, and she was one of them. Walter's misfortune was to be tied to her. It did not occur to her that a different partner might have drawn from her a different response.

She put cream and powder on her bruised face and brushed her hair forward before wheeling out her bicycle.

She had been right in suspecting that Walter might tip out all her clothes. The contents of her drawers were strewn on the bedroom floor and her few skirts and dresses were flung on the unmade bed. She didn't touch them before she left for work. Walter had done her a good turn, she told herself, as she was going to move everything into Jane's room. She'd put them away when she came home.

She changed into her working skirt and her fawn sweater. Jane's jeans hadn't been all that small; she might buy herself a pair of trousers. By the time she had pushed her cycle up the hill and was pedalling along the main road towards the turning for Prendsmere, she was feeling better. It was a clear, bright day and the sun made the cold seem less. She had pulled on a woollen hat and wore gloves; last week her ears had stung with cold as she rode along. Nigel had not given her a lift back again; each time she left Downs Farm he had been hard at work in his study.

Laura, unlike Theresa, left her no instructions and she had developed a routine, doing what seemed most urgent and fitting in extra tasks when there was time. Nigel expected her to put her head round the study door to say that she had arrived, and would leave her to get on with it, but he always made their coffee, and when it was ready would tell her to knock off for ten minutes. Then they would chat. He would stroll about the big kitchen, saying he grew stiff sitting at his desk for hours. She would ask him what he was working on and would listen intently as he described what he was trying to put across, and he was eager to hear tales of life in Merbury. She related how a woman who had made soft toys for years—teddy bears, ducks, rabbits—and sold them at modest prices in the village shop, had had to cease because of new strict rules about the materials used, although they were not flammable, nor were the eyes dangerous. Thus a useful and enjoyable occupation for an elderly person, which earned her a small income, had been curtailed at the same time as a local source of inexpensive presents for new babies and small children was lost. This gave Nigel an idea for one of his articles, and when he showed it to Hermione she was amazed at how he had elaborated on her simple theme, declaring that the active pensioner was now depressed and the would-be shoppers angry. He always asked her for her news, and she told him all she knew about village events. It seemed clear that he would disguise anything he learned from her, exaggerating and enlarging what to her had seemed a simple theme.

He saw the bruising on her face.

She'd thought of merely calling out that she was there; then he need not look at her. The arrangement was that if she had not arrived by ten, he would assume she was not coming, though she promised that she would telephone if anything were to prevent her.

"You might have a puncture," he said.

"Then I'd push my bike the rest of the way," she told him. "I would be late, of course." She looked at him solemnly as she spoke. There was no hint of levity in her voice or in her expression; he thought she lacked a sense of humour.

"I'd mend it for you during the coffee break," he told her gravely.

"Oh, I could do that," she assured him. "I've got a kit and I've mended plenty of punctures in my time." She'd always done it for the girls until she had taught them how to repair their own tyres.

"I think you're a very practical person, Mary," Nigel had said. "I'm surprised you do this job. Couldn't you find something more interesting?"

"It is interesting," she said. "This is a lovely house and you've got some beautiful furniture, and I'm well paid. Besides, there's nothing else I could do. I'm not trained for anything."

"You could put that right," he said. "There are heaps of courses geared to women whose children have grown up. The magazines I write for are full of details."

"I'd never manage that," said Hermione.

"You would, if you made your mind up to succeed," he said.

Hermione did not answer. What was the point of discussing something so impossible?

That was two weeks ago, and now she managed to announce her arrival while still keeping her face concealed, but when he came out to make the coffee she was taking the washing out of the dryer, and she kept her back turned to him as she folded garments and put them in the basket. Hermione was not normally doing this job at coffee time; more usually she was wiping down the work surfaces or had just swept the floor.

Today, she did not turn round as he boiled the kettle and put instant powder into two mugs, getting out the tin of biscuits with which he tempted both of them each week. She seemed to be making a business of folding up the clothes, and when he set the mugs down on the table, instead of sitting down, she picked hers up and said she'd take it upstairs to drink while she cleaned the bathroom.

This abrupt withdrawal was quite new; in past weeks she had seemed to enjoy their short conversations, relaxing more each time, sitting for ten minutes at the table. Surely she didn't suspect him of having designs on her, thought Nigel.

"No—you need a rest. Sit down. Have a break," he urged.

"It's all right," she said.

Her voice seemed strange and he looked sharply at her. Her head was still turned away so that he could see only one cheek, which was pale.

"What's wrong?" he asked. If he had given out some signals which she'd misinterpreted, he'd better sort it out at once; how could he tell Laura she had left because of his attitude?

"Nothing," said Hermione. "Really, it's nothing."

"You're not telling me the truth," he said. Perhaps Laura had been right and she should have had a contract. "Do you want to leave and you can't pluck up courage to say so? Is that it?"

"No! Oh, no!" came the instant protest, spoken from the heart, and without thinking she turned to face him.

Nigel's relief at this assurance was succeeded by shock when he saw the ugly mark, blue and blackening, around her eye and on her cheek. A quip about her having been in a fight came instantly into his mind, but before he uttered it, he realised it might be too close to the truth to be risked.

She had turned her face quickly away again.

"I'm glad you don't want to leave," he said. "Like in the song, I've grown accustomed to your face, but it seems to have been damaged. What happened? Did you walk into a tree?"

"Something like that," she said. "It's nothing. It looks worse than it is."

"It looks painful," he said.

"It was an accident," she said.

It might have been. People fell and hit their heads, sustaining black eyes and broken jaws without having been in scrimmages, but she had not wanted him to see her injury, and Mary was not vain.

"Sit down and have your coffee," he said. There was no point in embarrassing her by persisting with questions. Besides, he had something to ask her. "Laura and I want to beg a favour from you," he said.

It was a change of subject and Hermione seized upon it.

"Oh yes?" she asked. "What? I'll help if I can."

"It's next Wednesday night," said Nigel. "We're invited out to dinner, and we rather want to go, but our regular baby-sitter can't come. We've got another who can usually help us out, but she's away. Laura and I thought we'd ask you before we try scouring the neighbourhood for someone else."

Hermione did not answer at once. What a wonderful prospect! To spend an evening in this lovely house, basking in its atmosphere of calm, sounded to her like a glimpse of heaven.

"Wednesday, you said." She was thinking. "What time?"

"About seven-thirty. The children will be ready for bed, but they'll want a story and need settling. They're pretty good as a rule—it shouldn't be too arduous. We might not be back until after eleven, though."

Hermione's imagination—never vivid—had now placed her in front of the Wilsons' log fire, reading the latest copies of the magazines in which Nigel's work appeared.

"Let's see—it was the parish council last night, and I think it's the PCC next week—the parochial church council," she explained, in case he wondered what she meant.

"Are you on those?" he asked.

"No, but it means I won't be needed at home." Hermione was amazed at how easily this specious explanation came to her mind. "I'll do it," she decided. Walter would have gone before she need leave.

"I'll collect you and take you home," said Nigel.

"No—that's all right. I'll be able to have the car," she declared.

Walter went to all the village meetings on foot. He liked to see what was going on about him, he explained, if marvelled at for walking more than half a mile in a downpour. In fact he thought it wasteful to use the car for such short journeys, as, of course, it was. She could wait until he had gone, then drive over to Prendsmere.

"You're sure?"

"Yes. If there's hitch—like it won't start or something—I'll let you know," said Hermione. She could walk up the road to meet Nigel if he came to fetch her. The notion gave her a *frisson* of excitement, but she did not understand the true reason for that; she considered the whole undertaking somewhat of an adventure.

"Good," said Nigel. "Would you like some steak for your eye, or more seriously, have you bathed it with anything—witch hazel, for instance?"

"It's all right," she assured him. "No serious damage."

She hadn't known men could be as nice as this, anyway not since her father died.

9

Hermione collected her money from the kitchen dresser and left without saying goodbye to Nigel. He was so engrossed in his work that he had not realised how late it was; he had intended to put her bike in the Volvo and drop her off; it was the least he could do when she'd got such a bruiser.

Could her husband have done it? If so, it rather knocked on the head his theory that she was earning money for a special holiday or present. That evening he told Laura about the injury.

"It's a corker," he said. "A real black eye."

"And she said it was caused by some sort of accident?"

"Yes."

"Well, it could have been. People do get black eyes from other causes than a bashing," Laura said.

"But if she is being knocked about, it's terrible," said Nigel. "She's so shy and timid—like a startled mouse," he added. "It fits."

"Well, if your suspicions are correct, what are you going to do about it?" Laura asked.

"I don't know. Write a piece about concealed domestic misery and earn a quid or two," said Nigel. "What I ought to do is go and knock his block off, but I'm no hero, as you know."

"Passive rustic irony is more your line, isn't it?" said Laura. "You could do worse than explore marital violence. There's a lot of it about."

"You're right, I know," said Nigel.

"How would you conduct your research? You can't force Mary to describe her private life to you. You could visit a refuge for battered wives and hear the stories of the inmates."

"You make it sound like a prison."

"It is, in a sense," she answered. "They're really only safe inside. Their husbands or partners often track them down and try to get them back or beat them up again."

Nigel shuddered.

"I couldn't stand it," he said. "It churned me up just to think that some man might have done that to her. Why doesn't she turn him in to the police?"

"Assuming you're correct, and that her husband did do it, she probably blames herself," said Laura. "Women in her situation often do. They tell themselves that if they can only mend their ways—be better wives—please their husbands— the men will change."

"But that won't work," objected Nigel.

"Of course not, but the husband does blame her. There are plenty of people who go round blaming someone else for their own mistakes and failures. It saves facing facts," said Laura.

"Like saying, 'Look what you've made me do,' when you're interrupted and spill or break something."

"Yes."

"I asked her to baby-sit next Wednesday," he said. "I did it on the spur of the moment, because we're in a fix over it and she'd be much more reliable than Jessie."

Jessie was a girl they had used before; she always brought her current boyfriend and, as she was only sixteen, Nigel and Laura were not sure this was such a good idea. The boyfriends, who changed from time to time, always had cars and were rather old for her, Nigel and Laura thought, and they never had regular jobs. There was the fear that they might be thieves, or scouts for thieves, seeking targets, or in other ways undesirable. There were other objections, too; the last time Jessie and had come, with a young man in a leather jacket and very clean jeans, Laura and Nigel's bed had definitely been occupied in their absence. Apart from all other considerations, what if the children had caught the couple in it? Laura had not been pleased at having to change sheets in the middle of the night.

"Good," she said now. "I vowed never to have Jessie again, and I meant it. We'll have Mary and hope she'll be our future standby. Did she accept at once?"

"No. She worked out something in her mind connected with a village meeting and said she wouldn't be required at home—something like that," said Nigel. "She said she'd be able to have the car."

"That's fine, then," said Laura. She did not want to discuss it any more, but she made a diary note that on this day Mary had come to work with a black eye, allegedly sustained in an accident.

She still wished they had a contract. Mary might start saying she'd fallen whilst in their employ and seek damages.

Unless Nigel was right, and the cause of the injury was close to home.

Walter had been shocked when he saw that he had marked Hermione, but he felt no remorse. She'd got ridiculous thin skin which bruised easily; that was the trouble; he'd noticed it before. Now she'd be setting off for the coffee morning wearing not only her permanent patient martyred look but visibly injured. The bruise would soon fade; in memory he shrank it to the size of a small coin. He must be ready, if asked, to explain that she had had a fall.

Even if Hermione were to say that he had hit her, she would

not be believed, but then only he, Walter, knew how careless she was, how lacking in all the qualities he had a right to expect. What did it say in the Bible? That the price of a good woman is above rubies? Why, if Hermione were a housekeeper, she would have been sacked for incompetence years ago. Musing like this on the way to the station and in the train, Walter justified his actions as he mentally listed Hermione's many faults. He recalled burnt scones in the first year of their marriage; dinner often late when the children were young; plate powder left on silver; smears on windows; the tail of a new shirt scorched, due, she had said, to a defective thermostat on the iron when the real cause was her inefficiency. He remembered seeing his own mother spit on the iron when she was testing its heat before ironing his father's uniform shirts. He remembered the hiss and sizzle as she pressed his khaki trousers through a damp cloth. Walter himself would be under the table in his private hiding-place, fearful lest he incur his father's wrath for some misdemeanour. But the harsh punishments he received had taught him to mend his ways. When he was young, he had blamed his mother for failing to protect him from the beatings he was given; now he knew that they had instilled in him high standards. People who erred deserved punishment, and Hermione had failed, throughout the years, in every way.

Having satisfactorily resolved this subject, Walter turned his mind in the direction of the woman on the train. If he could have persuaded her to listen to him, if he could have got her to accompany him into the pub, let him buy her a drink and talk, she would have appreciated his sincerity and a meaningful relationship, as nowadays it was called, could have developed between them.

If it were not for Hermione, he would be free to seek other company, find another woman, one who would respond to him, someone who would offer him comfort and understanding. There were plenty of women about, but as he was married he was not free to pursue any he might meet. Why, there were Belinda and Rosemary at work, for instance, not that either was his type, and sometimes there was a female student filling in time, a young person who would be flattered if he paid attention to her. It was well known that young girls enjoyed the company of older men, just as Hermione had done when he first met her; then, she had been glad of his protection.

What if he were rid of her?

Walter brooded about what life could be like if he were not handicapped by a cold, pallid wife whose very expression invited punishment. She was like a cur—a dog cringing round its owner's heels until it had to be kicked away. The dog should sit subservient in a corner, waiting on its master's commands, and so should a wife, when not actively performing her duties.

Walter never thought about other people's marriages; for him, no one else's life held any interest; he did not even envy their circumstances if they were richer or more successful than he was, except to regard himself as having been dealt an unlucky hand of cards by fate. He was so self-absorbed that he thought only in terms of how he was affected by the actions of others and he never queried the impression he made on them; it did not occur to him that it might not be favourable.

At the office, the efficiency of his colleagues was his only concern, and often it was wanting. Belinda and Rosemary talked too much and spent too long in the cloakroom, but they were both unpaid and the director said that reproofs to voluntary staff were not in order. Casual helpers were worse still; they lacked all sense of discipline, and when Walter attempted to introduce some method into what looked to him like a muddled cheque-counting operation, Simon, the director, had dared to suggest that Walter's approach was less than tactful.

Walter was tolerated by the organisation because he was so

capable. He had good, practical ideas about how to run campaigns and he was an excellent book-keeper; accounting was his main task. He was not popular, but he was not actively disliked. Rosemary thought he was a heartless robot, but Belinda said you had to have a heart to work for their cause.

Rosemary did not agree. You might be of a certain age, as Walter was, and have found it difficult to get other, better paid work. Here, he was a large fish in a tiny pool; elsewhere, he might be merely a minnow.

Walter, at odd times during the day and in his study in the evenings, planned a future following Hermione's death. There would be a brief period of formal grief, then the enjoyment of his freedom and eventually another marriage with someone like the woman on the train, or indeed, the woman herself. The episode when he had spoken to the woman and had been rebuffed was expunged from his memory, written off as a misunderstanding because he had accosted her in the street. After her unpleasant experience with the louts on the train she was naturally nervous, and he had not made clear his honourable intentions.

His intentions: what were they, in fact?

He let his mind wander back to some of his encounters with women who took money for gratifying male desires; that was how he thought of them, those shady sisters of the twilight hours. When he read the newspaper definition of the recent murder victim, whose long hair had been twined around her neck, as a prostitute, he shied away from accepting the crude description. Some men were not adequately catered for at home, the right place for indulging their natural appetites; they were forced to look elsewhere and to pay for services which could be forgotten as soon as the transaction was over.

The woman from the train was different. She had style: that was it. She would regard him kindly when she understood the sort of man he was, how well able to take care of a wife and to provide for her. Hermione had never needed to earn a penny in the years of their marriage; she was able to enjoy all the leisure of a domestic life. Walter had long ago wiped from his memory that what was his had originally been hers.

The woman from the train would be grateful and kind, soft and warm, once she had learned to trust him. Walter's imagination projected various bedroom scenes in which he and she were entangled, and he grew excited at the prospects thus suggested.

Soon he would call on her again, and if the same elderly man opened the door, Walter would say that he was a friend of the man's daughter. If she were not at home, he would wait for her arrival.

10

Mrs. Fisher was very disappointed when Hermione did not
come to see her the following Tuesday. Already she had begun
to rely on these visits, which had been taking place for several
weeks. I mustn't start counting on her to come, she told
herself; she must not feel herself under any obligation. Even
so, she could not help wondering if all was well; Hermione
had said, "See you next week," when she left last Tuesday.
Wouldn't she have telephoned, if she could not come?

Probably not; younger people were less heedful of their
manners than her own generation and Wendy's. But Hermione
did not fit into the category of pushy, self-regarding individuals of whom there seemed to be so many. Probably she had
missed her usual bus and was late, but wouldn't she have
dropped in to explain?

Because she was aware that Hermione was working without
her husband's knowledge, Mrs. Fisher felt uneasy. Hermione
had simply said that he would not approve and that she was
working to gain some independent income, but Mrs. Fisher
sensed that there was more to it than she revealed. She sat
at home wondering if Hermione had been found out, and
worrying.

Meanwhile, Hermione was at Orchard House, busy with

her cleaning but with her mind full of the resentment that had filled every waking thought since Walter had hit her so hard. Why, he had taken everything that was hers, starting with the money from her father's house, and its contents. He had appropriated her father's desk for himself. At first, for a very short time, she had liked seeing him seated at it, going through his papers; later, she saw it differently.

Why shouldn't she use it for herself, she wondered, whilst admitting that she had no business papers to keep inside its drawers. Now, she realised that it was probably valuable; she could sell it; it was hers.

Such a thought was treachery, but it nagged at her as she vacuumed the pale carpets in Theresa Cowper's house. Her bruises were turning yellow and had begun to fade, but she had not had the courage to let Emily Fisher see them for it would have been difficult to lie to her convincingly.

She'd gone to church on Sunday, though Walter had suggested that she stay at home.

"I'd have expected you to want to hide your face—not let people see how stupid you've been," he said. He seemed to have forgotten about the coffee morning; there had been no questions about it, no comments.

"Stupid?" she said, outraged.

"It was your fault," he said, walking away, folding up *The Sunday Times* and taking it to the study—all the sections, even the children's pages.

No one in Merbury had seen her bruises until now, and several people asked about them as they left the church. Hermione smiled and said she'd knocked into something, turning away, walking off while Walter stayed behind to tidy up the hymn books. You went to church among people who professed to be Christian, and lied to them, and they believed you, Hermione reflected. Suppose she'd told the truth, would anyone have believed her? Walter would have said she was hysterical, neurotic, menopausal, and bluffed his way out of any awkwardness. People would have pitied him, saddled with a silly, useless wife.

But I'm not useless, Hermione told herself, wiping Theresa's kitchen window. I've got two employers and some new friends, for surely Mrs. Fisher and Nigel Wilson were her friends? She passed over her brief encounter with Jeremy; he wasn't quite a friend in spite of his casually intimate manner last time they met.

He came in while she was ironing one of his shirts. Hermione liked ironing; it was soothing, and she put the radio on while she did it, so she did not hear Jeremy until he entered the kitchen.

"Hi there, Mary," he cried.

She had no time to turn away and he noticed her face at once. "God, what's happened to you? Been in a punch-up?"

"An argument with a lamp post," said Hermione.

"I shouldn't have thought you were the drinking sort," he said. "I am surprised."

She did not answer, simply reaching out to turn the radio off.

"I hope you didn't mind me putting the radio on while I did the ironing," she said.

"Not at all," he answered. "If you like, I'll show you how to use the CD player."

"No thanks," said Hermione. "I wouldn't risk that. It's just nice company while I'm ironing." She set the iron down and said, "Can I get anything for you? Would you like some coffee?"

"I'd love a cup," he said. "I'll be in my den."

"Sugar?" she asked, as he left.

"Yes, please. Two."

She put the kettle on and found a cup and saucer. She'd make a cup for herself while she was at it. Getting it ready scarcely interrupted the smooth flow of her ironing. She took Jeremy his coffee, feeling capable and important, carrying it on a small round tray. Silly woman, she told herself; it's only a cup of coffee and he's your boss. But she always liked making tea for workmen when they came to the house, which was rare, for Walter did most of the repairs and painting. Luckily he never expected her to help him.

Jeremy looked up when she entered the room where he was looking at some photographs. She saw that they were of women—just their heads.

"Thanks, Mary," he said, and glanced at her bruised face again. He frowned at her and added, "I once fell down in the street and bruised my face. I had a black eye just as bad as yours and no one would believe I hadn't got it in a fight."

She tried a smile, but said nothing.

"Ah—that's better," he said, still looking at her quizzically. "That's a terrible haircut you've had," he told her. "It looks as if you did it yourself."

"I did," said Hermione, blushing, so that the bruising stood out oddly on her face.

"Why don't you go to a hairdresser?"

"It costs too much," she said.

"Don't we pay you properly?"

"Oh yes—I'm perfectly satisfied," she said hastily. It would be dreadful if he thought she was complaining.

"Let's go up to the bathroom," Jeremy said. "I'll see what I can do about it, but it needs to be a bit longer really, to be put right."

"You'll do what?" She stared at him.

"I'm a hairdresser. Oh—of course—you didn't know, did you? I have three salons, all doing quite well in spite of the recession, and I go to a health farm as their consultant. I flit round from salon to salon, a day here, a day there," he said. "I have my special clients, you see. They pay more for my personal skill. That's how I met Theresa. She has to look good for her job, but a decent cut is the right of every woman."

"I wore it long for years," Hermione said.

"And then you got fed up with it and decided to hack it off. I see."

In the bathroom, he made her bend over the basin while he gave her a quick shampoo and a rinse.

"I've just cleaned in here," she protested, half laughing but half upset as small splashes marked the big mirror.

"I'll explain to the boss," he said, putting a fluffy towel around her shoulders and brandishing a pair of scissors with long slender blades.

There was nothing for it. She submitted while he snipped and combed. As he worked he chatted away, telling her how he had begun with one small shop in Bromley after serving an apprenticeship. He had been fascinated by women's hair and what a difference a new style could make to their appearance. His own mother was always altering hers and perhaps that had influenced him; she was an actress who gave up the stage when she had her family of two boys and three girls. When young he had practised on his sisters' hair.

By the time he had finished cutting, her hair was almost dry, but he plugged in a dryer and blew it, curling it around a brush.

"I don't suppose you'll bother with this," he said. "But comb it into shape when it's damp and it will dry quite well. What you really need is a soft perm to give it body."

"I don't know what to say," said Hermione, when he had finished. There were so many mirrors in the bathroom that she could see all round her head without difficulty, but he brought in Theresa's hand-mirror to show her the back. "It—it's a transformation."

"So I should think. That would cost you thirty pounds in my salon," he told her.

She went white at this, and he put his hands on her shoulders, gently squeezing them, leaning his face against hers, both of them gazing at their reflections.

"Don't worry. I'm your fairy godfather and it's my prezzy at the christening of the new you," he said.

He forgot their conversation as soon as he departed from the house.

Mrs. Fisher ate her lunch slowly. She always had sandwiches on Tuesdays, to keep Hermione company, and this week hers were of smoked salmon for a treat; she had intended to offer some to her visitor, whose own were always filled with cheese. Now, Emily's seemed to taste of dust. She could not rid her mind of fears about Hermione. "Walter doesn't like the cinema," or "We don't have holidays now," were remarks she remembered Hermione making.

Mrs. Fisher did not know why holidays were once a feature in their lives but were no longer. Walter was not unemployed; he went to London daily and worked for a charity about which Hermione had revealed few details.

This week Mrs. Fisher had put out some old photograph albums, wanting to show Hermione the big old rectory where she had spent her childhood, and photographs of her first husband, who had died of pneumonia when her son Jack was only four. In those days people died of illnesses which nowadays barely caused a ripple of alarm, and people dealt with death as a matter of course. She had been left very badly off, and her second husband had given her and her son security. Wendy was their daughter.

She had told Hermione some of this story. There were no photographs of her first husband or of Jack in the drawing-room, but Mrs. Fisher had several in her bedroom, where she kept the albums in a drawer. Wendy would burn them after her death, Mrs. Fisher was sure. There was no one else who might be interested in them, no grandchildren to want them, but that was as much a disappointment to Wendy as to herself. Jack had joined the navy as soon as he was old enough and he was killed in the last months of the war.

She had better put the albums away. Wendy thought time spent looking at them was wasted, sheer sentimentalism which got one nowhere.

"You must go forward, Mother," she insisted, but Mrs. Fisher was eighty-six years old and there was only a short way left for her to travel. Wendy was so busy that she left no time for nostalgia in her life.

After she had put the albums safely away, Mrs. Fisher sat for a while in her room. It had a bay window overlooking the road. Sometimes she sat there, in her comfortable upright armchair, watching people pass. Mrs. Fisher had a small television set and a radio in her room, and a kettle to make tea. The day would come when she would be confined to this small area, but the moment must be postponed as long as possible. She could still get about and, like Hermione, show independence, even rebel.

For a while she stayed there. Often she dozed after lunch, but not today. She was obsessed with the thought of Hermione in some trouble. It was a dry winter's day, with low cloud massed grey above the roofs of Creddington; no rain had fallen for some time. Mrs. Fisher had gone shopping that morning to buy the smoked salmon and some fresh brown bread which she had sliced herself, wafer thin. She seldom went out so late at this time of year but there had to be exceptions. Mrs. Fisher put on her warm tweed coat and her felt hat; she found her gloves and her stick, and she set off along the road towards the church and Orchard House, where Hermione should be working.

As soon as she emerged from Orchard House with her new haircut, Hermione saw Mrs. Fisher standing on the opposite side of the street, under a lamp post. It was dusk now—almost dark—but she recognised the old lady at once and crossed over to her.

"Mrs. Fisher! What are you doing here? It's too cold for you to be out," she exclaimed, seizing the older woman's hands in her own, on which were shabby green knitted gloves.

Hermione looked into Mrs. Fisher's face, and Mrs. Fisher looked back at hers, and even in the dim light she saw the bruises.

"Oh, my dear," she cried. "I knew something was wrong when you didn't come today. What's happened?"

"Let's get you home," said Hermione briskly. She took Mrs. Fisher's arm and led her off, away from the revealing lamplight. They walked out of the close, Mrs. Fisher using her stick but grateful for Hermione's support, past large houses protected from the road by shrubs and hedges. Mrs. Fisher was wheezing slightly; the cold, damp air had got into her lungs. "You shouldn't be out so late," Hermione scolded.

Questions were racing through her mind. She must see the old lady safely into the house, unless Wendy had come home, as was possible; and if she had, wouldn't Mrs. Fisher be in trouble for straying? Might she be deprived of her key or in some other way restricted?

But the white car was not outside the house.

Mrs. Fisher had the key in her pocket. She gave it to Hermione, who unlocked the door and gently led her inside. The old lady was chilled through and shivering slightly, but Hermione did not realise that some of this was due to horror at the sight of her fading bruises. They went through the hall to the drawing-room and Hermione helped Mrs. Fisher into a chair. The room was quite warm, but she bent to light the gas fire which supplemented the central heating.

"Best keep your coat on for a few minutes, till you've warmed up," she said. "What about the key? Where do you keep it?"

Mrs. Fisher told her that it lived on a hook in the kitchen at the side of the sink.

"I'll put the kettle on. You'll feel better when you've had a hot drink," said Hermione.

She went out to the kitchen, replaced the key and found the tea things. While the kettle boiled, she went back to the drawing-room and found that Mrs. Fisher had taken her coat off.

"In case Wendy comes back," she said, looking like a small girl caught out in a prank.

"I'll put it away," said Hermione, who by now had missed her bus. Well, there would be another in an hour and she would catch that; she should still be home before Walter, unless he was early, which was most unlikely. On the rare occasions when it had happened in the past he had found her reading or watching television and she had been berated for wasting time instead of carrying out some household task. She hurried upstairs and hung Mrs. Fisher's coat in her wardrobe.

When the tea was made, she took a tray into the drawing-room and poured out two cups. What if Wendy came home now?

"Your face, Hermione. What happened?" Mrs. Fisher was determined to find out.

"I had a small accident," said Hermione. "I fell."

Mrs. Fisher was now composed again. The cup she held did not waver in her hand.

"You fell?" she said.

Hermione nodded, but she could not meet that steady blue gaze. She looked down at her own cup and saucer.

"It was an accident," she repeated.

"An accident?" Mrs. Fisher knew it was no such thing.

Suddenly it came out.

"He didn't mean it—he—I've never been hit on the face before," said Hermione. Tears sprang into her eyes but she blinked them back. There was no time to weep; Wendy could return at any minute, and what explanation for Hermione's presence would be offered to her?

"Your husband hit you?" Mrs. Fisher wanted to be quite sure.

Hermione nodded, tears now rolling down her face in spite of her efforts to hold them back.

"You're not the first battered wife I've met," said Mrs. Fisher gently. Such things had always happened.

Battered wife? Was that what she was? Hermione had read about them. She had always imagined their husbands were drunk but Walter did not have that excuse for his behaviour.

She pushed away the thought and stood up.

"I've got to go," she said. "I'm late."

She was running away, afraid to confess her plight to this sympathetic friend.

"You've missed your bus. You're to take a taxi," said Mrs. Fisher, opening her handbag which was beside her chair. Handing Hermione two ten pound notes, she said, "This should cover it. You can give me any change next Tuesday. That will mean you are sure to come." She looked straight at Hermione. "You didn't come because you knew I would ask about your face," she said.

Hermione nodded. She had wiped her eyes and blown her nose.

"I'm sure it won't happen again," she said, though the only way she could be sure of that was to keep a physical distance between herself and Walter, which could be difficult. "It's always my fault when he's cross, you see. I'm stupid and a disappointment to him."

Mrs. Fisher thought of the two kind husbands she had had in her long life, the first for so short a time and the second for more than fifty years; there had been arguments, even angry words, but these were few and soon over, with mutual forgiveness asked and granted. Things had been discussed and decisions made, with compromises on occasions but always with tolerance and understanding. Without kindness, she thought, no other quality was enough.

"What about your disappointment and unhappiness?" she said. "Don't you count?" She gave Hermione a little hug.

"Don't try to find excuses for him. There are none. Now, just take your cup away, my dear, and rinse it through. Then ring for a taxi. You'll find a card by the telephone."

With luck the cab would arrive before Wendy, who was late this afternoon. She was busy organising costumes for the Nativity play her pupils were putting on before term ended.

Hermione had just been driven off when Wendy returned and Mrs. Fisher had not had time to ask her about the bearded man who had driven away from Orchard House in a large black car shortly before Hermione emerged. He had been smiling as he came out of the house, a man who looked confident and successful; was he the lover of Hermione's employer? Mrs. Fisher wondered if he often called while Hermione was there. He looked the sort of man who would eat up someone like her for breakfast and never notice. Mrs. Fisher felt a great sense of foreboding; Hermione was very vulnerable, and danger came in many guises.

11

Hermione was looking forward to her baby-sitting session at Downs Farm, but it was unfortunate that when she first met Laura, there would be bruises on her face. She worried about it on Tuesday, riding home from Creddington in the taxi, which cost twelve pounds, with tip. She had plenty of change to give back to Mrs. Fisher next week. As she paid the driver outside No 6, Pam Norton, who lived opposite, saw her from her office window. She was a qualified accountant who worked from home, and was married to the manager of one of the banks in Freston. To Pam, the sight of Hermione alighting from a taxi was as unlikely a spectacle as a landing from Mars would be. Pam was very curious. Where had Hermione been, and why? She was perfectly entitled, of course, to travel in other ways than by bus and bicycle. It seemed that Hermione, now both girls had left home, was getting about a bit, which was surely good. She had been looking more animated lately and had lost some weight; indeed, both these facts had been mentioned at a preliminary meeting to arrange the date and venue for the village fête, the topic ending when the vicar and Walter arrived together. Someone had even wondered aloud, just for laughs, if Hermione had found a lover. Pam had noticed that she caught the noon bus every Tuesday. It was Tuesday today. Where did she go on Tuesday afternoons?

Pam decided that she must ask Walter if he knew. He was always so correct and it might shake his calm to learn that Hermione had a regular weekly engagement. Probably, she told herself, he knew all about it; he was quite a martinet; everyone knew that; but Hermione was rather a poor thing, with that hangdog look she often wore. She never had much to say for herself. Perhaps she wrote poetry in secret, or had taken up water-colours or sculpture, with classes on a Tuesday.

Pam had not been in church on Sunday and she had not seen Hermione's bruised face, nor heard any comments on it, for people who had noticed it were too shocked to want to know the truth, and did not talk about it.

There was no malice in Pam's heart when she resolved to ask Walter, at the PCC meeting tomorrow night, where Hermione had been today.

Walter was in a very dark mood when he returned that night, and Hermione need not have been anxious about being home first for he was very late. If she had not known that he was usually abstemious, she would have thought he had been drinking; his only words were to complain that his lamb in chutney sauce was inedible and to demand some bread and cheese, which she set down before him without speaking. His own words, instead of being clipped and precise, sounded blurred. She went out of the room, leaving him alone. Until a few weeks ago, she would have waited to eat until he returned; it was only since she had been going to work that she had been able to stand back and see how ridiculous it was for two people's food to be spoilt and to realise how unnecessary her company was to him.

Now he called her, peremptorily, and asked her where she was going.

"To do the ironing," she said, and he wanted to know why it had not been done earlier.

"Because I was busy with other things," she said, and walked out of the room before he could question her about her actions. She was shaking as she closed the door. Defying him was so novel that it still terrified her. I'll get better at it, she thought; this is just the beginning.

Ten minutes later she heard him leave the house. There was no meeting that night, as far as she knew, but perhaps he had arranged to see someone about a village matter. There was the vigilante scheme he was so keen on, she remembered; perhaps he was on the prowl, looking for vandals.

She did a little ironing; she had never been a liar and found even small social fabrications difficult. Then she unplugged the iron. She would have her bath and hope to be in bed before he returned. She had bought two new bolts to add to the one she had already fitted to Jane's bedroom door, where she now slept, just to be extra safe, and she had taken to keeping the rolling pin beside her bed.

Walter was not one to work off his bad temper by walking round the village. He took exercise only with a goal, as when he went jogging, but tonight he could not endure sitting in the house with his wife, even if she were in another room, avoiding him.

He walked round to Robert Mountford's house, and found two large cars parked in the drive. The Mountfords had friends to dinner.

"Is it important, Walter?" asked Robert, napkin in hand at the door. "House isn't on fire? No robbery? Nothing like that?" He frowned at his caller, feeling mild guilt because the dull Browns were never on the guest list for the dinner parties his wife, a superb cook, loved giving.

"No. It can wait," said Walter curtly. "If you've more important things to do than discuss village safety."

"We could talk about it before the PCC meeting tomorrow," said Robert. Such matters were parish council, not church concerns, and would not be on the next evening's agenda. "Come in on the way, if you like, and we'll thrash out then whatever's on your mind."

Robert saw that Walter was determined to implement his vigilante scheme although the local police inspector had given it the thumbs down. Neighbourhood Watch, yes, but men walking round looking for trouble and thereby perhaps provoking it, no, was the verdict. Robert determined to present a foolproof case at the next parish council meeting, so that Walter's ideas would be shot down in flames.

"Very well," Walter grudgingly accepted the other man's suggestion.

"Sorry I can't talk now," said Robert. "Helen's soufflé's just about to rise," and he firmly closed the door on Walter's peeved face.

He was pleased with this remark, and when they were going to bed, repeated it to his wife, who had not served a soufflé that evening but had made profiteroles.

"Man's got a bee in his bonnet about this," said Robert. "You'd think he'd have other things on his mind. It's not as if we had a serious crime problem here—not like Stappenford, for instance." There had been a nasty case of ram raiding in that town, where two youths in a stolen car had reversed into a shop window, smashing it, filled up the car with television sets and radios and roared off in minutes, hitting a bystander as they jumped some lights. The car had been found burnt out, and they had stolen another. "I suppose we ought to ask the Browns to dinner," he said glumly. "Or drinks," he added hastily, seeing his wife's expression.

"If we do, they'll have to ask us back and poor Hermione will be so flustered that she'll be bound to drop the best china or singe the potatoes," said Helen. "Then he'll give her hell."

"Will he?" Robert looked astonished.

"Why else would she look so defeated?" asked Helen. "He's bad-tempered and selfish. Hermione has looked very tired and drawn since Sarah went away—though I must say she's seemed a lot brighter these last few weeks. She's cleaned up that old bike they've got and goes off on it every Thursday morning. I pass her when I'm on my way to my French classes." Helen Mountford had a regular routine, with household shopping on Tuesdays, French on Thursdays, and swimming at a health club in Creddington on Wednesdays and Fridays.

"She must like Walter. She married him, after all," said Robert, earning a wry look from his wife who thought the hour too late to expound an alternative theory. "She's one of those little clingers," Robert went on, lining up the coins from his pocket in tidy heaps, as he did every night. Sometimes Helen wished he would scatter them, fling them down, even drop some, but he had always been meticulously tidy.

"She was very young when she married him," said Helen. "She's the same age as Angela." This was their daughter, now married to her third husband after two unwise earlier unions. "She hasn't escaped, that's all."

"Shouldn't think she wants to," said Robert. "Nice house, enough money, husband out all day—what more could she want?"

Love, thought Helen, but did not say so. She knew she was loved and appreciated, even if she was not understood, and was grateful.

Walter walked angrily away from the Mountfords' house. He had recognised one of the cars in their drive as belonging to a couple who had recently moved into Merbury Grange, which they had bought for a very large sum. Knowing them could bring advantages at work; he might persuade them to espouse some aspect of the research programme. They did not go to church and had so far attended no village function; it would be difficult to meet them socially without the aid of a mutual acquaintance. If Hermione were a different sort of woman, one who developed a circle of influential friends which would include people like Helen Mountford, she could have opened doors to a wider social life for him. Naturally, since she was so dull and unattractive, no one she met in her charitable works in the village wanted to cultivate her. The more influential women in Merbury directed the younger ones, and Hermione did as she was told by Helen Mountford and her cronies, but by now the Browns should be included when there were large drinks parties, at least. The new couple were in their late forties; it was not a generation problem; besides, Walter had all the *gravitas* Hermione lacked, if only he had the chance to display it.

Walking on, Walter found plenty of reasons to whip up his anger against his wife. And that evening he had failed to see the woman from the train though he had been to the house and rung the bell. Again, there was no answer, so he had gone to Stappenford Library, which was open until eight, and consulted the electoral roll, from which he learned that the sole residents of No 18 were George and Valerie Palmer. She must be their lodger, Walter had decided, one who had arrived too late to be included on the register. He wished he knew where she worked and why she kept such irregular hours.

If he could manage to be on the same train in the morning, he could follow her when they arrived in town. It should be possible. All he would have to do was to leave earlier than normal, alight at Stappenford and wait until he saw her on the platform. If he drew blank a few times, in the end he would coincide with her. He wouldn't sit next to her on the journey up; that would be too obvious. He'd travel in the next coach so that he could easily keep her in sight after the train reached London. He could afford to be late for work as it would be the first time ever.

Planning this, walking the quiet streets of Merbury, Walter passed The Grapes. Cars were parked on both sides of the road outside the old timbered inn, which allegedly served excellent steaks though he had never tried one. The Nortons sometimes went there on Saturdays, he knew, and Sarah and Jane had occasionally been in the bar with other young people, until he found out about it and put a stop to such goings on. Pubs were unsuitable places for his daughters.

Walter rarely thought about the two girls now; they had brought him nothing but trouble, leaving home in the ungrateful manner they had demonstrated, taking their fresh young presences away from him. He had liked watching them in their tight jeans—though he disapproved of their wearing them—with their long hair either loose or in pony tails. Their bodies were so trim and supple, a blend of flowing curves. He had become alarmed about his feelings towards them as they grew older and that was when he began regularly visiting prostitutes.

It was all Hermione's fault that he had these thoughts, these unsatisfied desires.

She could have an accident. She sometimes rode Sarah's old bike—Jane had taken hers away—and there was the long hill leading into the village where her brakes might fail, if he arranged it. Would that be enough? It would depend on the traffic conditions at the time, her speed, and other factors. He thought around the possibilities. Injuries might not be fatal and would be an inconvenience as she might be laid up in hospital, unable to carry out her domestic duties. Death was the only answer to his problem.

Fire would not do; it would destroy too much that was valuable. Some of that furniture which had been her father's had appreciated with age. He knew: he had read up such things.

When he returned home she was in the room into which she had moved all her belongings. He did not try the door; it would be locked. One day he might remove the bolts, but he knew she locked it from the outside with a key for he had tested it when she was occupied downstairs.

He opened the airing cupboard, which was on the landing, and took a clean shirt from the pile of neatly ironed shirts on the first shelf. Then he rubbed it against his shoe and replaced it. If she noticed the stain he had made before she put it away in his drawer, she would have to wash and iron it again, and if she did not, he would have a legitimate cause for complaint when he went to put it on.

The following morning he got off the train at Stappenford and waited for the next two to stop there, but the woman with the long hair did not catch either of them. He could not loiter any longer and boarded the second as it was pulling out. He was an hour late arriving at the office and made the excuse of an emergency dental appointment to explain the delay, then spent the succeeding hours harrying young Philip Shaw.

"What's got into Wally?" Philip asked Belinda, who was a friend of his mother's and responsible for his presence in the office. They had a big mail shot to prepare to catch any possessors of Christmas compassion, when people should feel guilt at hedonistic spending.

"Don't let him hear you call him that," said Belinda, but at the moment Walter was out of the office, presumably in the cloakroom.

"Sorry." Philip looked not a whit abashed. "Bit of an old prune, isn't he?"

"He's very competent," said Rosemary primly. "And he's probably still got toothache, or a numb jaw."

When Walter returned, Belinda brought him coffee and enquired if he would like an aspirin, which he turned down with a curt "No," not even, as she noted, a word of thanks. He never looked up as she set down the cup, and afterwards she wondered if he had even noticed who had brought it to him, but then he never looked directly at either her or Rosemary; they had discussed this and decided that he was afraid of both of them.

"We're hardly likely to fall on him, desperate with lust," Belinda had said. "Or utter cries of 'Rape,' " she added, for Walter never stood close enough to them to touch either woman.

"Play it cool," Rosemary advised Philip. "Just get on with what he's given you to do and don't cheek him."

"As if I would," said Philip, opening his large blue eyes very wide and looking like virtue personified.

After that, he addressed Walter as "sir" instead of "Mr. Brown" as hitherto, managing to utter the word in an extremely unctuous tone while wearing an expression of childlike innocence. This little charade was not lost on Belinda and Rosemary; they were entertained by the smirking response the bogus respect earned from Walter, who reflected that the young man had been well reared. If those yobs on the train had been disciplined as children, they would know how to behave now. He remembered the hidings he had received himself, his terror and the stinging pain. He could recall his mother telling his father that he had been rude, stolen biscuits, neglected his homework—any crime she suspected even if she had no proof that he was guilty. It had done him no harm; indeed, it had made a man of him, able to take and hand out punishment.

Belinda began wondering about Walter's wife, whom none of them had met, though Sarah had helped out for a few weeks in the summer. She had been rather quiet and had seemed to want to keep out of everyone's way. She had brought sandwiches for her lunch and had eaten them in the gardens near the office while Walter went to a café round the corner. Father and daughter were never seen talking together except in the line of duty. Then Sarah had simply ceased to come. There had been no explanation. Some time later, when Belinda had asked Walter about her, he had said that she had gone abroad, declaring that this was always the plan and that she had been merely filling in time with them.

But Sarah, when Belinda and Rosemary talked to her, had said that she had a university place promised. Had she thrown that up or decided to take a year out, which was often a good idea? Perhaps her A-level results weren't up to standard; neither woman liked to ask Walter and both soon stopped enquiring about her since he gave monosyllabic replies.

"You'd think he has no idea where she is or what she's doing," said Belinda after one of these attempts to show interest.

"Maybe he hasn't," said Rosemary in her flat, matter-of-fact tones.

Neither had any notion that Sarah had stolen from their funds.

Walter sent Philip out to buy sandwiches for his lunch that day; he must work through, because he had been late that morning due to the dentist. Walter never left anything in his IN tray at night.

"Is your tooth better, sir?" Philip asked. "Would you like egg? It's easier to eat than ham."

"Your concern does you credit," said Walter. "Egg will be appropriate, and a carton of orange juice, if they have it. Bring a receipt." He gave Philip three pounds for these expenses and had very little change.

Might have told me to keep it for my trouble, thought Philip, going off to eat the cheese roll and banana which he had brought from home for himself.

Belinda and Rosemary were followed from the office by Walter that night; he was always the last to leave and both he and the director had keys. The two women went a different way from Walter at the nearby crossroads, and this time they saw that he turned towards the bus stop for his station.

"He'll be home on time tonight," said Belinda. "No dates up west with the toothache. Let's hope his mood improves in the train."

They both spared Hermione a friendly, sympathetic thought before they parted.

12

Walter's train was on time. Hermione heard the car turn into the driveway and began dishing up their dinner. He would eat promptly so that he could be off punctually to his meeting, and she could go to Downs Farm to carry out her baby-sitting engagement. She could foretell his movements exactly: there would be the sound of the garage doors closing; then he would enter by way of the front door, using his key. He would remove his raincoat and hang it up in the cloakroom, twining his scarf round the hanger, and he would hook the tweed hat he wore in winter on a peg. After all these dispositions were made to his satisfaction he would go into the lavatory, where he would remain for up to ten minutes. This was his evening ritual.

The sound of water running in the cloakroom basin would be her signal that he would soon be on his way to the dining-room and the dishes must be on the table by the time he arrived. Everything had to be properly served up; no short cuts, such as putting the meal directly on the plates in the kitchen, were permitted. She was giving Walter a good dinner tonight: pork chops with parsnips. He would dissect the chop like a surgeon separating tissues, munch up the fat and the meat, his jaws moving with a circular motion as he savoured the flavour and the texture. She found pork rather rich herself and always bought one large and one very small chop. The pudding was blackberry and apple crumble, another favourite. It was wise not to try new dishes; in the past she had attempted recipes she saw in papers or on television, but Walter would always divide into sections on his plate fish or meat done in a new sauce, or vegetables he had not met before, and enquire sarcastically what she had been trying to achieve before dismissing such efforts with contempt.

He approved of parsnips and would eat a large helping. The potato was mashed this evening, smooth and creamy, done with a whisk—she had no food processor; Walter would have thought money spent on one wasted, when what was her time for but to use in performing domestic tasks? She was lucky, he said, that circumstances did not compel her, like many women, to work; they needed no second income and she could spend her time as she chose. Then he would add that a further reason to be grateful on this score was the fact that no one would employ her except possibly to wash up in a catering kitchen; she was, he would allow, reasonably capable as a washer-up.

She broke things, though. She grew edgy when he hovered near her, watching what she was doing, ready to criticise with regard to too few or too many suds, or anything else at which he could carp, or if she was in a hurry, as when the girls were younger and needed her attention.

Tonight he took his place at the table and served himself, heaping parsnips and potato round his chop, pouring on gravy. There should have been some green, she thought: spinach or sprouts to improve the colour scheme, and she had scarcely formed the thought before he put it into words.

"A drab spectacle," he said, stirring the gravy round his plate. "All beige and brown. Like you," he added, giving her one short stare from his pale eyes. She was wearing a beige sweater and a dark brown skirt, and her hair was brown. Was her face beige? Probably drab dun, she thought, but she was armoured against his insults this evening; soon she would be at Downs Farm, where she was appreciated and where no one would humiliate her.

She made no reply and ate her own meal, which tasted of nothing because fear deprived her of sensory perceptions others took for granted. This evening his taunts would be limited because of the time available in which they could be uttered. Soon he would leave; he was never late for a village meeting.

He ate his crumble without comment and went again to the cloakroom, this time for a brief visit to the lavatory and for further washing before putting on his country garb—his waxed jacket, with his tweed hat and his woollen scarf. Then he was gone.

Once the door had closed behind him, Hermione sped into action, clearing up quickly, putting the left-over vegetables away; there was very little surplus, for she gauged what was needed to perfection, then added a spoonful more, for otherwise he might complain there was not enough, but he was just as likely to rebuke her if she prepared too much.

"Mum eats the scraps for her lunch," Sarah had once said, in her defence. "She's got to be fed, after all."

Sarah, unlike Jane, was not overtly afraid of their father and she sometimes tried to protect her mother, but was reproved for being pert, and even dismissed to her room if Walter considered her comments rude. She had felt badly about abandoning Hermione, and though she did not confess her theft to her mother, had revealed her plans. Hermione encouraged her to go; it was her chance of freedom; Sarah would make something of her life. She worried about Jane, however; what future had she, living in a squat with young people, some of whom begged in the streets? Hermione hoped Jane had never done that. She seemed to drift from job to job with spells out of work in between. Hermione wished she would sign on for a training scheme or seek some sort of qualification, but she appeared to have no drive or ambition.

In her haste to leave, Hermione broke a glass. She cast the fragments into the bin without a pang. If Walter came home and found the least thing out of place or a worktop not properly wiped clean, he was likely to fling all the contents out of the drawers and take the stores from the cupboards, then expect order to be restored before breakfast. This had happened many times.

But tonight she would be in bed when he returned, or so he would think, though in fact she would still be at Downs Farm, but her bedroom door would be locked and she would have the key with her. Walter would bolt the front door after him, so she left by the back door, taking that key. It was her duty to lock the kitchen at night.

She set off eagerly. There was enough petrol in the car; Walter would never let the tank drop below the halfway mark; it was one of his maxims. There would be plenty left to get him to the station and back tomorrow. She closed the garage doors behind her; there was nothing to indicate that she was not at home, and by this time Walter's fellow councillors would be at the vicarage so that they would not recognise the Maestro passing through the village.

In less than ten minutes she had parked outside Downs Farm. She locked the car and walked towards the back door, her usual entrance, but the big oak front door was opened before she reached the side of the house and Laura Wilson came to greet her.

"It's good of you to help us out, Mary," she said.

"It's a pleasure," said Hermione.

"We'll try not to be very late," Laura promised.

"Oh, don't worry," said Hermione. The later she was, the more deeply asleep Walter would be.

"It's going to freeze," said Laura. "Will your car be all right?"

"Oh yes," said Hermione airily, not caring now, but of

course Walter would have seen to topping up the anti-freeze; he did much of the car maintenance himself.

James and Fiona were already in pyjamas and dressing-gowns, quite used to their regular baby-sitters and prepared to greet Hermione on the same friendly terms, and eager to exploit her good nature into reading extra stories once their parents had departed. This ploy was successful; Hermione struck a deal that if she indulged them, afterwards they would be perfect angels and go straight to sleep. Tired by that time, they did so, and peace prevailed.

Smoked salmon sandwiches and a large glass of white wine had been left for Hermione. Despite the pork chop, she was able to enjoy the sandwiches, and the wine made her feel relaxed and comfortable as she sat on the sofa by the fire. Now and then she rose and added a log, or stirred the ashes. Outside the house was a pile of wood from an old apple tree that had blown down in a gale, and when it burned it gave off a special fragrance. She left the drawing-room door ajar so that if the children called out or cried she would hear them.

She was asleep on the sofa when Laura and Nigel returned, but she woke at the sound of the car. They came in flushed and happy after enjoying their evening.

"It's nearly midnight," said Laura. "Oh dear, I'm sorry, Mary."

"That's all right," said Hermione, who wished she could stay for the rest of the night.

Nigel was standing behind Laura, one hand resting lightly on her shoulder. As Hermione gathered up her coat they turned to look at one another and Hermione knew that when she had gone they would make love together in the big bed in the room she cleaned and polished each week. Love, she thought; that was what they would share; mutual love for the joy of both, such as she had read about but never experienced. There would be no thought of rights to the body of another, as in theft. Or rape. Compliant rape; that was what she knew about, rape where the victim accepts it as her destiny and does not struggle, merely wishing it to end.

Nigel released his wife to hold Hermione's coat and help her into it; he saw her to her car and sprayed defrosting mist from a tin kept in the hall on to her iced-up windscreen and windows. Hermione drove off, aware with calm contentment that she would see him again in the morning. She had something to look forward to, now.

Laura had bundled some notes into her hand and when she reached home she found they had given her ten pounds. That was a very generous reward for enjoying an evening's peace! She would come any time, if she could manage to get there and back without Walter's knowledge.

She drove home with great care. It would be typical of her now to skid or do something stupid, even be stopped by the police and breath tested, though her single glass of wine should not take her over the limit.

Though beset by such fears, Hermione safely negotiated her journey and turned quietly in at the gate. She opened the garage and drove the car inside; the engine noise was slight, surely, she thought, not enough to wake Walter who was a heavy sleeper. After closing the garage, she walked softly up to the back door. The house was in total darkness but she had taken a torch with her and now she shone it on the door as she inserted the key.

The lock turned but the door did not yield. Slowly it was borne in on her that it had been bolted. Walter must have checked, found she had failed in her nightly duty of pushing the bolts across, and had made sure no one could easily enter the house.

She had thought letting herself in would be easy. How stupid she was; she saw that now. Walter probably often checked up on her, making sure she had rammed the bolts home, and had chosen tonight to do so again. Her happy mood dissolved as she stood there wondering what to do. She dared not ring the front door bell to wake Walter up; he would want to know where she had been and would be furiously angry. If she broke a window to let herself in, he would find out what she had done because he would be certain to see the damage in the morning, even if she managed it without making a lot of noise.

Oh, how silly she had been, not thinking her scheme through, making a better plan. There might have been another way. She knew she could not manage the long ladder Walter used when he cleaned out the gutters; it was an old wooden one, very heavy, and she had to help him carry it from the garage when he wanted to use it. What could she do?

After a while she returned to the car. There was a rug in the boot, kept there in case of breakdown or emergency. She pulled the garage doors to behind her, wrapped the rug round herself and sat huddled on the back seat, attempting to sleep.

It grew very cold.

Walter was listening for her return. He was in the bedroom, fully dressed, pacing up and down, seething with rage.

His bad temper had been fuelled at the meeting by Pam Norton, important behind her pile of papers, who had hailed him when he arrived. He regarded her as usurper of the position to which he should have been entitled; she was treasurer of this committee and had been appointed in spite of Walter, so experienced in money matters, volunteering.

"Ah, Walter," she had greeted him this evening. "Nice to see Hermione getting out and about."

Walter had immediately thought of Hermione's bruises which, apart from church, must have kept her at home, as she could not be anxious for people to see her looking so disagreeable. But she had been to that coffee morning, he remembered; Pam must have seen her there.

"Of course she's out and about," he said defensively. "Why not?"

"I meant getting out. Going off in taxis and on her bike.

She's got a whole new routine, hasn't she? I think it's splendid. She must miss the girls so much; she needs fresh interests. She's found new friends, I expect."

"New friends?" Walter's voice rose as he echoed her.

Pamela had wanted to disturb Walter's complacency and she had succeeded.

"She goes off on her bike on Thursday mornings and on the midday bus on Tuesdays," she said blithely. "But she came home in a taxi this Tuesday. Later than usual," she added.

There was no time for Walter to demand more information for the rest of the committee arrived at that moment, with the vicar wearing an anxious frown because there was sad news about the state of the church tower, likely to need expensive repairs. Walter was left glowering down at the papers before him, his head feeling as though it would burst. For the first five minutes of the meeting he sat in silence, as though not hearing a word being said, and this was very unusual for he always had comments to make at every chance there was. Robert Mountford reported to Helen, when he went home, that Walter's face had been purple for the first quarter of an hour of the meeting. He had not called in first to discuss his vigilante scheme as Robert had wearily been expecting, after the previous evening's exchange. Even though Walter might then have imagined himself snubbed or slighted by Robert's response, surely that was not enough to turn him into an effervescent beetroot, still sizzling nearly twenty-four hours later, Helen suggested.

"Pam Norton had been talking to him. Something about Hermione and a taxi. I wasn't paying attention," said Robert, who pretended he did not enjoy gossip.

"Good for her—Hermione, I mean," said Helen, mildly intrigued.

"He calmed down after a while," said Robert. "Perhaps he had a bad day at the office."

Robert's own tribulations these days were limited to tedious

time-wasting discussions at the various committees he felt it his duty to adorn, but he missed the stimulus of his earlier life as managing director of a light engineering company. His best hours, now, were spent at the golf club, where he went three times a week. The men he played with did not inflict their problems on one another, just as in his working years his colleagues had not wanted to talk about their home lives. Except for major events, such as weddings and births, and sometimes divorces, one kept one's private life just that: private. If you knew about people's difficulties, you were sometimes obliged to act, and Robert preferred never to interfere. Helen called him an ostrich, but he said that people should keep their troubles to themselves.

"I don't like Walter," said Helen. "He doesn't look you in the eye."

"He does me," said Robert, surprised.

It was women, then, thought Helen. Walter was not comfortable with women. Like Belinda, she had noticed it.

Robert offered Walter a lift home.

"Thank you, I prefer to walk," said Walter, wrapping his scarf round his neck before setting off.

It was freezing. He strode out, thinking about what Pam had said. Riding in a taxi, indeed! Hermione would have to account for such a luxury and give a good justification for her extravagance. And what was this regular cycling? And the weekly bus trips?

Pam Norton did not overtake him as he walked home; she had gone to The Grapes with two of the other councillors.

Walter did not expect to find Hermione still up; for years, now, she had been in bed whenever he came back from meetings, even though he had told her that his mother had always waited up for his father. The porch light was on for his return, and one light burned in the hall. None of the upstairs windows showed any illumination so she was not reading in Jane's room, though she might be feigning sleep.

He had felt her removal like a blow in the face. How dare she defy him? Her action shook him, too, because he had always been able to make her submit before. Unlocking the front door, letting himself in, he was ready to tear the place apart as his anger boiled up again. He was noisy as he moved about, banging doors. Let her wake up, if she was genuinely asleep.

He felt suddenly very hot, so he went to the kitchen to drink some water, gulping down two glassfuls. Then he glanced round, looking for some untidy factor which he could point out to Hermione next morning, but he could not see anything to criticise. He could arrange a flaw: smear a surface, splash some milk on the table.

In the cloakroom, hanging up his coat, something struck him as out of place. It took him a minute or so to realise what it was: Hermione's beige raincoat, which was what she always wore, even to church, since she had not had a new overcoat since they were married, was missing from its hook.

He made sure, but it was easy to check because all the coats hanging there were his, apart from an old anorak belonging to one of the girls which Hermione used when required to help him in the garden.

Perhaps she had taken it upstairs, hung it in the room she used now.

He went heavily up the stairs and rattled her bedroom door, calling out her name, but there was no answer. The door, of course, was locked. This was not surprising; the surprise would have been if he could have opened it, or if she replied. He banged again and went on calling. The total lack of response, the stillness when he himself was silent, made him suddenly certain that the room was empty. There was no sound of the bed creaking; her light was not switched on. Her coat had gone, and so had she. Walter was convinced that he was alone in the house.

It gave him a weird feeling, almost a sense of helplessness. She couldn't have left him, really gone, could she?

He searched the other rooms in the house, and when he thought of going out to the garage, he found the car was not there.

In the cold night air, Walter shook his fists at the dark heavens, studded with stars, and a great oath rose in his throat, to be bitten back, for sounds travelled at night and the neighbours might hear. The only person who ever witnessed his expressed rage was Hermione; even the girls never saw him really explode; they were only aware of his contained anger when his face darkened and he made biting, sarcastic remarks.

Walter closed the garage doors again. She had left him, taking the car. He had no way of knowing how many of her own possessions she had taken since so much had been transferred to Jane's room. He went to the cupboard where suitcases were kept and could not see any missing, but that meant nothing; she could have used plastic carriers, as the girls often did. He checked the bathroom. Her toothbrush and flannel were still there.

He went downstairs again, looking round for a note, usually left, he thought, by absconding wives. There was no note. Then he went out to the kitchen and something made him test the back door. The lobby door was not locked, and the back door, though locked, was not bolted, and the key was missing.

She had gone out and planned to creep back when he was innocently sleeping. Had she done this before, without his knowledge, in the time since she had been sleeping in another room? Before that, it would have been impossible.

He remembered Pam Norton's words about her expeditions and her taxi ride. Had she, oh inadmissible thought, found someone else? A lover? He recalled how Robert Mountford had remarked on her looking well; that was before she bruised her face. Now that he thought about it, she had seemed different, and indeed her rebellion was a sign of a change in her attitude. Unfortunately, so far, he had not succeeded in bringing her to heel, though that was only a matter of time.

Surely no one else would want her, plain as she was, and dull? But even Walter knew that there was no accounting for taste in such matters: somewhere there could be a man who had turned her head.

She was being unfaithful!

The words seemed to be printed in scarlet letters across his vision.

Methodically, he took cups, plates and saucers from the kitchen cupboards and stacked them on the table, separating each article from the next and pouring on to each one ketchup from a bottle; he liked tomato ketchup and Worcester sauce, and there was enough of both to ornament all the crockery. By morning it would have congealed and she would find removing it took a long time. He would have turned the boiler off and emptied the tank so that she should have no hot water for the task, but he liked a morning bath himself and would not go to work without a good shave. He might run the tank down when he had used what he needed, he decided, getting glasses out and arranging them on the worktop, where he ran a trickle of honey across them all. He liked honey for breakfast on Sundays as a change from marmalade. He poured more honey on the floor, away from where he would walk himself. It would take her hours to clean up the mess. He added flour and poured water on it to make it into sticky dough.

After that, having made sure that the back door was securely bolted, he extinguished the hall light and went up to his room where he alternately lay on the bed in the darkness, fully clothed, or walked up and down by the wall where there were no obstacles. He would not confront her in his dressing-gown.

He saw the car's headlights as she turned in at the gate, and he heard the faint sound of the garage doors as she opened them. She made no noise as she walked to the house to let herself in, but, now standing by the landing window, he saw the faint glow from her torch. Then, after her vain attempt to enter, he watched the thin silver ray flickering as she lit her way back to the garage. She closed one of the doors and pulled the other to, but it was not possible to shut them properly from inside and he was pleased about that; it would let the cold air circulate. It was a pity that there was a rug in the boot, but of course the car was properly equipped.

If it got cold enough, she would start the engine to get the heater going. Then he could go downstairs and close the garage doors, locking her in. She would suffocate very quickly, and it would be deemed suicide. The fact that before committing the act she had stacked china and glass all over the kitchen and soiled them with sauces and honey would reinforce the impression the coroner would certainly have that she had been out of her mind.

He waited for the sound of the engine starting. He might need to strike her, make her unconscious to stop her from realising what was happening and switching off before enough carbon monoxide could build up. On the other hand, if she were to fall asleep despite the cold, he could creep quietly down and make sure it happened like that.

It would be easy.

13

The temperature in the car fell steadily, and Hermione was already cold from shock. She drew the rug round her and tried to calm her rapid breathing; at least she could rest while the night wore on. But her mind raced round. How stupid of her to rely on Walter sticking to his usual routine. It was the story of her life. No wonder he was always telling her how incompetent she was. It was the truth.

He had treated the girls the same, though to a lesser degree, always seeking perfection and never commending effort. For a long time her attitude to them was the same, so indoctrinated was she by him. Then a teacher at the primary school they went to said that Jane seemed lacking in confidence, although she was a hardworking little girl and certainly at least an average pupil; praise and encouragement for any small success at home might help her.

Hermione had seen the truth of this and was horrified to think that she had contributed to Jane's difficulties. She was still haunted by the memory of times when, if not actively supporting Walter's mocking or even harsh comments on Jane's inability to swim early, read easily at six, even tie up her shoelaces, she had not defended Jane.

Lying curled up in the car, her feet icy, Hermione looked back on so many incidents when she should have coaxed her daughters on, applauded their successes. After the teacher's comments she had altered her own approach to them, and all three conspired to conceal setbacks and disasters from Walter, Jane and Sarah uniting to protect Hermione if they could distract their father's attention when she had broken or spilled something, or forgotten to put the salt or the butter on the table. It had been so damaging to them, Hermione saw.

Alone and cold in the dark, she lived again through times when she had cringed before Walter and almost whined like a beaten dog; she had certainly wept, in those early years. Later, she had developed an invisible shell, a carapace of armour to enable her to get through each day as it came. She worried more about Jane than Sarah; Sarah had been more resilient than her sister, and was safe now, in her job with an Italian family where the father was a lawyer. Jane needed support; she thought that she had found a prop in Felix, who had once brought her over to see Hermione in his cherished Morris Minor. Now that chapter in Jane's life was over and she was in this squat in Reading. Sarah had been to see her and had frankly told her mother that such a life was not for her.

"But they're a nice crowd," Sarah had said. "Clean, mostly. Some have jobs." She had tried to reassure Hermione, saying that Jane would sort things out for herself and that she had lots of good sense, but both knew Jane found decisions hard to make and that she was innately timid, like her mother.

Did Walter know she was out? At first Hermione had simply assumed that he had locked up, believing her to be in bed. How could she get into the house in the morning, without his discovering what she had done? Was there a window she could break very quietly so that she could open it undetected? Once Walter had gone to work, she could get someone to mend it straight away and pay him from her wages.

She knew it was impossible. There were security locks on all the windows.

She might try to pretend she had been unable to sleep and had gone out for an early morning walk, but he would see the bolts still pushed home on the back door and the chain up on the front.

What if she simply disappeared? Hid somewhere until he left for work and then came home? She had her key; she would be able to enter by the front door then. Where could she go? The church would be locked, and the bus shelter was on Walter's route to the station. He would go off as usual, she was sure. Would he make breakfast for himself? She spent some minutes working out various scenarios based on this solution, meanwhile getting colder all the time, and at last she decided to start the car to warm herself with the heater. Opening the rear door to let herself out, so that she could sit in the driver's seat, she pushed the garage doors apart to allow the fumes to escape. Walter would not hear the car; he slept so soundly, often snoring heavily, that he had never heard her on the many occasions when, unable to sleep, she had gone downstairs to spend what was left of the night on the sofa. This was not referred to the next day; she had always slipped back upstairs to dress while he was in the bathroom. The girls had sometimes known; she would tell them she had a headache and had not wanted to disturb their father.

She started the engine. It seemed very loud to her, but it had cooled down after being switched off and the automatic choke made it run faster than merely ticking over. It would take some time to warm up.

Suddenly a flash of light, reflected in the mirror, caught her eye. What made her instantly lock the doors she did not know, but she just had time to do it before the shape of Walter loomed up behind her. He walked all round the car trying the doors, while she crouched over the wheel, hiding her face from him, wailing softly and trembling with fear. Then she heard the garage doors bang shut.

There was a spare set of car keys, his, kept on his key ring with the door key. He could return.

She had the sense to turn off the car's engine. Then she tried the garage doors, but they were locked. She was a prisoner.

The air was already full of fumes. She got back into the car and locked herself in again, whimpering and shivering, waiting for Walter, but he did not reappear.

Morning came at last. By then, Hermione had drowsed into a sort of sleep. She heard a sound, and as she stirred a shaft of light pierced her dark prison. The garage doors had been unlocked and pulled an inch or so apart. By the time Hermione sat up and looked out, Walter had gone back to the house but she did not know that; he could be lurking outside.

No. He would want his breakfast. That would be the reason for her release. She reached up and fumbled for the car's interior light and glanced at her watch; it was six forty-five, his usual time for going to the bathroom.

Stiff, and chilled to the bone, Hermione uncurled her aching body and limbs and got out of the car. She put the keys in her pocket and her fingers met the comforting stiffness of the money Laura Wilson had given her in what seemed another life. She had that, and her other earnings, at least. She shook out the rug, folded it up and returned it to the boot. Then she pushed the garage door open far enough to let herself out and walked towards the house.

She knew he would have left the back door unlocked; why release her, otherwise? She let herself in through the lobby and into the kitchen, where she saw the mess Walter had made, but she was past caring. When her foot stuck to the honey spilled on the floor, she simply took off her shoe and continued out of the room and into the cloakroom, thankful to have the chance to relieve herself; during the night she had feared she might have to squat and foul the garage floor. Then she washed her face and hands and combed her hair.

What next?

Why, breakfast, of course.

When Walter came downstairs at the end of his morning's toilet ritual, some of the chaos in the kitchen had already been cleared up and his breakfast waited, as usual, on the dining-room table; the only break with routine was that Hermione had not laid a place for herself. She stood at the sink, still trembling and shaking, engaged in the task of washing up almost every piece of china and crockery they possessed whilst expecting him to come in and attack her both verbally and physically. She had closed the door so that she would have the warning of its opening and time at least to turn around and face him.

Nothing happened.

She continued with her work but she broke nothing. When it was time for Walter to go into the cloakroom, she paused to listen, and heard him walk through. Then she ran upstairs and locked herself into her bedroom until he drove away, leaving for the station at his normal time.

Walter had to know where Hermione had been.

He thought back to the remarks made by Pamela Norton, and Robert Mountford's earlier comment on Hermione's appearance. What was it that he had said? That it was nice to see her blooming. What an extraordinary statement. Flowers bloomed; women existed. As far as Walter could remember, he had replied that Hermione was always well. It was the truth; she was never officially ill though she sometimes had colds and made out that she was ailing. Apart from when the girls were born, for a few days after some of her miscarriages, and for several long weeks when she had her operation, she had carried out her duties more or less effectively. He had found a woman to come in every day to look after the girls and take care of the housekeeping while she was in hospital and for a while afterwards. He was never unwell himself; it was simply a matter of personal discipline; one ignored one's aches and pains.

He had spared her, during the night. In the end she would suffer the ultimate penalty, but that must happen at a time of his choice, not hastily. Meanwhile, he knew that being shut in, in the dark, would be a real ordeal for Hermione who did not like confined spaces and had once shrieked and screamed, showing total loss of control, when the lavatory door jammed at a guest house where they had stayed with the girls on holiday. At the time, she had made an exhibition of herself, shaming him and their daughters. He knew that she could not get out of the garage, once he had locked the doors; there was no window or pedestrian door. She might put the car light on and run down the battery, but he decided that even if she did, there was too little left of the night to endanger his morning departure.

Pam Norton had said that she caught the noon bus every Tuesday. She must mean the bus for Freston. Was she meeting someone for lunch? He had already dismissed as impossible the idea that she was meeting a man, yet she was refusing him his marital rights and wasn't that a sign of infidelity?

He would allow her some rope, follow her next Tuesday, and she would surely hang herself when he trailed her to her mystery assignation. He had every right to know where she went and what she was doing, spending his money on bus rides.

Driving along the road to Freston station, he recalled that she rode her bicycle somewhere on Thursdays. Today was Thursday and he could have prevented her from using it by letting down or puncturing the tyres. Still, she would be in no mood for riding about the countryside after her night out; she would be staying at home today, and he would attend to the bicycle before she wanted to use it again. Unless he had already dealt with the larger question of Hermione herself, snuffing out the nuisance of her life. It was so easy to do: pressure on the throat and it was swiftly over. But he must be more cautious with her, must plan and think of every detail so that it seemed to be either suicide or an accident. Murder must not be suspected.

He had made up his mind. He would do it. He would be rid of her hangdog, reproachful presence. The future would offer him a new, rich life with a partner worthy of him. Quite where he would go with this partner, he was not sure, but all things would become possible once he was free.

Walter thought of the woman he had strangled in that dark alley. She had recognised him from a previous encounter and had refused to accept him again as a client. This had happened to him before, and it enraged him. The women plied for trade; they should cater for all tastes. It did not do to oppose Walter Brown. When he had defied his parents, in his youth, he had been taught obedience and now, in his turn, he exacted it from those he controlled. A man was the head of the house; the women who lived there were subservient to him, their master. That was how the Bible had ordained things, though modern women rebelled against such precepts. It brought them no happiness. Divorce was on the increase, women and children left to fend for themselves or become an expense to the tax-payer. Youths grew up mannerless and undisciplined, stealing cars and thieving.

He had briefly forgotten the woman with the long hair, and it was a real shock when she got into the train at Creddington station and sat within sight of him, across the aisle but a row ahead. She never looked at him, nor at any other passenger. He did not know whether or not she had noticed him at all.

He followed her in London. It was too good a chance to miss. After all, soon he would be free of Hermione. Then he could devote time to persuading this woman that she had made a serious mistake in being so rude when he had sought only to apologise.

On foot and by tube, keeping his distance, he trailed her to a house in Kensington and watched her walk up some steps to its front door and press the bell. Moments later, she pushed open the door and entered.

He waited for a while, but she did not reappear. Still, he could return, now that he knew her destination.

14

Hermione was not going to be late at Downs Farm.

There was still a great deal of cleaning up to be done at home but it could wait till later. Walter had gone; she was safe until he returned, which would not be until half-past six at the earliest. She had not tackled the kitchen floor; the sticky mess of honey and flour would be difficult to remove. She had had to clean off a similar mixture before. This was an old trick of Walter's; the last time he had done it was when she defended Sarah's wish to go to a friend's party and stay overnight. Walter had come home to find Sarah gone without his consent. She had just managed to obliterate all signs of what had happened before Sarah's return.

Hermione's work satisfied the Wilsons, and also Theresa Cowper and Jeremy. Mrs. Fisher appeared to like her and Hermione knew that the old lady's regard was genuine, not due to her own isolation nor to sympathy because she perceived that Hermione was unhappy. Why should it be Walter who was always right and she who was in the wrong? What if she challenged him about shutting her in the garage all night? Asked him if he thought that was the right way to treat his wife?

He would turn it around. He would say that he had come

down to close the garage door unaware that she was there in the car. Why should he imagine that she had gone out while he was at his meeting? It was irrational behaviour on her part. If she wished to go out, she had only to ask, and if her request was reasonable it would be granted. She could construct the dialogue in her mind as though it was happening, but now she knew that he was the irrational one and that if any of their neighbours—the Nortons for instance—had known about her night or had seen the mess in the kitchen, they would wonder at her enduring such treatment.

These thoughts ran through Hermione's mind as, feeling grubby after her night's experience, she had a quick bath and changed her clothes. Then she set off on the bicycle, her mind still whirling with fatigue and confusing thoughts.

The journey seemed long today. It was still very cold, white rime like icing sugar on the grass verges and hedgerows, and lacing the bare trees. Her legs felt heavy as she pedalled along. She might sneak a cup of strong coffee when she arrived; Nigel wouldn't mind; he would attribute her need for it to the late night.

When she put her head round his study door to say she had arrived, he smiled at her. In spite of the weariness which threatened to engulf her, Hermione felt her heart lift. Life wasn't all Walter and woe.

"None the worse after last night?" he asked her, pushing back his chair which ran on wheels. "You're as punctual as ever."

"I hope so," she said, suddenly nervous in case she was a few minutes late.

"Of course you are," he replied. Her nervous response was not lost on him. "Everything all right?" he asked her, trying not to stare too closely at her pale face. Her bruises had faded, but there was still a yellowing smudge by her right cheekbone. Laura, having seen for herself these scars of battle, had admitted that she did not feel happy with the explanation of accidental injury which Nigel had been given.

Hermione wondered what he would say if she told him she had spent the night locked in the garage. The temptation was, for a moment, intense, but she resisted it.

"Yes—of course," she said quickly. "I'll get on," and she closed the study door on Nigel, who returned to his work.

How kind he was, she thought, getting the vaccum cleaner out and carrying it into the drawing-room where she had spent those peaceful hours last night. It was lucky she'd dozed off then; she'd had some sleep, at least.

Doing the fire and the floor, dusting round, she wondered about Nigel and Laura. Probably they had disagreements; everyone must at times, however well they got on together, but things could be worked out if there was tolerance.

She couldn't imagine Nigel hitting Laura if she burnt the toast or ironed his shirts less than perfectly—well, Laura didn't do a great deal of ironing these days as Hermione did most of it. Laura wasn't a good ironer; Hermione had seen evidence of that—or not good by Walter's demanding standards. She never baked cakes and made very few pies or puddings; that was obvious from the contents of the larder and fridge. Yet it didn't matter; the children and Nigel looked happy and so did Laura. Of course, she was clever and had a good career; she had undergone a very long training to qualify and must now earn a substantial salary.

Hermione, marrying Walter, had thrown away her chance of a university education and a career of her own. Maybe she wouldn't have got a degree; maybe she would have failed in a profession; but she hadn't even tried. Walter was going to take care of her, she had thought at the time, but in fact he was acquiring an unpaid housekeeper, she decided, mopping the kitchen floor with the new mop Laura had bought last week. It had long green and white fronds of some sort of fabric and left the floor almost dry.

Nigel wandered into the kitchen as she moved it over the last patch of floor by the Aga.

"I've come to walk all over your clean floor," he said. "But it's coffee time."

"It's all right. It's almost dry," said Hermione. "This mop's marvellous."

"Haven't you got one?" he asked, and when she said that she had not, he told her that she ought to buy one.

She could, from her earnings, but how could she explain that to Walter?

"Yes," she agreed. "I'll think about it."

While they drank their coffee he told her about forthcoming events at the children's school, the Nativity play in which James would be one of the kings and Fiona the angel Gabriel. Every child would perform, if only in a walk-on part as a shepherd or as a member of the choir. Some would play recorders or read appropriate verses.

"You always refer to your children by their names," she said. "I mean you never call them 'the kids.' "

"I hate that expression," he said. "I won't use it, but I often call them collectively 'the children.' "

"I used to refer to 'the girls,' " said Hermione.

It was the first time she had mentioned her family. Whenever it looked as though the conversation was heading in a personal direction, she had swerved away and either been silent or changed the subject. Nigel considered her as she sat looking down at the table, her hands, red and chapped-looking, clasping the pottery mug which had been bought on a holiday in Brittany. He and Laura brought back a mug from each place they visited and now had quite a collection.

"How old are your daughters?" he asked. He knew only that she had a grown-up family who had left home; she had told him that when applying for the job.

"Jane's nineteen and Sarah's eighteen," she said.

"They must have kept you busy when they were small."

"Yes. They were almost like twins," she said. There were less than eleven months between them, a matter which had sometimes provoked raised eyebrows or wry smiles when revealed. The girls themselves had noticed this and never volunteered the information. "They're great friends," she added.

"What are they doing?" he asked. "They must be at university, or perhaps the younger one hasn't started yet."

"They've both given it a miss," she answered. "Sarah's in Italy. She's learning the language." Hermione hoped that she was, though she was supposed to be teaching her charges English.

"That's good," he said. It seemed a sensitive subject, so he did not enquire about the second daughter. This odd, drab employee was beginning to interest him. She looked very tired today and he felt guiltily responsible for that, having been the cause of her late night, but then he was no more tired than usual, and Laura had gone off to work in her normal cheerful manner. It hadn't been so very late, after all. Mary, as Hermione was to him, seemed much more relaxed now than when she first came to the house, but she was still shy and too defensive; it was sad to see in a woman her age. In thinking this, Nigel over-estimated Hermione's age by almost ten years; later, people were to marvel at how relatively young she was, only forty years old.

"Sarah might go to university one day," Hermione volunteered. "She could, I suppose."

"Anyone can. You could." He floated the idea. "Or did you?"

"No. I married when I was only nineteen," she said. "Could I, though?"

"Could you what?" How long had she been married before the girls were born? Seven or eight years?

"Go to university. I had intended to," she said.

"Of course you could, if you've got the right A-levels," he said. "And there are arrangements for what are charmingly called mature students." Didn't she know all this? It wasn't exactly secret information.

What had worn her down so soon? Had she had a premature menopause? Nigel always read all the articles in the magazines for which he wrote and was well informed about female problems.

"I wonder what's happened to the art of seduction," he said suddenly.

"What?" she stared at him, setting her cup down.

"It used to happen. Seduction, I mean," he said, remembering how he had seduced Laura one evening when they were impecunious students and had been to the cinema together, then gone back to his digs to eat fish and chips. Two years later they had married. "I'm thinking of writing a piece about it," he invented quickly, and as he spoke the idea seemed a good one. "You see it on television all the time," he went on. "Not seduction. Its lack, I mean. We're shown instant sex of an aggressive kind. No finesse—no soft, romantic approach. Don't you agree?"

"Er—yes, I suppose so," said Hermione, not altogether sure she understood.

"Courtship has disappeared," he said cheerfully. "Walking out, as it was quaintly called in some quarters. Sometimes it went on for years. What a strain on all concerned." He laughed.

What would she do if he kissed her? He let the thought flit through his head to be instantly dismissed. It would be like taking advantage of a child, and she would leave. He knew it. Besides, he felt no desire for her, nor affection, merely curiosity.

He told Laura about his conversation that evening.

"Did you try anything on?" she asked at once.

"I was tempted," he admitted. "In the cause of research."

"You'll lose us a bloody good cleaner if you succumb," said Laura. "I'll fire her."

"Don't worry. I'll confine my experiments to conversation," he replied.

Hermione thought about it, too. If they'd been in a film or a book, he'd have made a pass at her. She wondered what it would have been like. Alarming, but in an exciting way, not a fearful thing. Pedalling home, she kept picturing Nigel's thin, sensitive face with the high forehead and the thick, fading hair that was streaked with grey, and his dark blue eyes, so different from Walter's pale ice.

She had forgotten all about the mess that was waiting for her when she reached home.

Walter did not speak until after dinner.

He had not returned until late, and as usual when this happened, after each succeeding time when she could expect him, half-hourly during the peak travel period and later at hourly intervals, Hermione relaxed for a short spell, tension building up again inside her as the next train was due. Whichever one he caught might be late; at this time of year there could be leaves on the line or ice in the points, standard explanations for delays, so she could never be quite sure that he might not suddenly arrive when she was off her guard. Tonight she was very tired, and after the buffetings of the past twenty-four hours she felt wretched. How could she go on living like this for the next twenty or thirty years? Yet if she left Walter, where could she go?

If she went out cleaning every day, all day, would she earn enough to rent a room and feed herself? Just about, she thought, but she could not do it in the Freston area; it would be too humiliating for Walter. Although why should she worry? He would have everyone's sympathy, left alone in the house. Soon he'd find some other gullible woman and marry again, and bring her to live in this house which by rights should be hers. Her inheritance had underwritten their lives from the day of their wedding. Now she understood why Walter had married her, but then, because of her youth, her inexperience and the fact that she was bereaved and mourning her father, she had not seen through his plan. An older girl might have suspected his motives, as, perhaps, her aunt had done. Probably he would have shown no interest in anyone who was penniless or without prospects.

How ignorant she had been, how trusting and silly! How Walter must have been laughing at her all this time. She felt chilled and shocked as she accepted the truth of what she had now realised was behind his pursuit of her, his courtship, Nigel might have called it. The conquest had been easy, but there had been no seduction. Her mind closed on that thought as sadness swamped her. She felt pity for the naive young girl she had been, and she wept a little, but then she stirred herself and put on the television for company; at least Walter had not denied the household that, as he liked watching certain sports. She took little heed of which programmes followed one another as the evening wore on, falling asleep for a time, and she did not hear the car. Her first warning that he was back came with the sound of the cloakroom door closing.

Heart racing, she turned off the television and scuttled out to the kitchen; he would expect his meal to be ready by the time he emerged.

Then she made a decision. Tonight he would have to wait, though she would be as quick as she could. She was not going to rush and scurry. If he couldn't take the trouble to telephone and tell her which train he was catching when he was late like this, why should she race about trying to give him the sort of service which could not be matched at the Ritz? At a place like that, you ordered your meal and waited while it was prepared, or so she believed; it would not be unreasonable for him to wait now while she cooked fresh vegetables instead of heating them quickly in butter in a saucepan. A microwave would do this for her: a microwave would revolutionise the problem of delayed dinners; his helping could be placed on his plate and heated up when he arrived, and she could eat her meal at a regular time every evening. Perhaps, when she had earned enough, she would buy one and pretend to Walter that she had won it in a competition.

These thoughts ran through her mind as she carried the chicken casserole, rice and sprouts through to the dining-room. Sprouts warmed up wonderfully in butter and retained their colour.

She had not felt hungry all day, and she pecked now at a small helping while Walter ate heartily as though he had no cares or problems. Her stomach was churning with fear; at some point he would start shouting at her, opening a post-mortem on where she had been last night.

The chicken was good; it was a new recipe which she had seen in the parish magazine. Walter soon realised that it was not her usual bland cream sauce with only a hint of mushrooms.

"What's in this? It's different," he said, pushing the food around on his plate. If he was hungry enough he would not throw it at her, she told herself, and he had been eating it with apparent appetite.

Hermione gripped the sides of her chair with her hands to keep herself steady while she answered him.

"It's a recipe of Helen Mountford's," she said, managing to keep her voice level. "It was in the church magazine. Under cookery notes."

Walter did not comment on this but ate on, chewing vigorously. She glanced at him from under her lids once or twice but he never met her gaze, his own attention concentrated on what was on his plate as he packed his fork neatly with individual portions of chicken, rice or sprouts. He never mixed things in his mouth. Sarah had once commented on this and he had told her that flavours were best enjoyed separately.

"I thought they were meant to blend in," said Sarah, who had been doing cookery lessons at school, and she had been sent to her room for impertinence.

After the pudding—apple tart, troublefree if served late—he laid down his spoon and fork and addressed her.

"Where did you go last night, Hermione?" he asked her. His voice was calm, dangerously calm. Icy fear filled her and she felt slightly sick.

"To visit friends." Her voice shook only slightly. She clasped her hands together under the table.

"What friends?"

"No one you know. They had been let down by their baby-sitter and I offered to help out," she said.

She had thought of this reasonable, almost true explanation that afternoon as she scrubbed the honey and flour from the kitchen floor.

"You never told me you wanted to go out." His voice was still quiet. She knew that tone; it terrified her, the lull before the storm.

"If I had, you would have forbidden me to go," she said.

"Am I so unreasonable?" he asked, and now he did meet her gaze. Her heart was thumping with fright and her whole body trembled as she tried to keep her voice steady.

"You never let me go on any outings with the girls when parents could accompany them," she said, unable to think of other occasions when she had really wanted to do something badly enough to seek permission.

"Such trips cost money we could ill spare. Besides, you were needed at home," he said.

"And you would have refused to let me go last night," she said. For a moment she wondered if she should say that her friends had only rung up after he had left for the meeting, but she knew she would never carry off even such a small deception.

"Who are these friends?" he asked.

"I told you, no one you know," she said, and then, bravely, went on, "Do you think it reasonable to lock me out all night and make all that mess in the kitchen?"

"You did wrong. You must be punished," he said, and now he stood up and moved towards her.

She was too quick for him. She went round the other side

of the table and dashed from the room, up the stairs to her bedroom.

She listened then, expecting him to follow, but instead she heard the sound of breaking dishes. He had never done that before, except by accident on very rare occasions; possessions were valuable. The dining-room would be in a dreadful state: the round rosewood table that had come from her own home might be ruined, the carpet stained, but she no longer cared.

15

What would Walter do next?

In her small room, the curtains drawn back, Hermione sat on her bed and looked out of the window across the street to the Nortons' house, where a rim of light showed upstairs at the window Pam used for her study. Was she working at this late hour? What was Desmond doing? Wondering whose overdraft to crack down on, whom to give credit to? Were the Mountfords preparing for bed? Was the vicar writing his sermon? Only a few yards away there were other people living their own lives, not under threat, but Hermione might as well have been on an island with Walter for all the use they were to her. How could she ask anyone for help? If she opened the window and screamed, would anyone hear? What if she ran from the house and pounded on Pam Norton's door, telling her Walter was mad? Pam wouldn't believe her, and was it even true? He knew what he was doing; he was only mad with anger, and that was because she had broken his rules.

Pam's study light went out and the bedroom light came on, glowing faintly behind the lined curtains. Hermione imagined her undressing, getting into bed—probably she creamed her face first, Hermione thought. The figure of Desmond floated vaguely in the background of the scene she tried to picture. She put him in pale green pyjamas, unaware that Desmond slept naked.

Helen Mountford, she thought, would wear a long-sleeved night-dress with tiny tucks down the front and lace at the neck. She and Robert would sleep in single beds, each with their own lamp, and would civilly wish each other good night, possibly exchanging a chaste kiss on forehead or cheek before composing themselves for sleep. Their teeth might rest in tumblers in Steradent, as some of Walter's did.

Thinking like this, trying to imagine the mundane activities of people she knew, calmed Hermione and distracted her. She sent her mind along the road, calling in at each house and inventing night scenes for the occupants. She could recognise everyone who lived in the village even if she did not know all their names, but none was her friend.

It's me. I can't be jolly, she had told herself a long time ago, wondering why she drew back from involvement apart from playing a humble part in communal activities. No one will want to talk to me, I'm so dull and stupid, she would think to herself, functioning efficiently but in silence as she washed up after a village function or sorted jumble, and all the while she retreated further into her isolation. Now she realised that in the last few weeks she had been interacting with other people—having conversations, especially with Nigel and Mrs. Fisher, and even Jeremy had concentrated on her, cutting her hair and telling her she looked pretty when she smiled.

She didn't feel like smiling now.

If, last night, she had left a note for Walter, telling him she had gone out and might be back quite late—the sort of thing that would be a normal action for most people—he would not have locked her out and the fearful hours she had endured could have been avoided. She would have received a lecture, of course: a hectoring monologue when she came home or over breakfast the next day, but nothing as dreadful as the hours she had spent shivering in the garage.

He might have locked her out just the same. He would have been so angry at her act of rebellion, as to him a simple show of independence would seem, that his reaction might have been no different. She would never know, now, but she had been very stupid not to think of a way of getting back into the house that did not depend on luck.

She would never dare to baby-sit again.

She had been sitting there in the darkness, gazing out at the street, for a long time when she heard the front door open and close and a few minutes later Walter drove away in the car.

Where had he gone? She used to wonder if on his night trips he visited The Grapes, met the regulars, but it was so unlikely. Walter never enjoyed any sort of social encounter, though he insisted they go to those to which they were invited and all the village fêtes. He would talk grimly to people he thought important, at the same time watching her so that later he could criticise her behaviour.

While he was out she had a chance to do something about the dining-room, perhaps save the table from permanent damage.

She was still dressed, and she hurried downstairs. She could lock Walter out now, she thought, put the chain up, ram home the bolts. What would he do then, when he came home?

Tempting though it was, she rejected the idea and concentrated on what she intended to do. The mess was not as bad as she expected because the smashed plates and dishes had been empty and there were only smears of sauce on the table, cool and congealed by this time. Walter had left nothing intact to wash up, only the cutlery. Would he give her the money to buy more?

She was too tired to worry about that now. She washed the knives, forks and spoons and put them away, swept up the broken glass and china—luckily he had finished his glass of mineral water, and the bottle from which it was poured had been made of plastic; it was tightly screwed up and he had left it untouched on the sideboard.

She seized her chance to use the bathroom while he was still out, and when at last he came home she was asleep. He made sure of waking her up, banging the front door loudly. It was four o'clock in the morning.

Breakfast was silent.

Surprisingly, Hermione had slept soundly after Walter had stopped crashing about. He had thumped around in the kitchen, and had been noisy in the bathroom, but at last he had given up and, she assumed, gone to bed. Even in his anger he must need some sleep.

She expected to find more chaos in the morning and it was a relief to discover that all was orderly, except for a frying pan on the cooker and a plate, knife and fork with egg and grease stains on them by the sink.

How extraordinary! He had cooked a meal when he came back! But he had already eaten a substantial dinner. She had never known him cook before, not even to make a cup of tea if she was unwell. He had used the bacon she would have cooked for his breakfast, and two eggs. Several slices of bread had gone from the loaf; he'd fried it, she saw. Her careful allocation of supplies was now upset and she would have to buy some more.

She did not care. She had some money. With that, little though it was, came liberation from her constant nagging worry about balancing the books. If only she had thought of this solution sooner! There was always domestic work to be had, and it was peaceful in someone else's house where there was no fear of enemy attack. That was how she thought of Walter now: as the enemy.

She felt a sudden surge of power, a recognition that she

would one day summon enough strength to find a way to freedom. Other women did; there were several in Merbury who were in the course of second marriages and a few who had separated from their partners. But if she managed to break free, how would she ever start a new life on her own?

I'm not fit to take care of myself, she thought, grilling tomatoes and putting eggs in a bowl ready to scramble. So many eggs couldn't be good for Walter; only two or three a week were recommended. Well, let him eat himself to death.

Once again she did not eat with him, going upstairs to make his bed while he had breakfast. Would he yell at her to come downstairs? Would he complain about the lack of bacon on his plate?

Her heart was pounding away as she pulled the bottom sheet taut, tucked in the top sheet and the blankets. None of them had ever had a duvet; the expense was not justified for the girls, Walter had said, and he would never use one. Hermione was glad of that; it had been difficult enough to keep some space between them in the bed as it was; a duvet would have made it harder. It wasn't easy to sleep in a room with another person when you were used to your own. Being alone in Jane's room was wonderful; whatever Walter was doing somewhere else in the house, however cruel he had been, she had made that place her sanctuary.

She listened for his voice but there was silence; he must have decided not to make an issue about her presence at breakfast, and that was a small victory in itself, but it was unnerving. He would find a way of getting back at her in the end.

She locked herself in her room, sitting quietly on her bed to wait till he left the house. She was getting quite good at dodging him, she thought, briefly forgetting her cold dark night in the garage.

Today she must shop, prepare for the weekend. How would they survive two whole days when Walter would be at home? She remembered that the Girl Guides were holding a jumble sale tomorrow. She could ring up their leader and offer to help. She was sure an extra pair of hands would be welcome, and Walter could not object when he was so eager for her to take part in any village activity which would reflect creditably on the family and therefore on him.

As far as she knew he had no plans; there was no note on the diary beside the telephone, but he often went out and did not say where he was going.

He could easily have another woman, she thought, and she, Hermione, would never know. It would account for his late nights and might explain his impotence. The possibility gave her an extraordinary feeling of hope. If they wanted to marry, Walter would seek a divorce! How wonderful that would be! This happy fantasy kept her going through the morning until she caught the bus to Freston for the weekend shopping.

She might meet someone she knew who would give her a lift home so that she would not have to struggle with her heavy bags from the bus stop. Helen Mountford went in on Fridays and had brought her back several times. Hermione decided to look out for her as she went round the supermarket.

Strangely cheerful, sure that she had solved the puzzle of Walter's late hours, Hermione set out on her expedition.

That morning, Walter was punctual arriving at the office, and he was in a better mood than for some weeks. He even commended Philip for his efficient tidying of the office files.

"Must be in love," said Philip, grinning at Belinda when Walter thanked him for bringing in his mid-morning cup of coffee and one digestive biscuit.

"Got his dental treatment finished, more likely," said Belinda. "Toothache would make a saint swear."

At lunchtime Walter astonished her and Rosemary by asking them if they would care to accompany him to Le Bistro down the road, where he planned to eat.

"You sometimes go there, I believe," he said.

Both declined, saying they had shopping to do, though in fact they had other plans.

"Was he going to treat us?" asked Belinda as they walked away, stifling their laughter.

"Never. He just wanted our company to demonstrate his new mashers," said Rosemary.

"He's got no new mashers," said Rosemary. "He's already got almost a full set. I guess it was his last remaining molar, anchorage of his plate, which was infected. Now it's been saved."

"How do you know all this about his teeth?" asked Belinda, intrigued.

"It's my artistic eye," said Rosemary. "When he bares his teeth at you, they're too perfect. He shows a lot of gum. I can tell."

Belinda was laughing at Rosemary's description of Walter's grimace when he may have meant to smile.

"Wonder if he ever unbends," she said, and they spent some minutes suggesting possible occasions.

Walter almost always went out to lunch, only rarely, when work had accumulated, sending Philip out for sandwiches. There were several cafés and small restaurants in the neighbourhood, some rather down market, and Rosemary and Belinda had been surprised to find Walter in one of these on a day when they were treating themselves to toasted sandwiches and coffee. They both thought he would prefer slick salad bars like Ann's Pantry.

"Too chilly for him. He likes roast meat and two veg.," said Philip, to whom they mentioned this. "I've seen him settling down to bangers and mash and shepherd's pie."

"Not together?"

"No!"

The two women had discovered it was Philip's birthday and were treating him to spaghetti Bolognese at the nearby Trattoria Fiesole.

"Why doesn't he go to the Hen and Chickens?" wondered Belinda.

"I can't imagine. Maybe he's teetotal," Philip said. "He never comes in here. Doesn't like what he calls messed up foreign food."

"You're an observant infant, aren't you?" remarked Belinda.

"I try to be," said Philip modestly. "I'll need my wits about me in the big wide world, won't I, when I've left you two and your gentle guidance?"

"We'll miss you," said Rosemary. "You cheer us up."

"These are happy days," said Philip, who, though speaking flippantly, meant what he said. "My carefree youth and all that."

The evening paper, out on the street when they walked back to the office, had a piece on the front page, jostling for space alongside news of a city scandal, reporting the discovery of a woman's body in a ditch. Belinda bought the paper and, back at her desk, read the item aloud. A motorist who had stopped at a lay-by on the A1 had seen a pale object among undergrowth below the embankment where he had parked. He had investigated and had found the corpse. What he had seen was her naked leg. Few further details were released; her identity was not yet known, nor the manner of her death, but the police were treating it as suspicious.

Walter returned to the office as Belinda read out a description of the dead woman's clothes; she had been wearing a short leather skirt and patterned tights, and one high heeled shoe, small size, had been seen by the journalist.

"Dreadful," said Belinda, folding up the paper. "Probably a hitchhiker. What a shock for her family when they hear what's happened to her."

"She was a prostitute," said Walter. "Dressed as you describe, she must have been. Short skirt, fancy tights, high heels, didn't you say?"

"Well, Walter, that's a bit sweeping, isn't it?" said Rosemary. "Lots of girls wear short skirts and high heels and aren't on the game."

"She meant to be provocative," said Walter. "She knew the risks she ran." He looked pointedly up at the clock on the wall and stalked into his own small cubicle. The others glanced at one another and Belinda folded up the paper.

"There was a prostitute killed about a month ago," said Rosemary. "There could be a connection, if Walter's right."

"She wasn't ripped up," Philip said. "Wasn't she strangled with her hair, or something?"

"I wasn't thinking of Jack the Ripper," said Rosemary. "Just of someone with a habit."

"I wonder if this one had long hair too," said Philip.

Belinda gave herself a shake.

"Look at us all, horribly intrigued by something dreadful," she said. "We ought to be ashamed."

"We're shocked," said Rosemary. "Shocked that somewhere outside these windows there's so much evil, men who can do such things."

She bent over her work, unwilling to prolong the talk, aware that Walter, if he heard them still discussing the murder, might come out and wear his disappointed frown as he suggested it was time they got on with all the tasks that waited for them.

Walter, however, had put the whole thing out of his mind as he studied a graph representing the rising needs of the small medical team whose research they sought to finance. He heard the murmur of their voices, nothing more.

After work that evening, Walter returned to the house in Kensington, to which he had followed the woman from the train. Was she there now?

He loitered opposite. It was a pleasant house, built in a more spacious age and well maintained, with a cream painted exterior and a gleaming black front door reached by a short flight of steps. Many of the neighbouring houses had been converted into flats and a few were offices. Walter crossed the road and walked slowly past the railings which separated the basement from the pavement. Glancing down, he could see a kitchen, brightly lit. The sink was beneath the window and its stainless steel gleamed. He walked past again to give it another approving glance. The house must be worth a great deal of money. He contemplated ringing the doorbell and carrying out the same ruse as he had used in Stappenford, declaring that he was collecting for the appeal. There was a big brass knocker, beautifully polished, on the door, and just one bell, so it was a single household. Perhaps it was some sort of clinic; he had decided that she must work on a shift system, and it was possible that she was a nurse. Would a nurse have remained so impassive during the verbal assault by the louts, the first time he had seen her? Who else worked odd hours, in a dignified building like this?

He moved away up the street, then walked back, and as he drew near again, the front door opened and, in a pool of light, a man emerged. As he did so, sounds of music issued with him, a male voice singing and the notes of a piano, and then the door, closing, cut it off. Music meant nothing to Walter; he simply noticed that this did not sound like the radio.

He waited outside for another ten minutes but no one else arrived or left. It was very cold, and at last, still baffled, he abandoned his vigil. There would be another time, another night.

He was not worried because his second victim, the girl he had strangled instead of Hermione, had been found so soon. He had picked her up in the car and had driven her to a quiet street, killing her quickly after their hurried coupling on the back seat. She had been terrified in the brief minutes before he choked out her life, and that had made him feel wonderful. He had covered her with the rug from the boot and driven northwards, dumping her where she had been found.

When he reached home, he had been ravenously hungry, so he cooked himself eggs and bacon, making a lot of noise in the house to ensure that Hermione was disturbed. His only regret was that she had not been his victim, but her turn would come and she would suffer first, understand her fate.

Unless he were suspected of the murders, and that new test done on his blood, who would ever consider Walter Brown, charitable worker and pillar of his village community, a person worth investigating? He would keep away from prostitutes until the immediate hue and cry had died down. He might not need another, once he had put paid to Hermione and when he had got past the defences of the woman on the train.

16

Going home in the train, Walter looked at the evening paper, ignoring the report on the murder which had so intrigued Belinda and Rosemary. If only they knew, he had thought, for an instant wanting to wipe out the smooth expressions of superficial concern on their faces and replace their detached interest with terror.

He studied the financial reports, then put the paper away to consider the various ways by which he could rid himself of the encumbrance of his wife.

People in the village realised that she was inadequate and immature—almost, he thought, a case of arrested development. A fatal accident or suicide would not come as a great surprise to those who knew her, and he could easily recount tales of past incompetence to explain whatever had happened, pretend he had loyally covered up for her all this time by making good her deficiencies.

Repeating Wednesday night's incident with the car seemed to Walter to be the best method to use. Then he could say that it had happened before but that he had found her in time to save her, and naturally had not told anyone about her attempt on her own life. He would not have to lure her into the car; he could use some sort of sedative to make her fall asleep, then, in darkness, carry her out and put her in place. There was no need for all the rigmarole with hosepipes connected to the exhaust; once she was shut in, with the engine running and the car windows open, it would soon be over. What more likely than that she should take pills herself to hasten the process?

Would aspirin do, or codeine? Which was stronger? Walter did not believe in drugs and had never, in his adult life, swallowed as much as one aspirin, though sometimes, and especially lately, he had had severe headaches.

He knew there was Anadin in the bathroom cupboard. Hermione and the girls had various aches and pains from time to time and such remedies had to be paid for in the interests of keeping them on their feet. Living was certainly cheaper now without the girls. He had not forgiven Sarah for costing him so much money; indeed, he would forgive neither of them for their ingratitude. Walter had not read or seen *King Lear*, but his emotions were similar to those of the angry monarch who railed against Cordelia. If Hermione heard from them, as he suspected, he did not want to know. They had had their chance; both could have continued their education. He would have been gratified if he could refer to his daughters at college. He had never foreseen their rebellion, and to think that his own daughter was a common thief—well, it was intolerable. Of course, Sarah might not be his daughter; Hermione could have betrayed him. But even Walter was brought up short at that, remembering what had happened when Jane was only a few weeks old, with Hermione protesting that it was too soon and that it hurt, that she would be damaged.

She had never been the same again. After Sarah's birth the sequence of miscarriages had begun, and the long years of Hermione walking about like a pale, reproachful ghost, with her brown hair, which reached below her shoulder blades, in a knot at the nape of her neck. He had liked to take hold of it, jerk back her head. Then, one day, she had cut it off and ever since then her hair had been short, trimmed in a jagged untidy bob. He had refused her money to spend at a hairdresser having it styled. He liked long hair and had told her to grow it again. That had been her first defiance.

What was going on? Why was she behaving like this? What had happened to make her so undisciplined, daring to take the car without permission and shutting herself up in Jane's room?

Her conduct was intolerable.

Adding up in his mind her various shortcomings, Walter gave no thought to the skinny, harmless girl, younger than Sarah, whom he had deprived of life and left in a ditch as carelessly as if she were a spent cigarette or some old shoe.

He would never be suspected of her death, nor that of the other woman whom he had dumped behind a hoarding near an empty warehouse.

There would be another death, and soon, but this time it would not look like murder.

While in Freston that morning, Hermione had bought some material to make Jane a skirt, red corduroy with a pattern of small flowers. By the time Walter came home, she had cut it out and was well on with putting it together—not difficult, since it was simply gathered into a waistband and hemmed, but she had included a pocket in the seam.

Although she still felt very tired, she had a curious sense of elation because she had avoided a confrontation with Walter both the previous evening and this morning. She sat up in her room, as she now thought of Jane's former bedroom, working at the sewing machine which she had kept there since Jane left, balancing it on a piece of old blanket on rather a nice table which had been in her old home and which Jane had used as a desk.

She had decided to go and see Jane the following week, and she must plan her excursion carefully without making a silly mistake which would give Walter more grounds for finding fault. If Jane seemed happy and well, it would help Hermione decide what to do about her own future, for with every day that passed she felt less able to continue living in this atmosphere of fear. She would find a way to earn a living. Sarah had secured a post as a nanny without any training and at the age of only eighteen. Hermione would not choose to look after children herself, but she could be somebody's housekeeper, and why not abroad? She ought to see a bit of the world. By the time she was ready to break away, Theresa Cowper and the Wilsons might be willing to act as references. Sarah had obtained character references from school and from the vicar; they wouldn't have recommended her if they had known of her theft. Hermione, hearing about it from Walter, had been both horrified and admiring of Sarah's behaviour; she had gambled on her father covering up for her. Sarah had not yet paid back much of her debt to him; what did it matter if she never made it up? She had got away and was keeping herself, which was what mattered. A little courage was all that was needed, Hermione thought, and surely she could find enough to free herself?

She had made a fish pie for dinner. It would dry up if kept hot long, even in a low oven, but there was some extra sauce which could be poured over it if Walter was very late.

He was home by nine o'clock and was eating his meal at nine-fifteen, savouring the pie, with Brussels sprouts, and finishing what was left in the dish. He was greedy, thought Hermione, who had never noticed it before. There was raspberry fool next, made from frozen raspberries grown in the garden, with sponge finger biscuits and cream. Walter had beer with his meal, an indulgence he allowed himself on rare occasions though they never had wine. Hermione was not encouraged to drink.

Hermione had fixed a small mirror on the wall by the sink, one from a handbag, secured with Blutack. It would give her some warning—not much, but a little—if he were to creep quietly up behind her, intending to use his superior strength to make her do as he wished. She had made up her mind that he would never touch her again.

Hermione did not lay a place for herself at the breakfast table the next morning. She came down before Walter stirred and had toast and coffee in the kitchen; the Girl Guides' sale would be her excuse for an early start to the day.

But he did not ask her for one. When he came downstairs, she made his tea and set it before him, with kippers, which was what he always wanted on Saturdays though he would not eat them on a working day; he said they tended to repeat. She poured him out a cup of tea and left the room. The sale did not start until two, but jumble was being assembled and sorted all morning and she could be useful then as well as later. She would take sandwiches so that she need not come home, and would leave Walter a cold meal. If he complained, and he probably would, she would let it wash over her as of no importance. She had resolved that although she was still very frightened of Walter, she would not let him bully her into a state of hysterical submission ever again. Bullies need victims, she told herself, and I won't be one any longer.

To avoid that fate, she must keep out of his way. By evening, when she would have to come back, it might be difficult to dodge him, and it would be dark, when hostile scenes were more alarming than during daylight hours. She went upstairs to make the beds and clean the bathroom, then came down again hoping that Walter would have finished his breakfast. If he hadn't, she would call out that she was off to the sale and would clear up when she came back. Screwing herself up to utter the words, she went into the dining-room, to find he had gone.

He was in his study, the door closed. He would be sitting at her father's desk doing his accounts or sorting his papers, whatever he did in there.

She sighed with relief. He must never be disturbed when

he was in the study; he had made that clear years ago. She loaded a tray with the things from the table, wrinkling her nose at the smell of kippers, which she had once liked but had gone off during her first pregnancy when Walter had insisted on her cooking them every week, although they made her feel sick.

She put out a plate of ham, with sliced tomatoes, beetroot and potato salad, and a bowl with some of the raspberry fool left from the previous night, covered them over, and wrote a note which she stuck to the cloakroom door with Blutack. He would be sure to go in there during the morning and so could not fail to see it.

Just as she did this, he came out of the study and saw her in her raincoat.

"Where are you going?" he asked, glaring at her.

"To the Guides' jumble sale. I've promised to help," she said.

He had forgotten that it was to be held today.

"You're going nowhere until you've prepared my lunch," he said.

"It's ready," she told him. "It's in the dining-room." Now her courage began to falter and she started to tremble. Movement would help. "I'd left you a note, as you were busy," she began to explain, and pulled it off the door.

"Give it to me," he said, holding out his hand.

"You don't need it, now we've spoken," she said.

"I told you to give it to me," he repeated.

She handed it over and turned away. She would go, quickly, before he thought of another excuse to delay her.

Walter was left holding the sheet of lined paper with the message in Hermione's rounded childish hand. He had almost no examples of her handwriting because they were never apart and her accounts were the only things she wrote for him.

How could he use this? He could trace the words, copy them carefully, compose a suicide note which he would then declare to be in her writing. No one would challenge his statement, and if they did, the likeness would be almost exact.

I have to go out, she had written. *It's the Guides' sale. Lunch is in the dining-room. Hermione.*

How could he change it?

I have to go. It's my fault. Forgive me. Something like that. There were no Fs in her note but perhaps in her household accounts there would be some to copy, flour, for instance, and fish.

When Walter had paid a visit to the cloakroom, he returned to the study and to his plans, copying her message, practising her signature. After a while he put his various efforts and her original in an envelope and sealed it, placing it in a file under the miscellaneous heading. Then he opened the locked bottom drawer of her father's desk and took out the magazines he kept there for his solitary enjoyment.

Dinner was eaten in silence that night. Weeks ago, Hermione would have attempted to tell Walter about the sale, and its success or otherwise, then waited for his scathing comments on her statements. Now she made no such effort.

When the meal was over, he went out in the car. He drove to Stappenford and parked outside the house where the elderly man in the cardigan lived, to which he had trailed the long-haired woman from the train. Lights were on in the house, and he walked up the path and rang the bell. He heard it echo inside the house, but no one came to the door. He rang again, pressing the button down, hearing the shrill sound, so loud that it must be heard if anyone were at home. To make certain, he walked round to the back of the house where there was a solid door, painted green, and as he approached, a halogen light came on, flooding him in a fierce white blaze.

They were very security conscious, he thought, leaving lights on to indicate that someone was in, and with an effective intruder deterrent at the rear. He approved.

They'd come home in the end. He went back to the car to wait.

17

On Sunday morning Walter decided to work in the garden after church, which was at half-past ten. The weather had grown slightly warmer but it was fresh and crisp outside as he swept up a few last leaves and inspected shrubs, deciding which should be pruned and when. Hermione was never involved in these decisions but she was expected to wheel the full barrow and empty it when he was mowing, and to weed.

They walked to church together, which meant Walter always striding in ahead of Hermione, something Helen Mountford had noticed years ago and now watched for; it was one thing if you were the Prince of Wales; then protocol might dictate precedence, but otherwise wives should be followed by their husbands. She watched Hermione trudge down the aisle behind him—early, because of his sidesman's duties, though before a service these were negligible as the church wardens, of whom Robert was one, dealt with most things. Helen was playing the organ today, deputising for the regular organist who had flu. From her seat, using the mirror which was needed for weddings and funerals so that the organist could observe the church door, she was able, as she improvised melodiously, to see what went on as people arrived. Yesterday at the Guides' sale, Helen had noticed Hermione's new, improved haircut. It made quite a difference to her appearance, and though she still looked pale and had the faint trace of bruising on her face, she seemed somehow more alert. A mild curiosity about her entered Helen's mind. She must miss her daughters. Perhaps she would like to come to lunch one day; there would be no need, then, to invite Walter.

Side by side the Browns occupied their pew and sang of blessings for which they must give praise. Side by side they prayed. After the service Hermione went home alone as Walter stayed behind to put away hymn books and hassocks. Robert Mountford locked the church; it could not be left open for fear of vandalism or theft.

Hermione had lunch to prepare, roast pork today, and steamed treacle pudding. She could spin out her tasks, ensuring that she stayed in the kitchen where Walter rarely came unless with the express intent of scolding her, or worse. When she saw him go down the garden she relaxed. He often washed the car on Sundays, but as it was so cold, she thought he would leave it for a week. He never told her to wash it: she could not be trusted to do it properly.

How would he occupy himself today? Everything was tidy. She saw him light a small bonfire. In Merbury, people respected one another's comfort but Walter, on the question of fires, considered no one but himself and lit his whenever he chose, even when Hermione had washing on the line. However, this morning there was no wind; no one could object.

He came in for lunch and the glass of sherry he drank every Sunday before the meal. He never offered Hermione one, and she had long ago given up noticing this or even thinking that she might enjoy some, though when they went on rare occasions to other houses in the village, she eagerly accepted wine or vermouth.

After lunch, Walter took the paper into the sitting-room and Hermione went upstairs. She had the portable radio there, a very old one that her father had given her after her mother's

death. It ran off batteries or the mains. Her library book was
a fat volume about a pioneering family in New South Wales.
She would be safe in her room, reading and listening to the
radio, until it was time for tea.

Downstairs, Walter read a short paragraph about the murdered prostitutes; by now the second victim had been identified. The two cases were thought to be linked. The first girl
had some children, it seemed. Fancy a mother going on the
game, thought Walter, rattling his paper; how obscene. He
read about proposed army cuts, which he deplored, and explor-
ations overseas, and eventually he slept. He had arrears to make
up.

Hermione came downstairs at four-fifteen. If afternoon
tea—scones with butter and home-made jam, and cake—was
not brought in punctually at four-thirty on Sunday afternoons,
Walter would complain and scold, might even rant around
and damage something.

When she wheeled in the tea trolley he was asleep with the
paper lying across his chest, his half-glasses still on his nose.
He started up as soon as the sound of the trolley penetrated
his subconscious and at once looked at his watch, ready to
comment if she were even a minute late, but he did not snap
back into alertness and he did not remove his glasses. He was
so vain that he tried never to wear them in front of other
people, even her. She supposed he must have to let his office
colleagues see them.

He drank three cups of tea—one more than usual—and ate
a scone and a slice of Victoria sponge. Then he went out in
the car.

He must have got a mistress. Surely it was the only explanation
for all these expeditions in the dark. Hermione automatically
plumped up the cushions on the chair he had just left and
almost smiled. Outsiders would say he had been driven to it
by her conduct, but so what? The mistress was welcome to

him. Maybe he would want to marry her; that would be a wonderful solution.

But he did not approve of divorce and remarriage. People made their beds and must lie in them, he often said, using those very words; standards must be maintained and examples set. But what sort of example did Walter think he set, with his overbearing ways and his unkindness? Perhaps he was nicer to the mistress, who might be poised and elegant. Maybe she was better at sex, too; she must be, otherwise what was in it for her? Well, wherever Walter was, at least it meant that Hermione could breathe calmly for a while—till supper time, at least. He might come back then.

On impulse, she went into the study to see what Walter had been doing. Occasionally, though very rarely, he left papers out if he intended to work on them again that day. This was not so now; everything was neat, the desk that had been her father's was closed. She opened the flap. Inside, each pigeon-hole had its appointed contents, envelopes and writing paper, an address book. She pulled this out and looked at it; it contained very few entries, but beside some names was a big letter C in red. She knew what that meant; it was his Christmas card indication. Walter always wrote their cards, not trusting her selection or her competence. The various chosen names covered anyone who lived in a large house in the village and his fellow members of the committees on which he sat, people whom he might consider in some way influential. She was familiar enough with this list since it was her annual duty to deliver the envelopes round the village. His snobbery was ridiculous, she saw, and in the same instant realised that he was a failure. He had not been able to follow the career he wanted in the army, and he had held only minor posts since then. His present work was useful and worthwhile; there was no doubt about that; but anyone with a head for figures could have done it.

Walter would never be the head of a big firm, nor own a

mansion, nor hobnob on equal terms with people he thought important.

Hermione put the address book away and closed the desk; then, almost without thinking, she tried the drawers. She had never done this before; Hermione did not pry.

She saw ledgers, files, spare stationery, but the bottom drawer was locked.

Where was the key? It was not in the lid, nor, she soon saw, in any of the small interior drawers. Why had he locked that particular one? What was so secret? He knew she did not poke about among his things.

She pulled out the drawer above the locked one and set it on the floor. It was heavy, but she managed it. Now the next drawer's contents were revealed. There were several large manila files inside. She lifted one, and underneath it saw the magazines. Slowly, incredulously, Hermione took one out and opened it.

Once she had understood exactly what they were, had gazed in shocked dismay at the explicit photographs inside, her one thought was to restore them before Walter could come back and catch her looking at his private library. One of the files caught against the drawer she had to replace, but she managed to restore everything as it had been before. With her sweater sleeve she rubbed at the front of the desk in case she had left it smeared by her hands, now hot and sticky. She could not wait to get out of the room, away from those revolting images.

Outside the study door she stood panting, breathless with the shock of her discovery and filled with anger at this desecration of what had been her father's property. How could Walter enjoy looking at such things and how dared he store them in her father's desk? He must be sick, mad, or both. She felt soiled herself, just by looking at them fleetingly, and on impulse went up to the bathroom to collect the dirty washing. She could do it now, and save some Monday chores.

She piled all Walter's soiled garments in the machine; none of hers were in the bin. Lately she had felt unable to wash her things with his; she did them separately. Now she tossed in a splash of Dettol with the wash; everything he touched or wore was contaminated and needed disinfecting.

With the machine turned on, she went outside, into the garden, and stood breathing in the cold, raw air. It was a damp night, not freezing, and there was no wind. Clouds hid the stars. She thought of Jane and Sarah, embarked alone on life, and knew that each was better able to steer her course than she had been at the same age. They had each other, she thought, even if she had failed them both and could not help them in the future.

She was too distressed now to cry, and at last the cold drove her back indoors, into the sitting-room where the fire—a gas one resembling coals installed by the previous owners—was still burning. She felt shivery though the room was warm, and pulled her chair up to the fire, huddling there, her mind a blank. She prayed that Walter would not return till late; how could she look at him, after what she had seen?

Eventually she felt calmer, and went to make herself a cup of tea, only being deflected as she passed the dining-room by thinking that sherry might be nicer.

The fruity taste of Harvey's Amontillado warmed her in an amazing way. She refilled her glass and sipped it by the fire. Then her glance fell on the paper which Walter had left on the coffee table, and, to distract her mind, she picked it up. The world news was depressing; politicians seemed to spend their time and energy fighting each other instead of setting things to rights, and there seemed always to be small wars. Hermione skipped this dispiriting stuff and, on an inner page, saw the report of a murder. The death was compared with an earlier one because both victims' long hair had been twined round their necks after they were strangled.

It was horrible. Hermione remembered how, when her own

hair was long, Walter had wound it round her neck, pulling it tight, once almost choking her, but that had been an accident, of course. Men liked long hair. In novels there were descriptions of women with their hair spread like sheets of silk on pillows, and you saw girls on television with billowing manes teased into styles which made them look top heavy. Theresa Cowper's was like that. Both Jane and Sarah now had short hair; Walter used to tweak their plaits when they wore it long and they had soon decided that short hair would be easier to manage. They had never grown it again.

He had hurt them, obviously; Hermione had known it at the time, though it was never discussed. She had taken them to a hairdresser and added the cost to her accounts; Walter had not queried the expense except to say that a woman's hair was her crowning glory and they had made a serious mistake.

She watched *Songs of Praise* and then went to get supper; a cold fish mousse made from the same mixture as the fish pie, with tomato salad and baked potatoes. If Walter wanted more, he could have cheese or fruit, or both.

He did not come home. She left the meal waiting, with the potato shrivelling in a low oven and a note by Walter's plate telling him where to find it.

Hermione was not hungry. At nine o'clock she had a cup of soup, with some bread, and then she went to bed.

Walter's vigil on Saturday night had, in the end, given him a result, though not the one he wanted. Eventually, the elderly man who lived in the house outside which he waited had returned, and with him was the woman from the train. They had stepped out of a taxi together, some time after midnight. The woman had walked up the short drive and opened the door while the man paid off the cab; then they had entered the house and were briefly illuminated by the light from the hall. The watcher saw them talking and smiling. He stayed in the car and waited while a cold understanding chilled him as he saw the downstairs lights go out and another come on in the upstairs bay window. She was his wife, the woman listed on the electoral roll as Valerie Palmer, not a daughter, a friend, a niece. She had married that old man who must be thirty years older than she was; he was balding and had a paunch, while she was at her peak of beauty and desirability.

The discovery made Walter feel as much betrayed as if he were her lover whom she had cuckolded. In his mind he had formed a relationship with her, assuring himself that it would become fact as soon as he had overcome her irrational rejection of his approaches. Perseverance on his part was all that was needed; she would see what sort of a man he was—experienced and in control, able to care for and protect the woman he chose to benefit in such a manner.

His disappointment pierced Walter in a way few other setbacks in his life had done, and there was no one to lash out at and to blame. Before, he could hurl abuse at Hermione, imply that with a more presentable wife, promotion, not redundancy, would have been his experience. Now, the one he wanted to punish was inside the house where she lived with her ageing husband.

He went home at last, but on Sunday, after tea, unable to endure remaining in the house with Hermione's silent presence in her room upstairs, or flitting round, keeping out of range, he went out again and drove to Stappenford.

Valerie Palmer, singing the soprano solo in Vaughan Williams' setting of *O Taste and See*, from Psalm XXXIV, and accompanied at the organ by Patrick Porter, choirmaster at St. Bartholomew's, had noticed the man sitting behind her husband. As she resumed her seat after her solo performance, she glanced at him again; where had she seen him before? He was a little taller than George; she saw grey hair. Though she could not place him, a vague disquiet seemed connected with him.

After the service, George waited for her by the door, while

the vicar stood in the porch speaking to the departing flock and receiving congratulations on the music, always good at St. Bartholomew's but especially so tonight. People wanted to tell Valerie how much they had enjoyed her singing, and it was a little while before they could escape. Valerie did not notice that, as they walked home, they were followed, but when she went upstairs to put away her coat and change into other shoes, for some reason she drew back the bedroom curtain and looked out.

A car was parked on the far side of the road and, because the street was quite well lit, she could see that someone was sitting in the driver's seat. She knew very little about cars; it was a medium-sized saloon, dark red or black, she thought. She let the curtain fall, frowning.

Later still, at bedtime, the car, with the man inside it— she was sure it was a man—was still there.

In the night she woke up, suddenly remembering who the man in church was: the persistent, tiresome man who had tried to apologise for not helping her the night she had been harassed by louts on the train. She knew she had been rude to him when he pursued her from the station, but he had been almost as annoying as the yobs.

She thought she had seen him recently, in London, near the house in Kensington where she rehearsed with a quartet who gave concerts and occasional broadcasts; she also sang with a London choir and it was after their performances that she travelled home on a late train.

Until her marriage two years ago, she had lived in Pimlico. She had met George on a music-lovers' holiday in Italy. He was a widower, a civil servant working for the council and near retirement. He did not want to move to London and she had made the adjustment, travelling back and forth several times a week as, apart from her singing, she taught music part-time at a school not far from the house where her group met to rehearse. The scene on the late train had been her first bad experience of that kind. She had not known how to deal with it and had decided that ignoring it was the best method; reacting might prove provocative. However, she had felt that the other passengers, and especially the men, had acted cravenly during the verbal assault. It had been a relief to her when her tormentors stayed on the train after she got off. If they had followed her, she would have been very frightened.

She had said nothing to George about the incident. He did not like her travelling alone late at night and usually went with her when she was singing at an evening concert, but on that occasion he had had a bad cold and had stayed at home.

She was content with him. He was kind and gentle, and he made her feel secure. When he retired next year, they were going to move to somewhere with a large garden, set apart from neighbours, where she could have her grand piano which was now in store, and where they could enjoy musical evenings together. He played the clarinet, not very well, but with time and practice he might yet improve.

On Monday morning the watcher in the car had gone. She wondered what to do about it, whether to tell the police. It seemed weird. But if she reported it, George would have to know, and that might make him worry. She did nothing.

18

An hour after Walter left on Monday morning, Hermione set off to cycle to the station. She had done the washing the night before and this morning she had simply washed up and made Walter's and her own beds. The rest could wait. She was going to see Jane.

The station was quiet now, between trains, and she put her bike in the rack, chaining it up. Then she walked along the rows of parked cars till she came to Walter's Maestro. There it sat, its nose to the hedge separating the parking area from the gardens of some houses beyond the station yard. There was no attendant, no one to see her as she unlocked the car with the spare key, got in and drove off.

She couldn't have done this before, even if she had thought of it, because she could not have afforded to pay for the petrol she must put in the tank to replace what she used, so that Walter would not find out what she had done. She hoped he had not noticed the mileage on the clock; he had been out so often late at night himself that perhaps he would be less observant now about such details than in the past.

The tank was well down, which was unusual. He must have driven a long way in the night and perhaps found few pumps open, as it was Sunday. His rule was to fill up as soon as the gauge reached the half-way mark. She stopped at the first pump she saw and put in five pounds' worth; it might be enough to take her to Reading and back; if not, she would stop again, being careful not to go over the low indication showing when she took the car. Walter must be expecting to fill up when he came home, even though it meant making a detour as there was no pump between Merbury and Freston station.

Would he visit his mistress again tonight? Hermione wondered what she was like: was she young and pretty—a bimbo? It was difficult to imagine him with such a girl, but she had been very young when he married her; an older and more experienced woman would, she saw now, have been too much of a challenge and he would have been alarmed lest he could not control her. Walter had to be in charge.

After a while she put him out of her mind to concentrate on the journey. Would Jane be at the squat when she got there? She might be working now. Still, she could deliver the new skirt for her, and leave a message.

The road was clearly signed. She had come this way from time to time when the girls were young; the shops were good and Walter had approved expeditions to buy their clothes. Now she found a major road improvement scheme in progress and there were delays at traffic lights, but eventually she reached the outskirts of the big sprawling town, crossing under the railway bridge and going past the prison. Poor Oscar Wilde, she thought, incarcerated there; what a dreadful fate.

She had consulted a street map, and with some difficulty she eventually located the road where Jane was living. There was a sale board attached to the gate post of the house; that meant Jane and her fellow squatters would have to move. Or did it? Was that why they had been able to appropriate the house? It seemed rather dreadful. How could it be sold while they were there?

There were no curtains at the ground floor windows, which were dirty. Hermione pressed the bell push but could not hear it ring so she thumped the big knocker, painted black but, like the railings separating the house from the pavement, rusted.

Nothing happened, and after a while she knocked again, with more determination. Soon she heard the sound of footsteps on bare boards. Bolts were drawn, the door was opened a few inches on a chain, and she looked into the questioning face of an unknown young woman with red curly hair.

"Jane Brown. Is she in? I'm her mother," said Hermione in an anxious tone, and her pale face flushed as she regarded the stranger.

"You're like her," said the young woman. "She's out, but come in. I don't think she'll be long." She unhooked the chain and opened the door. Hermione entered the hall, which was quite bare except for tea chests which were upturned and on which were piled papers and print-outs of various kinds. The wallpaper was peeling, and the place was very cold. The young woman locked the door behind Hermione. "Can't be too careful," she said, and Hermione, looking at her as she turned back, saw that she was heavily pregnant. "Come into my parlour and I'll make us both some tea," said the girl.

Hermione followed her into a room at the back of the house. The walls had been painted white; in one corner there was a mattress covered with a duvet in a dark cover. A threadbare curtain, too short, hung at the single window, which was clean. The floor boards were swept and had been stained. An electric kettle stood in the fireplace, and on a tea chest were two mugs and a bottle of milk.

"Sit down," said her hostess. "I'm Mandy, by the way."

"I'm Hermione."

"Gave your girls plain names, didn't you, when you've got such a grand one," said Mandy, plugging in the kettle. "It's only just boiled," she added. "I was going to have a cup myself, as it happens."

"That's why," said Hermione. "Why they had short ordinary names," she enlarged. "Because mine was more difficult."

"The Winter's Tale," said Mandy, surprising Hermione, who
had been named after the daughter of Menelaus. "A much
wronged woman," went on Mandy.

"Yes," agreed Hermione. She watched while Mandy made
the tea, with a bag, in the mugs. "How many of you are there
here?" she asked.

"Eleven at present," said Mandy. "Mostly in couples. It
varies from time to time. We don't all have rooms to ourselves," and she laughed.

"But your baby—you can't—" Hermione stopped.

"Where else can we go?" asked Mandy. "We can't find
anywhere to live. I'll probably get a flat when the baby's
born—you do—the council's obliged to house you—but I'll
wait and see. I like it here. Of course, we may be evicted
before then." She sounded quite cheerful about it. "We're not
breaking the law," she said. "We've done no damage. Funny,
isn't it? You can take over someone's house and they can have
problems about getting you out. But usually we go quietly, if
they want it, and move on. There's always somewhere else."

"But it's not yours," said Hermione.

"We've changed the locks and got keys. We take care of
it," said Mandy. "I've painted this room. Nice, isn't it? I've
only been here three weeks, and I'm thankful, I can tell you.
It's good here. I'm not in a couple," she added. "My bloke
took off when he found out about the baby. Doesn't like kids.
He'd left his wife because she'd got three of her own by her
first husband and he couldn't take it. But he was decent
enough. Gave me some money. The kid should be fine. I want
it," she said. "By the way, do you take sugar? Sorry, I should
have asked. I haven't got any but someone else will have. We
muck in together and we all use the kitchen, but it's handy to
have some of your own things."

"I don't take sugar, thanks," said Hermione. She took a sip
from her mug. "It's good," she said. "I needed that." Then
she asked, "Jane's not pregnant, is she?"

"No. Or not to my knowledge," said Mandy. "She's a nice girl, Jane. Steve's all right, too."

"Steve?"

"Her boyfriend. Didn't you know? He's a paint salesman. Got a good job," said Mandy. "She's going to move in with him."

Hermione did not know whether or not to be pleased at this news.

"What about you?" she said. "Can't you go home to your parents?"

"Not really," said Mandy. "My mum's gone to live in California with a toy boy, and my dad's second wife is a cow. Wants him all to herself and their little nippers. They've got three, all under six."

"But even if the council does give you a flat—" Hermione's voice trailed off.

"They give you furniture, too," said Mandy. "It's all right, you know."

"But the baby will grow up—have to go to school—" Hermione wondered if a similar future lay in store for Jane, if her paint salesman didn't like children either.

"There are worse fates than having a single parent," Mandy told her. "I'll find work. There'll be something I can do. I'll put the nipper in a crèche or find a cosy minder for him. It'll be OK."

"How old are you?" Hermione asked faintly.

"Nineteen last week," said Mandy.

Hermione buried her nose in her tea. One day Mandy would find out all about maternal anxiety.

Hermione had been Mandy's guest for almost an hour before Jane returned. In that time she had learned a lot about Mandy's life and her separated parents who had no time for her. For a while there had been grandparents on both sides but now the two grandfathers and one grandmother were dead, and the surviving grandmother was in an old people's home where Mandy visited her when she had enough money for the travel involved.

"Jane and Sarah have no grandparents, either. They never have had," said Hermione, at which Mandy looked sad. Hers had always made her welcome, she said, and she felt their loss keenly.

"Your grandmother knows about the baby," said Hermione. "What does she think about it?"

"She said that sort of thing happened in her day, too, and often ended in a hasty wedding," Mandy answered. "She didn't recommend that. Said it was a desperate remedy leading to years of regret." She grinned at the memory of her small, shrunken grandmother whose cheeks had grown hollow with age and who walked with a stick, but whose hearing was acute and whose eyes still sparkled with delight when enjoying a racy conversation or a stimulating discussion.

"She was right," said Hermione.

"Why do people get married?" Mandy asked. "Why did you marry Jane's father, for instance?"

What a question!

"Because he asked me and I thought I was in love," Hermione heard herself say.

"And you weren't?"

"I was very young—about your age—and my father had just died," said Hermione. "I suppose I was excited and flattered." Why was she telling Mandy this? She had never discussed it with a soul before, not even Mrs. Fisher when admitting that Walter had hit her.

"It answered your problem of what to do next," said Mandy, who suspected that her own pregnancy fell into this category.

"Maybe." Hermione clasped her hands together and tried to look old and wise, but she was already sure that Mandy knew more about life and was wiser than she. "I thought you were the one with problems," she said.

"There had to be a reason why Jane left home," said Mandy.

"Yes," Hermione agreed. She looked down at the bare floor. Near her feet a long dark stain, ink or something similar, made a weird shape. How had it got there? When was it made?

"And Sarah," said Mandy.

"Their father can be difficult," Hermione confessed.

"How long are you staying?"

"Till Jane gets back—unless she's very late. I'll wait outside," said Hermione, rising. "I'm sorry, Mandy. You've been very kind. Thanks for the tea."

"I don't mean now," said Mandy. "Do sit down again, Hermione. I mean at home, where you live. With Jane's father. You're just a drudge, aren't you?" She spoke brutally. "Jane's very sorry for you. I wouldn't be surprised if they both thought that by clearing out, you'd have a chance to go too. You wouldn't have to hang on because of them. After all, you're not really old."

"I suppose not," said Hermione, and felt a wild impulse to laugh, but at the same time her eyes filled with tears.

"Things aren't like they were in my grandmother's day, you know," said Mandy sternly. "Women have rights. Everyone does, even Jasper here," and she patted her stomach.

"Jasper?" Hermione snatched at the diversion.

"I'm sure it's a boy, and if so, that's his name," said Mandy. "You mustn't mind me telling you what I think, Hermione, but strangers can speak their minds and Jane and I have had several long chats. She's nice. A bit lacking in confidence, but she'll be all right."

"So will you and Jasper," said Hermione. "You've got guts."

"And you think you haven't? You might surprise yourself," said Mandy. "You've come here today, haven't you? How did you manage that? Jane says he doesn't give you any money except for food and such."

"I took the car from the station," said Hermione. "Biked there and drove off, while he's at work in London."

As Mandy praised this show of initiative, they both broke into laughter, Hermione's of a near hysterical variety, and she was wiping her eyes, still trying to regain control, when Jane arrived.

She had seen the car in the road, recognising its number with disbelief, and had come rushing in, wondering what had happened.

"Mum! It's you," she cried, and hugged her mother warmly.

"Who else?" said Hermione, falsely bright.

"It might have been Dad, come to drag me back by the hair," said Jane.

"You haven't enough of it," said Mandy. Jane's hair was almost cropped.

"You've had a good cut at last, Mum," said Jane, now looking properly at her mother. "And you've lost weight."

"A bit," Hermione admitted.

"Where did you go for your hair?" Jane wondered if she had sold some more books to pay for its styling. She and Sarah, as beneficiaries, were both aware of her mother's small disposals to raise funds.

Should she tell them?

"Oh, to a little man I know of," said Hermione, deciding that she could not confide in the girls.

"Mm, how mysterious," said Mandy.

Hermione produced her parcel.

"It's for Christmas, a bit early," she said. "I suppose you won't be coming home?"

"I'm going to Steve's," said Jane. "Sorry, mum. His parents have asked us. I'm moving out of here on Saturday, into his place. Maybe we could meet you somewhere, when we're settled. I'll phone."

"I'd like that," said Hermione, but she looked anxious.

"Don't worry, I'll pick a safe time, like I always do," said Jane. "If I get it wrong and Dad answers, I'll hang up, and if you answer but he's there and you can't talk, you can pretend it's a wrong number. I'll understand. Steve's got a nice flat. I'll be fine. We're not getting married," she added. "Nothing like that."

Neither she nor Sarah would ever trust marriage, thought Hermione.

"I've got a new job," Jane went on. "In a shop selling toiletries. What a word," and she giggled. "I start there on Monday."

"Well done," said Hermione. Jane's last shop job had been stacking shelves in a supermarket.

"What do you think your mum did?" said Mandy. "Nicked the car and drove over."

"Did you really, Mum?" asked Jane, astonished.

"I borrowed it from the station," said Hermione. "I'll put it back and he'll never know."

"I hope he won't," Jane said to Mandy, when she had gone. "He won't like being outwitted."

"Your mum's on the turn," Mandy said.

"On the turn?"

"The worm, you know," said Mandy. "She's getting her act together."

Jane frowned. What if Walter realised and took steps to safeguard his comfortable life? He wouldn't want things changed.

Curiously, when she left them, it was of Mandy that Hermione thought, not Jane. What would happen to her and Jasper?

When she arrived back at Freston station, Hermione could not remember exactly where the Maestro had been parked that morning, except that it had been facing the hedge. Perhaps its original space had been occupied by another car, meanwhile. There was a gap between a red Metro and a grey Sierra, and she put it there, with a little more petrol in the tank than when she had driven away, but surely even Walter could not know precisely how much there had been.

He was late again that night.

She was glad, dreading more than ever the prospect of another tense, silent evening confined together in the house.

Her time with Mandy, and later with Jane, had affected her deeply and she saw that she had fled into marriage expecting to continue the somewhat protected existence which she had been leading with her father. She had been able to use him as an excuse to avoid difficult socialising with her peers; theirs had been a happy prison but she had exchanged it for a grim one.

Mandy had as good as told her that she ought to leave Walter, and that Jane and Sarah would be glad if she did; in her own mind, after his recent behaviour, she had begun to think so herself. A first step would be to find out the legal position, what claim she could make on the house. She could ask at the Citizens' Advice Bureau.

She would do so, when she next went to Freston.

19

The police had made small progress in their search for the killer of the two prostitutes but they were convinced that the cases were linked. Swabs from the victims' bodies could help identify a suspect, but each had had other clients on the nights of their deaths and such evidence might be inexact. Both had been manually strangled, and the hair twined round their necks was merely a garnish; a trademark, said Detective Superintendent Ronson at a briefing. Any murder was, to him, one murder too many, prostitute or not, but the media rarely showed as much interest in their deaths as in those of victims considered to be worthier citizens. It had to be agreed that the women's occupation put their lives at risk. It was all too likely that this man would repeat his crime if he were not caught first; he could be a serial killer starting out on a sequence of punitive deaths, for he hated women; that was certain.

Much of the investigation was routine, often tedious. Prostitutes who worked in the same areas as the dead girls were questioned about clients who showed particular interest in women with long hair.

One woman spoke to the police about a man who had been very rough with her some weeks before; he had accosted her again on the night the first girl died and she had refused to go with him. She had known the dead girl; that was how she remembered which night it was, for she had wondered about the man and whether he could be the killer.

Detective Inspector Ferrars was very interested in this woman's statement and she was asked to help the police artist make a sketch of the client.

Monday's tabloid papers carried an artist's impression of a man the police wished to interview in connection with the murders. It was an unremarkable face: the eyes were set very straight in the head beneath indeterminate brows; the mouth was small. He had rather large ears with big lobes, and was aged between forty-five and fifty-five.

Belinda Arbuthnot noticed the drawing on the front of the papers when she stopped to buy a magazine which featured beautiful houses set amid several acres, tastefully furnished with pretty prints, and equipped with copper saucepans in their commodious kitchens. She secretly dreamed of living in a small version of such a place instead of in the house in Wandsworth which had been her home for more than twenty years. When her husband retired, which would not be for ages yet, they might move to the country, though a flint cottage in Norfolk was more likely than a manor house. She enjoyed her dream, however.

Something about the sketch in the paper caught her attention and she knew at once whom it reminded her of; she read the caption underneath the picture but she did not buy the paper, nor did she mention it to Rosemary when she reached the office. Poor Walter, he might be prickly and extremely pompous but he was hardly a patroniser of prostitutes, much less a murderer. She knew that identification of suspected criminals was a thorny subject; there were people who resembled one another and could be wrongly named.

During the day, the sketch came into her mind again. She studied Walter, when he left the room and returned. His ears were large. His eyes were very level in his head. She had not read the full description so did not know what colour the wanted man's were alleged to be. Going home that evening, she remembered once seeing him heading away from his direct route to the station. Which night was that, she wondered idly; did it coincide with the murder of either of the women? Was there any way in which she could manage to remember? At the time, she'd mentioned it to Rosemary; they'd joked that he might be bound for a massage parlour. Perhaps they had not been far off the mark.

She could ask Rosemary if she remembered when it was. Between them, they might pinpoint the date. She'd collected some shoes from the mender's, she recalled, but she hadn't kept the ticket.

Vaguely troubled, she decided to talk to Rosemary about it in the morning, and she wished that she had bought the paper. There was a reproduction of the drawing in *The Times*, which her husband had brought back with him from the office; it was a much smaller version than the other, but it still looked like Walter. The eyes, she read, were very pale blue. So were Walter's; scarcely blue at all: like ice.

She cut the picture from the paper.

Walter, returning late when there were only a few cars left in Freston station yard, did not notice that the Maestro was several yards away from where he had left it that morning. It had had plenty of time to cool down after Hermione's trip to Reading and back. He knew he needed petrol, made a detour through Freston to a pump that stayed open late and put in ten pounds' worth. The tank was not as low as he remembered; maybe the gauge was becoming faulty. He did not notice the increased mileage although, on Tuesday morning, it showed a higher figure than he expected. Still, he had not noted down the distances he had travelled on his night excursions; perhaps he had driven further than it seemed at the time.

He did not want to go home. Seeing that woman singing in the church, discovering her duplicity—how was he to know that she was married?—had upset him. Now he no longer saw her as Hermione's successor; she, too, had become a target for revenge. With the tank full, he drove round the district for a while. When at last he felt unable to stay out any longer, he found that Hermione had gone to bed, leaving a note to say that his dinner was in the oven.

It had been arranged on a single plate: there were no dishes, no correct servings. The plate, balanced over a soup bowl full of water in a low oven, had to be carried by Walter to the table. Its underside was wet. It was hot, and he burned his fingers touching it without the oven glove.

He thought about shouting at her to come down, but since she was locked in her new room he could not physically force her to obey, as would have been easy if she were in the bed they should share.

Walter would not risk a confrontation in which he might be the loser. Grimly, he ate his pork done up in sauce, the remains of Sunday's roast, with winter fruit salad to follow. That, in a bowl above the oven, was pleasantly warm, but skin had formed on the custard. Walter ate it all. Then he went up to bed.

Passing Hermione's door, he paused on the landing. She might be asleep now, but soon she would pay for her conduct. Tomorrow he intended to see where she went on the Tuesday bus.

The next morning Walter left for the office as usual. He was always in before Simon, opening the office, though both had keys. He sorted the mail and, when the director arrived, after exchanging the usual formal greetings with which they opened their day's contact, Walter explained that he must, unfortunately, beg to be released at ten o'clock as he had to return to Freston for a most important business meeting which could not be arranged at a more convenient time. He was deeply apologetic about once again needing time off—his recent dental trouble having led to two late arrivals—and of course he would make up the time.

Walter was so conscientious that Simon never doubted the veracity of his statement. Of course he must go, and he was not to worry about making up the lost hours.

The previous evening, Walter had cleared his desk and dealt with some telephone calls to companies which had promised donations not yet received. He had set in train various matters connected with the appeal that would go out straight after Christmas.

"People feel guilty after spending large sums gratifying their own greed," he told Philip. "Now, get these done by the end of the day," and he gave instructions about sending receipts and returning unsigned cheques with requests for amendment. It was surprising how many were received; people were very careless.

"Do you think he's been behaving oddly lately?" Belinda asked Rosemary, when Walter had gone. Bidding them farewell, his manner had been that of a schoolmaster obliged to leave his class unattended; while his back was turned, they must behave, was implied.

"He's had toothache. That's enough to make anyone touchy," said Rosemary.

Belinda had remembered Walter's remarks about prostitutes when they discussed the girl found in the ditch. He had said that they were provocative and knew the risks they ran.

"Do you remember which night it was I saw him heading towards King's Cross instead of going his own way home?" she asked Rosemary. "We wondered if he'd gone to a massage parlour."

"I do remember," said Rosemary. "At least, I remember that after you'd mentioned it, the next night I stopped for a carton of milk at Mr. Patel's on the corner, and Walter came in and bought a Mars Bar. I was surprised. Didn't I tell you?"

"No wonder he's having tooth trouble, if he snacks on sweets when our backs are turned," said Belinda. "Why did you need milk? Haven't you got a friendly neighbourhood milkman?"

"Yes, I have, and he's marvellous—never makes a mistake—but we needed extra because Hugh'd rung up to say his daughter was coming that night with her infant. She was going out somewhere and couldn't get a sitter. It was all fixed at the last moment. I can find the date in the diary at home; Hugh will have written it down. Or Anna will remember." Anna was her step-daughter, a solicitor who had decided at the age of thirty-six to have a child despite being unmarried. She had not told Hugh who the father was, only that he was intelligent and healthy. Toby, the result, an angelic baby, was looked after in the daytime by a nanny Anna shared with another mother. "Why are you so anxious to know when it was?" Rosemary added.

Belinda showed her the small clipping from *The Times*.

"Who does it remind you of?" she asked.

Rosemary studied the sketch in silence and read the short report below it.

"It's just like him," she said in a low voice. "But then, it could be hundreds of other men, too."

"I know. I was just wondering which night it was that he sloped off. Whether it was around the time that first girl was found," said Belinda.

"Well, the second one must have been dumped from a car," said Rosemary. "Walter comes up by train."

"What's to stop him driving up one night, if he got the urge?" said Belinda.

"I'll check in the diary," said Rosemary. "But *The Times* doesn't say when the first girl was found."

"Some other paper will. Or its news desk will, if we ask," said Belinda.

"Don't let the child see it," said Rosmary, nodding towards Walter's office, wherein Philip was busy printing out pages of appeal literature. "I'll tell you tomorrow about the dates."

"I'm not sure if I'll ring the police, whatever you say," said Belinda. "It would be awful if they came down on Walter and gave him a hard time when someone else was the real murderer."

The two women stared at each other.

"He can't be," said Rosemary. "It's ridiculous."

"I know," said Belinda.

Afterwards, she was to regret bitterly the fact that she had not telephoned the police the moment she saw the resemblance. After all, Walter could soon have proved his innocence, if innocent he was.

Several times that Tuesday evening she almost lifted the telephone to make the call, and she did ring Rosemary to confirm the date. After a night in which she woke up more than once wondering where her duty lay, she called the police early on Wednesday morning. She told them where Walter Brown, a man very much like the one shown in the sketch, could be found, and she asked for her identity to be kept confidential.

Travelling to work, she looked ahead to the moment when several large uniformed officers would invade the office, handcuff Walter and take him away to be questioned.

But it wasn't like that at all, because Walter did not turn up, nor did he telephone to say why he would not be coming in.

Simon was sure that Walter would arrive with a valid explanation—a train accident, or at least one that was cancelled; such things frequently happened. Belinda, however, feared that the police had traced his home address, gone down to Merbury and arrested him there, even kicking down the door of his house at dawn. She felt very uncomfortable as she sat putting leaflets in envelopes with extra zeal to atone for her interference, but she had scarcely begun before Detective Inspector Ferrars and Detective Sergeant Hooper came to the office wanting to speak to Walter. Their calm manner and their sober dark suits were so unlike what her imagination had thrown up that she almost broke into giggles and had to blow her nose to regain her composure.

They spoke to Simon in private, and he looked grave when he reappeared to ask Belinda to go into his room as they wished to talk to her.

The two detectives told her that she had acted correctly and that if Walter was not involved he had nothing to fear. There were other reports of men looking like the one in the picture; all must be followed up, but the team investigating the London murders would instigate enquiries into where Walter had been on the nights in question.

The director had mentioned Walter's business appointment which had allowed him to come in for only an hour or so the day before.

"On past form, I'd have expected him to arrange it either first thing in the morning, or during the afternoon so that he would spend the best part of the day here," he said. "He finds it difficult to delegate, but he's most conscientious. He implied that the timing was not in his power and he had to fit in with whoever else was involved."

They spoke to Philip, who soon understood their purpose, and he agreed about the likeness. Of all of them in the office, Philip was the only one who thought Walter really could be the murderer.

Valerie Palmer had also seen the drawing in the paper. She thought the wanted man was very like the one who had travelled on the train with her and had pressed his company upon her so unpleasantly. This person had been in church on Sunday night and had sat in a car outside her house afterwards.

Could it be the same man, the one who travelled on the London train? If she told the police, they could check up on him. But if she had noticed the resemblance, so would others, and someone else would report it. She decided to do nothing.

20

Sitting in the bus on Tuesday, Hermione thought of a missed opportunity. She should have cycled to Freston station and helped herself to the car again. Still, the bus journey was, in the long run, quicker, and she had no lights for the bike, which she would have needed as it would be getting dark by the time she reached home.

She sat at the front, looking out at the landscape which was shrouded in misty fog today; it was lucky the visibility yesterday had been good for her trip to Reading.

The bus stopped outside the Town Hall in Freston, where a number of passengers got off and others boarded. Hermione, waiting for it to continue on its way to Creddington, did not see Walter lurking near by in a doorway, his coat collar pulled up and his green tweed hat pulled down. He held up a newspaper to guard his face, waiting for Hermione to descend so that he could follow her to her mystery destination.

Returning from London on a morning train, he had decided to waylay the bus, not follow it from Merbury where his actions might be noticed, if not by Hermione, by someone else who would recognise him.

When the bus moved on, still carrying Hermione, he had to dash to the car which he had left in the market square park, safely protected with a two-hour parking ticket. He panted back, startling Helen Mountford who was returning to her own car, left near his, and whom he brushed against, almost knocking her off balance. In his haste he did not notice her, intent only on catching up with the bus.

He knew it went on to Creddington, but it strayed into villages on the way, picking up and setting down passengers. Hermione might get off anywhere on the route, and he kept his distance, so that she should not see him. When she dismounted, he planned to follow her and catch her *in flagrante* of one kind or another, but if she saw him first, he would challenge her and very soon she would tell him where she was going. It wouldn't take long to break her down; his hands tightened on the steering wheel as he anticipated the short contest there would be. But he wanted to find the other party, her partner in deceit, for he must be dealt with, too, and surprising him would be better than forcing Hermione to disclose his name. By now he had convinced himself that another man was responsible for her conduct, perhaps also for her rebellion at home; no other explanation seemed possible.

She stepped off the bus in Creddington outside a row of shops, and, walking a short way, turned into a florist's. Walter was able to slot the Maestro into a nearby parking space when another car pulled out, and he saw Hermione emerge carrying a small package wrapped in florist's paper.

Walter got out of his car and followed her on foot. She never looked round, walking briskly up the hill in her beige raincoat, wearing jeans, he saw with horror.

She went down a side road and turned in at the gate of a large house. Standing opposite, again hiding behind his paper, Walter watched her ring the bell; then the door opened and a small woman with white hair was revealed. As Hermione entered, the two embraced.

Walter felt a distinct shock, almost a sense of disappointment. This was not a lover. He had not catered for a different scenario and he needed new plans. Even so, it was a deception; he was entitled to full knowledge of all Hermione's movements when he was out of the house, and she must explain herself. He waited for a while in full view of the house, but she did not reappear and after a time he retreated to the car to plot his strategy.

She would have to come back this way to catch the bus home. He saw the stop, on the far side of the road, and watched one bus bound for Freston and Merbury depart. He did not care if she saw him; she would know her hour of reckoning had arrived. He would bundle her into the car, force her to confess to her actions, then deal with her once and for ever.

Two more buses came and went with no sign of Hermione, who by this time was busily cleaning Theresa Cowper's house.

Now cold and hungry, Walter had had enough. He drove to the house he had seen Hermione enter and rang the bell to demand the return of his wife.

Mrs. Fisher opened the door on the chain, as she always did when alone. She saw an angry middle-aged man, wearing a dark green tweed hat which he did not raise or remove.

"Yes?" she said, thinking he was probably selling life insurance or double-glazing, even Biblical tracts.

"I have reason to believe my wife is here," said Walter. "I wish to remove her."

"Your wife?"

"Hermione Brown. She entered this house at twelve-forty precisely," said Walter. "Kindly fetch her at once."

So this was Walter! Mrs. Fisher clasped her navy knitted jacket across her chest with one hand while the other still held the door. She was enormously shocked. How had he found out about Hermione's visits?

She must have been careless, made him suspicious. Had he

learned about her trip with the car? She had described it to Mrs. Fisher with glee, though why shouldn't she take it to visit her daughter?

Should she deny all knowledge of Hermione? Mrs. Fisher dismissed the idea at once; one lie always led to another and was no solution.

"She is not here, Mr. Brown," said Emily. Her voice was calm but her heart was leaping about like a trapped bird.

"I don't believe you," said Walter. "I saw her come in and she has not caught the bus home."

"She is not here," repeated Emily Fisher.

"Don't lie to me," said Walter, and he scowled at her. "I demand to come in and find her."

Mrs. Fisher did not know what to do. He had thrust his foot through the door so that she could not close it. He could not get in unless she unhooked the chain, but how could she force him to leave? She could call the police and have him forcibly taken away, but that would not help Hermione, who at least was now safe in Orchard House. Thank goodness he had not followed her there, where she would be alone and defenceless.

"You may come in and see for yourself," Mrs. Fisher told him, with dignity, and she opened the door.

Her stick was resting against the wall, where she had put it while opening the door, and she picked it up, leaning on it as she led the way into the drawing-room. Because of her concern that Wendy should not discover she had been entertaining, all traces of Hermione's visit had been tidied away. The freesias she had brought could be explained as Mrs. Fisher's indulgence to herself. Their scent lent fragrance to the air as Walter followed her into the room.

"As you see, I am quite alone, Mr. Brown," she said.

Walter would not believe her. He had seen Hermione enter. What game were they playing?

"This room is empty," he allowed.

"Look in the kitchen. Search the cupboard under the stairs," Emily invited, leaning on her stick, looking him in the eye, daring him.

Walter would not meet her gaze. He walked out of the room to the kitchen, where he opened the back door and glanced outside. Hermione could have left that way, he decided, slunk off over the garden; that must be the explanation, but he intended to make sure.

Returning, he looked in the cupboard, which was tidy enough to please even him. There was no hidden cranny behind clutter where Hermione could hide.

"There are two bedrooms upstairs, mine and my daughter's. Look there if you wish," said Emily. "Forgive me if I do not escort you, but I suffer from arthritis and the stairs are not easy for me. The rest of the house is reached by another entrance. There are two flats." She would not tell him that by day they were unoccupied; let him think that the tenants might rush to her rescue if she screamed.

She did not think he would accept her suggestion, but he did. She watched him bustle up the two shallow flights and then heard him opening and closing doors. He was some time. Presumably he was looking in the wardrobes to make sure Hermione was not skulking among the clothes.

It had become important to delay him. Any minute now Hermione would be walking down from Orchard House to the bus stop. Mrs. Fisher must try to detain him until that peril was past and Hermione was in the bus. After that, there was no more she could do to protect her friend.

Walter came downstairs at last. His face was flushed and sweating.

"You don't look well, Mr. Brown. Come and sit down until you feel better," said Emily.

She had felt quite faint herself, while he was upstairs. The thought of him rummaging through her and Wendy's cupboards was sickening, but she had sat down, tried to breathe calmly and evenly and regain some composure. Wendy would be back very soon, and if Walter Brown were still here, there would be no chance of concealing Hermione's visits from her, but it was now more important to win time for Hermione to arrive home first. Faced with Wendy, blustering Walter Brown might crumple, for Wendy could frighten her mother and might awe him. At the same time, Mrs. Fisher realised the extent of Hermione's plight; her situation was desperate.

Walter certainly did feel odd; he was clammy, and he thought his head might burst under the pressure inside his skull.

"Sit down," repeated Emily, pointing to a chair with her stick.

Walter found he was glad to obey.

"Hermione and I met in a shop some weeks ago," Mrs. Fisher told him. "Knowing it is difficult for me to get about, she kindly comes to see me on Tuesdays. We have a light luncheon together and then she leaves." Sitting in a chair facing him, Mrs. Fisher waited for Walter's response to this true statement.

He opened and closed his mouth several times, like a fish gasping for air. Finally he spoke.

"She never told me," he said.

"Because she feared you would object. You do object. That's why you're here," said Mrs. Fisher, refraining from adding comments on his outrageous behaviour. How had he found out about the visits?

"How does she pay for her fare?" he wanted to know.

"I'm aware that you keep your wife so short of money that she hasn't enough to travel to Creddington once a week," said Emily. "But you are scarcely a poor man, Mr. Brown."

"She has to record her expenses," said Walter. "She must be falsifying her accounts."

"I give her money for her fare," Mrs. Fisher lied. She glanced at the clock. Hermione would have left Orchard House by now, but she would not be home for a while. Mrs. Fisher was afraid for her; the man was clearly unstable. She decided to let him understand that she knew something about his treatment of his wife. "She had some nasty facial bruises when she came two weeks ago," she said.

"So?" Walter glared. "She had a fall."

"So she told me," said Mrs. Fisher. "But I didn't believe her, and if she has any more bruises I shall want to know why."

"It's none of your business," said Walter truculently. His high colour was fading now and he was breathing more evenly.

"Hermione is my friend and her welfare is my concern, especially as her own parents are no longer alive," said Mrs. Fisher.

"She has me to look after her," Walter said.

"And do you?" asked Mrs. Fisher.

Walter's whole manner suddenly altered. He rose to his feet, holding his hat, which he had not taken off until he sat down.

"I must apologise for taking up so much of your time, Mrs. er-?" he said, and bowed slightly from the hips.

"My name is Fisher," said Emily. "You are leaving, then?"

"Indeed, yes. You may expect to see Hermione next week and I shall see that she has her fare. And enough to buy more flowers." He glanced at the freesias and his features stretched in what was meant to be a smile, but it frightened Emily. "Please don't trouble to see me out," he added, and he walked across the room to the door.

Emily struggled to her feet and followed him. She was panting when she closed the door behind him and put up the chain, afraid he might have a change of mind and return. Something had bothered her all the time they were talking, and especially after he had removed his hat; she felt she had seen Walter somewhere before, but where could it have been? Perhaps it would come to her, if she let the question linger in her mind.

As he had gone before Wendy came home, there would be

no need to explain after all, but something must be done to help Hermione. The man was unbalanced and a threat to her; he was very dangerous.

On her way back to the drawing-room she paused, feeling giddy as she remembered where she had seen Walter, or his double: it was in a newspaper. The police wanted to talk to him about some murders in London.

When Wendy came home a few minutes later, she could not get into the house with her key because the chain was across the door, and through the gap she could see her mother lying in an unconscious heap on the floor.

21

Unaware of what was happening to Mrs. Fisher, Hermione was happily cleaning and polishing at Orchard House. That morning, after Walter left, she had washed her hair and combed it down so that it dried while she carried out her normal tasks. It lacked the bounce Jeremy's blow-drying had given it, but it was still a big improvement on its earlier state. She hadn't cared about her appearance for years, for Walter never made comments that were not derogatory, and all she could hope for in company was to be overlooked. Perhaps Jeremy would come in today; though it must be part of his job to flatter his female clients, nevertheless he had taken the trouble to make her feel good: automatic it may have been, but it was nice.

She worked methodically, thinking, some of the time, about Emily, who that afternoon had shown Hermione prizes Wendy had won at school for science and mathematics. Wendy had always been very practical, Emily had said, and though she seemed stern and austere, beneath this she was wise and kind, and the rules she made for her mother were for Emily's good, as she saw it.

"But I lost my independence when her father left her the house," said Emily. "I'm dependent on her for my home, though I still have some money of my own. It all made for sensible long-term financial planning, which was what her father thought important."

Hermione had murmured some reply, thinking of herself. It would be foolish to give up all claim to the house because she could not go on living with Walter. Perhaps, she thought now, polishing Theresa's dining-table, we could go to some of those people who help you, be counselled; maybe they would help her to make fewer mistakes and persuade Walter to be more tolerant.

It was a vain notion. He would never agree that they had any problems which could not be solved by her submission. The idea withered immediately.

She finished her work, looked round to make sure she had left no duster or tin of polish out, picked up her money and left, walking quickly down the road to the bus stop. It was still murky, now nearly dark; the fog had hung about all day and no doubt would come down hard later.

So far she had had a day free from fear. She had begun to count off time in segments, some slices calm and others full of tension. She could classify those portions: her dread at hearing Walter's key in the door; the sick feeling in her stomach at the sound of his steps in the hall; the frightening sight of his frowning brows and his scowl, and of his short stubby hands with the dark red hair on the backs and on his fingers. It was odd that his bodily hair was red when that on his head, now greying, had been brown.

She had Thursday to look forward to, when she would go to Downs Farm and see Nigel. She was smiling at the prospect as she walked from the bus stop back to the house and turned in at the gate. Pam Norton, opposite, working upstairs in her study, saw her, the mist around her, entering the drive.

Hermione let herself in and hung up her coat in the cloakroom. There was plenty of time to get dinner, which was home-made fish-cakes served with mashed potato already prepared, needing only to be heated up with added milk, and carrots which would cook in a few minutes. There were stewed pears and custard for pudding.

She went out to the kitchen and crossed to the sink; she had time for a late cup of tea before she need start cooking.

Walter was waiting for her behind the kitchen door. He caught her by the arms and twisted them upwards behind her, very painfully, so that she screamed, and he let go with one hand to clamp the other over her mouth.

"And where have you been?" he snarled at her, his voice thick, almost unrecognisable. "To a lover, after visiting that old lady you use as an excuse? Tell me his name."

She could not answer. She wriggled and squirmed and made desperate sounds in her throat, and he cuffed her on the side of her head, so that her ears rang. Then he hit her again, and when she fell to the floor, he kicked her hard in the ribs.

Walter had passed Hermione's bus before it reached Freston but he did not know she was on it; he expected to find her already at home, and when he discovered the house was empty, his simmering rage flared again. Was she visiting more old ladies? Spreading sweetness and light without reference to him? Or was she seeing a man? How long had this sort of thing been going on?

How should he deal with her now? Turning the cupboards out was monotonous and familiar; she needed much stronger punishment for her new, grave offence. Letting her come in unawares, imagining she had got away with her afternoon's exploit, would be a good way to begin. He put his coat and hat in the study, so that she should not realise he was already home, and he waited for her in the dark. She was sure to go into the kitchen almost at once, for she would have to prepare his dinner, so that was where he concealed himself. He was very hungry, having eaten nothing since that morning, and he always developed an appetite after what he described to himself as upsetting or emotional events. He would make her cook his meal before he dealt with her, and he would terrify her before he killed her, for that was what he was going to do; she would be dead by morning. By her actions today she had signed her own death warrant, and there would be no stay of execution. He must, however, plan coolly, not let his natural distress disturb his judgement.

Now, having hit her, he looked at her cowering on the floor with a hand up to her face to shield it from further blows, her frightened eyes staring up at him between her spread fingers. He loved to see her like that, utterly broken.

"Get up," he said, and reached down to pull her arm. "Look at you, in jeans like a student. Is that any way for my wife to dress?" he demanded.

She did not reply. Her head was still ringing and her heart was hammering away in her chest like an overworked piston engine. As roughly as he had thrown her down, he now dragged her to her feet.

"Get over to the stove," he said. "Cook my food," and, as she still cowered by the wall, he opened a drawer and pulled out the first knife that met his hand, a long slender one, thrusting the point towards her. He did not intend to use it; that was not in his plans; but she wouldn't know that. He had ruled her by fear all these years and he would rule her by fear till the end.

Hermione felt giddy from the blows and she was more afraid now than she had ever been before, even on the night she spent in the garage. Half sobbing, she made her way to the cooker and turned on the burners to fry the fishcakes and heat up the vegetables. She was shaking with terror while she tried to think of a way to save herself, for she knew now that he meant to kill her; she had seen it in his eyes.

All the time she was moving from fridge to stove to sink and back again, he was close behind her, and more than once she felt the point of the knife against her sweater. By the time everything was ready and she had carried it into the dining-room, with Walter, still holding the knife, padding behind her, she was almost gibbering with fear.

They sat down, and Walter laid the knife on the table close to his hand. Hermione put three fishcakes on Walter's plate. He helped himself to carrots and potato and poured tomato sauce from a bottle over them all. Hermione was thankful that she had remembered to replace it after Walter's extravagant use of their stock the week before, though much good that would do her now.

"You are to eat," he ordered, when she made no attempt to put any food on her plate.

"I'm not hungry," she croaked. She would die that night, she thought: she would never see Jane or Sarah again.

Walter leaned forward and put a fishcake and some vegetables on her plate, then began to eat his own. Hermione pushed back her chair, wanting to take her chance of getting away, but at once he picked up the knife.

"Sit down and eat," he thundered.

Hermione sank back and picked up her fork to chase some food round her plate. She would gag if she ate anything.

Walter had eaten quite a lot of his meal very quickly and he had had a change of plan.

"Put my plate in the oven to keep warm," he said. "And since you aren't eating and I abhor waste, put your portion on my plate. I shall eat it all by and by."

Hermione was past wondering at his reasoning. She moved the fishcake and vegetables from her plate to his, then picked up both plates.

"Leave your plate here," he said.

She did as she was told, and carried his laden plate through to the kitchen. The food was piled high and her hand was shaking; two pieces of sliced carrot slipped to the floor on the way. She put the plate in the oven, uncovered, then stood up and faced Walter, who had followed her.

He held the knife out, its blade facing her.

"You are going to kill yourself tonight," he said. "In the garage, with the car, like you nearly did once before. I shall tell the police about that earlier attempt when I find you in the morning, and I shall tell them how strangely you have been acting lately. I'll be rid of you then, you dry, feeble thing, and I'll find myself a real woman. But before that happens, I'll have my rights. Upstairs you go, Hermione," and he advanced towards her, the knife extended.

Hermione could not retreat because the cooker was behind her. She pressed her hands against it and somehow found the strength and purpose to lash out with her leg. She caught Walter on the thigh, and it was enough to halt him and make him retreat a pace, but he trod on a piece of carrot and lost his footing. Suddenly he was on the floor, the knife falling from his grasp, and before he could seize it again, she had snatched it up and held it over him. It wavered in her trembling hand. The heavy fall had shaken Walter, but he began hauling himself up, swearing, using words she had never before heard him utter. His back was half turned to her as he struggled to his feet and she shut her eyes, holding the knife with one hand clasped over the other and pushing it forward. It met little resistance as it pierced his clothes and slid between his ribs, and he made a gurgling sound, an expression of total astonishment on his face when Hermione dared to look at him. Horrified herself, she pulled the knife out; it came easily enough. Walter staggered about the kitchen for what seemed an endless time but was in reality only seconds; it was as though everything was happening in slow motion. Then he blundered towards the lobby, gasping something about air. He opened the door and staggered through, then slithered to the ground with a long sigh and was still.

Hermione had not moved. She looked at the knife grasped in her hands. Its long, thin blade was stained with Walter's blood and a few drops fell on the floor. Close to them was a small orange smear: the carrot pieces which had fallen from his plate and on which he had slipped.

She took the knife to the sink and held it under the running tap until it was clean, all the time gasping and shuddering with shock. Then she turned to the door. He'd be back as soon as he came round, for of course he was not badly hurt.

She locked the lobby door, leaving him in darkness. Then she sat at the kitchen table, facing the door. She stayed there for a long time.

Much later, Hermione noticed a smell of burning coming from the oven, where the food Walter had told her to put there had dried up. She turned the oven off but left the plate where it was; he might demand it when he recovered. Then she remembered the stains on the floor and wiped up the blood, now dried, and the carrot. It never occurred to her to ring either the police or for an ambulance. She was in a state of numbed suspension when time did not exist and she was incapable of thought. Her mind would not even replay to her the struggle she had managed to survive. Eventually, she went up to her room, walking heavily, dragging herself upstairs by the banisters. She bolted herself in, so that she was safe, and lay on her bed, fully dressed, only kicking off her shoes. She did not sleep until just before dawn, when she lapsed into a heavy slumber and was eventually woken by loud banging on the front door and the sound of the bell pealing through the house.

It was broad daylight. Walter would be late. She must cook his breakfast. Slowly, as if they weighed a ton, she slid her legs over the side of the bed and stood up.

The noise at the door continued, and without pausing to pass a brush through her hair, she went downstairs to hear a male voice calling, "Police, open up."

Hermione opened the door, which was not on the chain, nor bolted, as she had not locked up when she came home the day before, leaving it for Walter to do, as usual.

Two men, one in a tweed jacket and dark trousers, the other in jeans and an anorak, stood on the step.

"Mrs. Brown?" asked the older of the two. "Detective Sergeant Bagley from Creddington police station," he said, and showed her his warrant card. "This is Detective Constable Vincent. Is Mr. Brown at home? We'd like a word with him."

Hermione stared at them blankly. What were they doing here?

"Walter?" she asked.

"Walter Brown. You are Mrs. Brown?"

"Yes," she agreed, and made a huge effort to pull herself together. "I don't know where he is," she said. "I—I was late last night. I've only just woken up."

She must have dressed while they were battering at the door, thought Bagley, but later he discovered her bed, dented on the top, the nightdress still beneath the pillow.

"I'd like to come in, Mrs. Brown," he said, stepping firmly over the threshold.

"Oh—of course. But I expect Walter's gone to work," she said. "Unless he's still—" and she stopped. Hadn't she locked him in the lobby? She remembered now.

"Still what, Mrs. Brown?"

She gestured vaguely.

"Still out there," she said, pointing to the kitchen.

The two men went past her, and seeing the kitchen empty, opened the door that led to the rear lobby, where they found Walter.

They were not unkind. One of them sat down with her in the sitting-room; they did not want her in the kitchen, she was told. The second one had gone out to their car.

"Your husband's dead, Mrs. Brown," said Bagley, the one who remained. "Didn't you know that?"

"Is he?" Hermione showed scant interest. "I thought he was just unconscious." Then she looked at the detective again, with more attention. "Dead, did you say?" and added, "I didn't think I'd really hurt him. There was only a drop or two of blood. I wiped it up."

At this, Bagley cautioned her, but she scarcely took in what he said. All she had absorbed was the fact that Walter could never threaten her again.

"Dead," she repeated, and volunteered, "he fell. Some carrots had dropped from his dinner and he slipped on them. I wiped that mess up too," she went on, her voice now like that of an eager child insisting it had made amends for some mistake. "His dinner's in the oven," she continued. "And mine. I didn't want any and he told me to put mine on his plate and he'd eat all of it later. Oh, I'd better clear the dining-room. My dirty plate's in there."

Bagley had already noticed the dinner-table, still with one soiled plate and the empty serving dishes. For that reason he had taken her through to the other room.

"That's all right, Mrs. Brown," he said. "It can wait."

At first glance, Walter's wound had not been obvious. Most of the bleeding had been internal and the two officers had not been certain, until Hermione spoke, that there had been a murder here. They had come on behalf of the Metropolitan Police to question Walter about the two dead prostitutes, knowing only that he had not turned up at his office, had been mysteriously absent most of the day before, and resembled the man wanted for those murders.

Hermione did not say that Walter had intended to kill her.

"The knife's on the drainer in the kitchen," she said. "I rinsed it. There was blood on it."

22

Pamela Norton, at her study window, saw the activity at the Browns' house opposite. An ordinary saloon—a Vauxhall, perhaps, she was not sure—and two police cars were drawn up; several uniformed officers moved round the outside of the house which was soon separated from the road by tapes, and a constable stood on guard.

Then she saw Hermione leaving, being helped into the back of one of the police cars by a woman officer.

Pam was out of the house and across the road as fast as a runner breasting the finishing line, just in time to see the car containing Hermione drive off.

"What's happened?" she asked the policeman on the gate.

"There's been an incident," he said.

"What sort of incident?"

"I'm afraid I can't answer any questions and I must ask you to leave, madam," said the officer, a very young man with freckles on his nose.

At this point, an older man in plain clothes appeared, accompanying another who carried a small bag. Pam rushed up to both of them.

"What's happened?" she asked them. "I saw Hermione— Mrs. Brown—going off in a police car. Is she all right?"

"Why shouldn't she be?" Detective Sergeant Bagley enquired.

"Oh—I don't know," said Pam. "I wondered why you were taking her away, that's all. I live there," she added, pointing to her own house.

"Please go home then, madam," Bagley said.

She would be interviewed later, asked about anything she heard or saw during the night, when more was known about how Walter Brown had met his death, though the dead man's wife had admitted killing him. There was no mystery here about what had happened, only about the events that led up to the stabbing.

Pam had no choice but to obey Bagley's instructions, but she went slowly, and was able to see Bagley bid goodbye to the police doctor who had certified that Walter was, indeed, dead. He had taken the deceased's temperature; time of death might be important and the pathologist who would do the post-mortem would be glad to have this information. He would soon be coming to the scene, and the forensic team who must find the evidence to prove the case.

Through her window, Pam saw the Scenes of Crime Officer arrive, and, unable to contain her curiosity, which was tinged with concern about Hermione, she telephoned Helen Mountford to tell her what was happening.

"Is an ambulance there?" asked Helen, who was in her bedroom.

"No," said Pam.

"Have you seen Walter?"

"No, but he must have gone to work. He leaves about seven-thirty," said Pam. "I sometimes see him go when I bring in the milk."

That reminded her of something. She had noticed a milk bottle on the Browns' front step when she looked across, much earlier. Hermione always took hers in promptly; that was odd. It had gone now.

"I hope he hasn't punched her in the eye again," said Helen, and then thought that was an indiscreet remark to make to, of all people, Pam, who could never keep gossip to herself.

"What?" Pam was exclaiming.

"Well, she said she'd had a fall, but she had a real black eye," said Helen. "Didn't you notice it?" Helen had noticed it in church.

"No," said Pam. "When was this?"

"Oh, a couple of weeks ago or so. It's faded now," said Helen. "Perhaps it really was an accident."

She wanted to end the conversation, find Robert, who was probably reading the paper downstairs, tell him what Pam had reported. She remembered seeing Walter in Freston the day before, when he had almost knocked her over and had not apologised. Usually he was painfully punctilious.

"I wonder where Hermione goes on Tuesdays," Pam said now. "Perhaps it was something to do with that. Except there's still a lot of commotion over at the house."

"Does Hermione go out every Tuesday?" Helen asked.

"Yes," said Pam. "On the noon bus. And she bikes off somewhere on Thursdays, too, much earlier, and comes back round lunchtime."

"Pam Norton's a walking encyclopaedia about Hermione's movements," Helen told her husband when she had at last managed to end the conversation. "What can be going on? I hope Hermione isn't in any sort of trouble."

It wasn't very long before rumours began to run round the village, for someone saw the van arrive to take Walter's body to the morgue.

Though no announcement had been made, soon people had begun to say that Walter Brown was dead.

After the police had left Walter's London office, the director had called the staff together and suggested that they should keep the reason for the visit to themselves.

"Walter will be able to prove where he was when the women were killed," he said. "And he'll probably soon arrive with an explanation of why he's late today," Simon added. "He would be justified in being angry if he knew the police were here asking about him. They'll no doubt send someone to his house to check that end, if he doesn't turn up here." Simon had agreed to ring a number given to him by Detective Inspector Ferrars if Walter came in later. In fact, when the two detectives had discovered that he was not in the office, Detective Sergeant Hooper had slipped out to put through a call which led to the Creddington police going to Walter's house before he and Ferrars had finished talking to Walter's colleagues.

By the end of the morning, when Walter had still not arrived nor telephoned to explain his absence, Simon rang his home number.

An unfamiliar male voice answered the telephone, and when Simon, in some surprise, asked to speak to Walter, he was told that was not possible. Simon explained who he was, and was passed on to a second male voice whose owner said he was Detective Sergeant Bagley. He told Simon that Walter was dead. He would not reveal any details, but he wanted to know the address and telephone number of Walter's work place. Simon, deeply shocked, supplied the information, and his own private address and telephone number; then he asked for condolences to be passed on to Hermione, who, he was told, was not available to come to the telephone herself.

"How is she taking this?" asked Simon gravely.

"As well as can be expected," said Bagley.

When their conversation finished, Simon called the other members of the staff in to tell them the news.

"What happened?" asked Belinda.

"I don't know. The police wouldn't say," said Simon.

"Perhaps he had a heart attack," said Rosemary. "He sometimes went very red in the face. How dreadful!"

Simon exhorted them to carry on with extra zeal. His mind

had already moved on to the problem of what to do about replacing Walter. A retired officer from one of the services might be the person to aim for, he thought: male or female; naturally either would do. Such a person might be better at staff relations than Walter had been. And someone must go to the funeral, whenever that took place; it would please the widow. He made a note on his pad not to forget.

"Perhaps he topped himself," said Philip, when he and the two women were out of Simon's earshot. "Before the police got him, I mean. He must have seen his own mug shot in the papers."

"We can't be sure that was him, Philip," said Rosemary. "It was just someone like him. That's all we know."

"Well, I can't feel sad," said Belinda. "He wasn't very nice, even if he wasn't the murderer." At least, she was thinking, Walter had not discovered that his name had been given to the police.

"If Philip's right, and he committed suicide, he must have been," said Rosemary, not altogether logically.

"It's only Philip's suggestion," said Belinda.

"Funny the police being there," said Philip. "If he just died, I mean. Had a heart attack. Something normal."

"Sudden death. There'd be an inquest," said Rosemary.

"I wonder if anyone will shed a tear for him," said Belinda. "Perhaps the girls were fond of him. He was their father, after all."

"Hermione'll have her chance now, won't she?" said Rosemary. "Her chance for life, I mean."

But Hermione was to spend that night in a cell at Creddington police station.

"Can't I go home?" she had asked Police Constable Karen Hunt, who had come to the house to escort her when she was arrested.

They had made her change her clothes before she left the house. For some reason, having established that she had not undressed since the day before, they wanted what she had on, and Karen Kent put all the garments in polythene bags as Hermione took them off.

When Hermione stripped, Karen Kent saw purple bruises along her rib cage.

"When did that happen?" she asked.

"Last night. He—he kicked me," said Hermione. "He hit me and I fell down, and he kicked me, and then he got the knife."

"Did you tell Mr. Bagley this?" asked Karen.

"I don't know what I told him," said Hermione, who could not believe that all this was not a dream.

She had wanted to have a bath, but they would not allow that; however, they let her wash and clean her teeth and she felt better when she was dressed in her best tweed skirt, warm tights, and a blue sweater she had bought in a sale.

When she was leaving the house she suddenly said, "What about Walter?" and Karen Hunt told her not to worry, that the police would see to everything.

It was strange to be driving to Creddington in a police car instead of travelling on the bus. They turned off before reaching the row of shops where Brenda's café was, and the florist's; only yesterday she had bought freesias there for Mrs. Fisher.

The modern red brick police station was a short distance up the road. Hermione was taken to a room where there was a table and some chairs, and, though she did not notice it until later, a recording machine. Karen Kent stayed with her and said that soon Mr. Bagley or one of the other officers would be along to talk to her.

They would want her to tell them what happened, she supposed: how she had killed Walter for of course that was what she had done, though not on purpose. It was all because of the carrots; if Walter had not slipped on them, he would have killed her. They had saved her life. She almost laughed at the thought.

She should be doing all sorts of things today; there was the ironing to finish, and there were Walter's soiled shirts to wash, and many other things to be done so that she would be ahead with her work for tomorrow, Downs Farm day.

Then she realised that none of it mattered. Walter would want no more shirts. He would never scold her or shout at her again. It was over.

She was cautioned once more, as it seemed that she had not properly taken in what was happening before, and during the rest of the long day, with intervals when she was taken to a cell, given food, and locked in, she was questioned. She understood that the interviews were recorded. A middle-aged man with thick grey hair, Detective Inspector Windsor, seemed to be in charge, but Detective Sergeant Bagley was there for much of the time, and Karen Kent. They told her she was entitled to a solicitor, but she didn't know who Walter's was and saw no reason to bother one. Why shouldn't she answer their questions? There was no need for silence. She told them that she had been out the previous afternoon and when she returned, not expecting Walter to be back from work, he was there in the kitchen, in the dark, waiting for her.

"Waiting for you?" said Karen Kent.

"Waiting to pounce on me," said Hermione. She put a hand to her head. It was tender under her hair and, feeling the spot, she looked somewhat bewildered. "I suppose it's all right to mention it, now that he's dead," she added. "He hit me."

"On your head?" asked Karen Kent.

"It's a bit tender," she said. "It's not bad. Not as bad as last time."

"When was that?"

"About two weeks ago. I had a black eye." She gave an

embarrassed laugh. "After that time, I moved into Jane's bedroom."

"People noticed your black eye?" asked Karen Kent.

"Yes. I said I'd had a fall," Hermione replied. "I couldn't let anyone know what had really happened. It was my fault, you see."

"Why do you say that?" asked Detective Inspector Windsor.

"Because I wouldn't do what he wanted."

"And what was that?"

Hermione murmured and muttered, and Karen Kent helped her.

"Sleep with him, do you mean?"

Hermione blushed and nodded, and they coaxed her to say enough to get it recorded.

"I was bad at things, too," she said. "I wasn't efficient."

"And last night he waited for you, to surprise you?"

"To frighten me," said Hermione. "He liked doing that. He didn't know I was out."

"Where were you?"

"Here—in Creddington. Just up the hill," said Hermione. "I've got friends here, and a job. You will let me go home soon, won't you? I have to go to work tomorrow."

"Who are your friends," asked Bagley. "And where do you work?"

She told them. It needn't be secret, now.

"The Wilsons will be expecting me tomorrow morning," she said. "I can't let them down."

"I'm afraid you won't be able to go," said Windsor.

"But why not?"

They were not ready to charge her yet. Before they did so, Karen wanted her to describe in detail what had happened before she stabbed Walter.

"Tell us again about how he hit you," she said.

"Well, I fell down, and he kicked me," said Hermione. She

rubbed her hand against her side. "I've got some bruises," she added. "You saw them."

"Yes, I did," said Karen Kent. "You should have a solicitor, Mrs. Brown. It's in your own interests. We can find you one."

Hermione had begun to look on Karen as a friend. Her advice must be good; she had better accept what she said.

"All right," she said, then added, "I didn't mean to hurt him, but he said he was going to kill me and eat both our dinners later. He wanted me to go up to the bedroom with him, and I couldn't do that. Then he fell and dropped the knife and I picked it up."

"What happened next?" asked Windsor.

"I pushed it towards him to stop him getting at me," said Hermione. She was sure she could not be in any real trouble; she had only been defending herself.

When she was back in her cell, Windsor said to Karen Kent, "There have been cases of murderers eating large meals after killing their victims. Haigh, for instance, and Jeremy Bamber. The late Mr. Brown seems to have anticipated an increase in appetite. Nevertheless, he was the one who was killed."

"She's looking at manslaughter, isn't she?" Karen Kent said.

"She's looking at murder," said Windsor.

23

Hermione had begun to feel very frightened. It was not like the fear that she had had of Walter: no one was going to hurt her physically while she was in the police station, but she had lost what control she had ever had over her life. She was a prisoner, although she had not yet been charged with any crime.

It was going to happen, though. The solicitor, Carol Glossop, a little younger than herself, had explained it to her. Hermione had not denied killing Walter; indeed, she had admitted it. The fact that it had been done in self-defence would entitle her only to plead provocation; it would not exonerate her. There would be evidence to convict her. The knife, though washed, was on the drainer and bore her prints. It could be matched to the wound. Other factors would be discovered, and, indeed, later reports showed that some blood spots were found on the floor leading towards the lobby.

"It's a pity you cleaned up the carrots," said Carol Glossop, hearing that part of Hermione's story. "They'd prove he fell." There might be traces on the soles of his shoes. She would ask for tests to be carried out but it might be too late; no one else would have thought of protecting the shoes from contact with other surfaces, though they would have been bagged and labelled. Any carrot vestiges might have been lost when the body was moved.

Carol had other matters to deal with: she needed to find out if the two daughters knew about their father's death and Hermione's arrest.

"Must they be told? Can't we wait till it's cleared up and I'm home again?" Hermione had asked. Of course Jane and Sarah must eventually learn that Walter was dead and she supposed they would want to know how it happened.

"I'm afraid this won't be sorted out in five minutes," Carol told her. She could see that Hermione was still in shock but that could last for days, or even weeks. Soon she would realise the gravity of her situation.

"The Wilsons," Hermione mumbled, and Carol agreed to to tell them that she could not come to work the next day; she would paraphrase the message because Hermione would not be going there for a long time. Carol wanted to talk to the Wilsons; they might know something about the private life of the Browns. At this early stage, Carol had already assessed Hermione as the real victim and meant to find every possible piece of evidence there was to support that opinion.

"What about the house?" she asked. "Is there a mortgage?" For if there was, and payments ceased, Hermione and the girls could lose their home.

"No," said Hermione. "Anyway, by rights it should be mine."

She told Carol about her inheritance of the original house, and Carol nodded. This information, released in court, would help to establish Walter's attitude, if by astute questioning the defence barrister could get Hermione to reveal it at her trial.

"I'll be seeing a lot of you," she told Hermione. "And I'll do everything in my power to help you."

It was thanks to Karen Kent that she had got the case. The two had met on other cases and Karen had contrived to let her know that there was an interesting client in their custody. Carol had acted in domestic disputes and incidents involving children. Her crisp, matter-of-fact yet sympathetic manner had won confidences out of unlikely people and Karen thought Hermione would speak more freely to her than to a male solicitor. She had told Carol about the carrots, and the plate of supper with both portions piled on it as if Walter planned to have an extra large meal.

"And Hermione's plate, soiled but with no food on it, as if she had eaten, was on the dining-table," said Karen, who had seen it. "And there are the bruises."

"Bruises?"

"Awful ones on her ribs. He hit her on the head and knocked her down, then put the boot in," said Karen.

"Thank God you told me," said Carol, who was on her way out of the police station. Now she turned back to insist that a doctor be called to examine her client and report on what injuries were found. She remained at the station until this was done, saw the bruises herself, and required them to be photographed.

There would be a lot of work involved with this case and she must not miss a single detail, however small, which could prove Walter's intent to kill. Even so, it was most unlikely that she would be able to get bail for Hermione. She was no danger to anyone else, but the police might argue that she could harm herself, or seek to influence possible witnesses.

Carol would have to go through all the papers in the Browns' house, to prove Hermione's claim that it was hers. She made a note not to forget.

Because of the delay over the doctor, Hermione was not charged that night, which meant she could stay in the care of the Creddington police.

Detective Inspector Windsor had formed a not inaccurate picture of what had really happened, and by now had been in communication with the Metropolitan Police about their suspect. Anxious to solve their own case, they had asked for Walter's car, which they needed to examine, and they wanted to view the body and take away some of Walter Brown's clothing. The London victims had had long hair; it was possible that there were strands of hair which could be matched in the car, or on some of his garments. Neither victim had bled, and because of their profession, genetic fingerprinting of semen found in their bodies was not likely to yield definite proof that he had had intercourse with them; sufficient other evidence must be found to confirm his guilt, if he was their man.

It was agreed that two officers would come down the next day and meet Detective Inspector Windsor at the Browns' house. They could remove whatever they wanted as long as it was not required as evidence in the case against Hermione, and they could have a look at Walter in the morgue.

"We'll take a picture. Show it to the witness who described him," said Detective Inspector Ferrars.

By that time the post-mortem would be over, and they could have a copy of the pathologist's report. If Walter was the London killer, he would claim no more victims.

That evening, Carol Glossop telephoned the Wilsons, intending to make an appointment to see them in the next few days, but as a result of the conversation she had with Nigel, they arranged to meet at once. He and his wife, he had told Carol, had both seen Hermione with bruising from a black eye and he suspected that it had not been caused, as she alleged, by an accident. He would check the date and then, as he was a journalist and had many contacts, he would take steps to spread some details which could be reported before Hermione was charged and the case became *sub judice*.

Meanwhile, the solicitor had learned that the police had gone to the Browns' house about another matter and had then discovered Walter's body. Hermione, of course, knew nothing about the Metropolitan Police's wish to question him about the prostitutes' murders. With Nigel sitting in Carol's house, nursing a cup of strong coffee, they discussed how releasing this information might help Hermione.

"He can't be libelled as he's dead," said Nigel with satisfaction. "Poor Hermione—she told us her name was Mary—trapped in that prison of terror." He could see the headlines in his mind's eye; what a feature he could write when this was over; it might even make a book. "She was too scared of him to say she was working. And I wondered if she was saving for a surprise holiday for them both." He was determined to do what he could to help her now, though it would be little enough. "What are her chances?" he asked Carol.

"Not great," said Carol.

"Well, let's see what we can do to win public opinion to her cause," said Nigel. "I'll get going. We'll be in touch."

He could be a useful ally. Carol was aware that he saw there could be something in it for him, but he was informed; she had not had to explain that the dice were loaded against women who killed their brutal husbands, while men who alleged their wives drove them to commit the ultimate act were treated with sympathy by the courts.

So far, the only information which had been released about Walter's death was that a man's body had been removed from a house in Merbury and that a woman was helping police with their enquiries. No names, at this juncture, had been given.

"The worm was beginning to turn, you know," Nigel said, as Carol saw him to the door. "She was looking better. She'd lost weight and had a decent haircut. She'd even been talking about doing some sort of training—maybe a degree course."

"I wonder what the daughters are like," said Carol. "I hope they won't go to pieces and add to her problems."

"You'll soon know," said Nigel. Then he added, "A case like this is a shot in the arm for you, isn't it?"

"A challenge, more likely," said Carol. "I get to see a fair number of battered wives, but not many who've got themselves charged with murder, I must admit."

"She'll need a bloody good barrister," said Nigel.

"She'll have one," Carol assured him.

Jane was told the news that night.

A policewoman called at the squat and was let in by Mandy, who felt anxious. Visits from the police were not welcomed by tenants who were paying no rent. Jane was round at Steve's flat, but Mandy knew the address and the woman officer went off at once, her present mission more urgent than investigating any possible irregularities here.

Jane was not told that Hermione had killed Walter, simply that he was dead and her mother was helping the police find out what had happened. Jane wanted to go to her straight away, but the officer said it would be better to wait until the morning.

"You might not be allowed to see her," she said.

"Why not?" asked Jane, and then the realisation swept over her.

"You don't mean she's—?"

"Your father was stabbed," said the policewoman. "The circumstances aren't quite clear just at present."

"You mean my mother's in prison?" gasped Jane.

"No. She's in Creddington police station assisting with enquiries," said the policewoman doggedly.

"Oh God—she couldn't handle it any longer, I suppose," said Jane, and burst into a storm of noisy weeping.

The policewoman stayed until she had calmed down and had agreed to put off going to Creddington until the next day. When she had gone, Jane told Steve that she must telephone Sarah at once.

"She'll come home now," she said. "We both left because of Dad. Mum's going to need us."

Steve had seen that he was no longer the focus of her interest. "I need you too," he said, but faintly.

"You're not in a police cell," said Jane. "Can I use the phone to ring Sarah? I'll pay you back."

24

In the morning, Jane was allowed to see Hermione.

Both wept, clasped together, and watched over by Karen Kent.

"It was an accident," Hermione kept gasping, while Jane scarcely heard her words, patting her and trying to speak reassuringly.

"Sarah's coming home," she said. "She's catching the first possible plane."

"But how will she pay for her fare? She won't have any money," said Hermione. "She hasn't finished repaying—" and she stopped. Jane did not know about Sarah's theft.

"I don't know how she's fixed it," said Jane. "Maybe the British Consul is stumping up, or her boss is paying to be rid of her."

They both giggled weakly at this suggestion, but then Hermione began to cry again.

"Oh, I'm so sorry," she said, amid sobs.

"It's over, Mum," said Jane, who could not imagine what situation had sparked off the final scene. It must have been dreadful. "I'm going to see your solicitor and she can explain everything. Don't worry about anything. You'll be out of here in no time. I'll see to the house, and I'll come and see you again as soon as I can." Or as soon as they'll let me, she thought, suddenly aware that her mother was caught in the toils of a remorseless bureaucratic process.

Hermione looked so small, as though she had shrunk in the few days since they last met, but she was not broken. She seemed dazed, but not as cowed as Jane had often seen her.

"I slept well last night," Hermione volunteered. "Isn't that weird? In a police cell," and again she laughed, as though she was really amused. Jane realised that her mother's laugh was something she had rarely heard. "I'll be home tomorrow, if not later today," she added.

"She won't, will she?" Jane asked Karen Kent on the way out, and Karen shook her head.

"I'm afraid not," she said.

"Dad was a shit," said Jane. "He made all our lives hell. That's why Sarah and I both left. If we hadn't, Mum mightn't have flipped."

"She didn't flip," said Karen. "He did."

Wendy Tucker had broken the chain that held the front door; she had damaged the door, hammering at it with a heavy stone from the path until eventually the screws holding the chain tore away. Her mother had begun to recover consciousness while this went on, and when the doctor arrived he did not think she need go to hospital. She had not had a heart attack, simply an attack of faintness. Had she had a fright of some sort?

Emily admitted that she had opened the door to a man who resembled someone the police wanted to interview in connection with two murders.

"He was rude and aggressive," she said.

"No wonder that frightened you," said the doctor, wondering why the man had called at this particular house. It was probably of no significance; he was unlikely to have been the wanted man. There was no need to pursue the matter.

He reassured both Emily and her daughter. Wendy would take time off from work to care for the invalid, and would not return until next week at the earliest. She saw the doctor out and then went back to her mother's room.

"You didn't let that man in, did you?" she asked. The door, after all, had been securely on the chain when she arrived home herself.

"Yes," said Mrs. Fisher. She had decided that the danger to Hermione was so great that she must confess the truth to Wendy, who would have to tell the police about Walter's likeness to the man shown in the papers. But it would have to wait until she had regained a little strength.

Philip Shaw, in Walter's office, had thought he could be the murderer: Mrs. Fisher was convinced that he was the wanted man. She had known, during their minutes together, that she was in the company of a truly evil person.

Mrs. Fisher had slept for most of the next day. On Thursday, Wendy listened impassively while her mother revealed that Hermione Brown had been visiting her every week.

"She was a lonely woman," said Mrs. Fisher. "And frightened, as I began to realise. Probably you don't remember our meeting that day at Primmy's; we had a little chat while you were paying for our lunch and she had finished her meal just as you reached the table, so there was no occasion for you to talk to her." The tiny, face-saving fiction was necessary. "Then we met by chance at Brenda's." She must trust Wendy now. "Hermione has a part-time job in Creddington," she said.

"Why didn't you tell me about her before?" asked Wendy.

"I thought you might not approve of our friendship," said her mother, and improvised, "You might be afraid she would tire me. But she did me good. I enjoyed her company."

She waited for the scolding that must follow and there was a pause while Wendy considered her response. She was profoundly shocked that her mother should conceal something that was clearly of great importance to her.

"She might be out for what she could get from you," said Wendy, whose husband had spent many years in a near missionary role but who rarely believed the best of people.

"Oh Wendy, my dear, what could she get out of me? A cup of coffee? A little conversation? That's scarcely a threat to you," said Mrs. Fisher and her voice quavered as she felt a pang of disappointed anger.

Wendy's face reddened.

"Do you think that's why I've discouraged you from having visitors?" she said.

"What else should I think?"

"I wanted to protect you," Wendy said. She had been terrified when she saw her mother lying crumpled on the floor the day before. What would be the purpose of her life if—when— her mother died? She often had that nightmare.

Mrs. Fisher was silent. Perhaps what Wendy said was true. She could not risk a scene, however; she had strength enough only to deal with a limited amount of emotion. Even so, there were things that must be said, steps that must be taken. She had felt too weak until now to warn Wendy that Hermione could be in danger; no more time must be lost.

"The man who came here yesterday was Hermione's husband," she said. "He's exactly like a man the police are looking for, for murder. He didn't know she had the job here and another nearer Merbury, where they live. He hit her only two weeks or so ago— she had a black eye. I was going to ask you what she ought to do—who could help her. You know about these things."

"But you didn't," Wendy said.

"I was going to choose my moment," said Mrs. Fisher.

"Am I such an ogre that you have to humour me?" Wendy burst out.

"Your work is tiring," Mrs. Fisher temporised.

"You would have had to tell me what you've told me now— about her visits," Wendy said. "You were frightened of me."

Mrs. Fisher clasped her hands together, gripping them for courage.

"You can be quite formidable," she declared.

Wendy could not answer this. She looked away and swallowed, then created a diversion.

"How did the husband know that—er—Hermione was here?" she asked.

"I don't know. Perhaps he followed her," said Mrs. Fisher. "Anyway, Hermione needs help. What can we do for her?"

Wendy got up and left the room. She returned a few moments later with a newspaper.

"You'd better read this," she said. "It's too late to help her, if these are the same Browns."

The paper—one of the better tabloids—contained a photograph of Walter Brown—an old one, shown in grainy reproduction, taken at a village fête in Merbury. A contact of Nigel's on the *Freston News*, a weekly free paper, had unearthed it and had sent it out by fax. This was the man, said the report, whose dead body had been found when police called at his house to interview him about a serious crime. A woman was helping police with their enquiries into his death.

"Is that the man?" asked Wendy.

"I'm not sure—it could be," said Mrs. Fisher. "It says here that the body was found in Merbury." She looked up at her daughter. "Walter Brown is dead?" She could not believe it.

"So it says," said Wendy.

"Not Hermione. Thank God. That man had murder in his heart when he was here," said Mrs. Fisher.

"This report implies that she may have killed him," said Wendy. "She must be the woman who is helping the police."

"Oh no! Oh, she wouldn't," said Mrs. Fisher. "She's much too frightened of him to do anything like that."

"He came here looking for her. They must have met again

at home," said Wendy reasonably. "That is, if he didn't waylay
her on her way back. It may be important for the police to be
told that he came to see you, and what his manner was," she
went on. "And the fact that he alarmed you so much that you
collapsed when he had gone. I'll go and telephone them. I
think you ought to make a statement, when you're up to it."

"Yes," agreed Emily. "You're right. And I'm up to it now."
She had to be. Too much time had been lost already.

Later that day a constable came to hear what Emily had to
say and to take her statement, but by then Hermione had
already appeared in court, charged with murdering her husband.

"Oh, poor girl," said Mrs. Fisher when they heard the news.
It was on the local radio station, to which they listened in case
it was mentioned.

"She's hardly a girl, mother," said Wendy. "But I think we
should find out who her solicitor is and make sure he knows
what happened here, in case the police don't think it relevant.
You can tell him—or her—about his ill-treatment of his
wife."

"You don't think she killed him?"

"I don't know the facts. She may have had to, to save
herself," said Wendy. "I'll go and do some telephoning—see
what I can find out. Do you know who her employers were?"

Mrs. Fisher did.

"She likes the Wilsons, at Prendsmere," she said. "The
husband's a free-lance writer of some sort. They might be more
helpful than the other household."

"I'll try them first," said Wendy.

By being busy, she could delay facing squarely what she had
learned today: that she was guilty of frightening her mother
who saw her as a despot.

Nigel's contacts had, as he said later, "come good," and several
of the daily papers featured the Merbury story in vague terms,

always including the information that the police had visited the house in the course of investigating another matter.

Hermione, however, knew nothing about these prompt and subtle efforts on her behalf.

After Jane's visit a steely calm had come over her. The tears she had shed had been for herself, for her fears, and from shock, but she had not shed one for Walter, nor would she. She was glad that he was dead. The pity of it was that she had caused his death, albeit accidentally, and she must face the consequences, but once it was understood by the court—she knew now that she must go before the magistrates that morning— that her action had been necessary to save herself, they would understand and free her. After her surprisingly restful night on the hard bunk in her cell, she looked forward to returning home. Jane would want her own room; Sarah might be back later that day. With clean sheets on the big bed, she would sleep peacefully there, alone. She planned her actions, waiting for the next event in her day.

Carol Glossop arrived before Hermione left for the court, and broke it to her that she would be charged with murder.

"I'll apply for bail," she said. "But I'm sure it won't be granted. You'll go to prison on remand, Hermione. I can't save you from that."

Hermione stared at her. She had never imagined this could happen.

"But it was an accident," she said. "I didn't mean to kill him. I'll explain."

"You can't, now," said Carol. "You'll be able to later." Hermione would be her own best witness. "You'll plead not guilty, and when you come to trial we'll plead self-defence and provocation." Carol did not think Hermione, at the moment, was capable of understanding that a plea of guilty to manslaughter might save her a more serious conviction. When the evidence had been assessed, counsel's advice on this would be important. It was possible that the Crown Prosecution Service might adjust the charge when they had seen the papers. "I must warn you what to expect, Hermione. You'll cope. I'll help, and so will your daughters. You won't go to pieces."

Carol said this firmly, not entirely sure that it was true because prison would be a shattering experience for Hermione, as it was for everyone.

Hermione pulled at a thread on her sweater.

"I don't suppose it will be for long," she said. "And Walter won't be there."

If only Hermione had good, solid parents—such as they must, in fact, have been—into whose care she could have been released! But without that sort of guarantee, there was no way she would be allowed bail. Moreover, she would be in prison for months before her trial. She would find out about that soon enough from other remand inmates when she was taken away and locked up.

Carol told her what to expect in court.

"It won't take long," she said. "And Jane and Sarah will be allowed to see you afterwards." She had already spoken to Detective Inspector Windsor about this. "And they'll come and visit you, and so will I, and other friends. There's no restriction on visitors for remand prisoners." She patted Hermione's arm. "By the way, Nigel and Laura Wilson sent their love."

Nigel. Hermione had almost forgotten him. She should have been at Downs Farm today. How remote it seemed.

"What about money for the girls?" she asked. "There's my wages." She told Carol where she had hidden her savings.

"Don't worry about that now," said Carol. "We'll sort something out." The fact that there was no mortgage on the house removed one big problem while Walter's estate was frozen. If Hermione were convicted, she would not be entitled to any of his property, but it would go to the daughters, obviously. No one had yet seen his will. Meanwhile, the girls could live in the house and work, or if not, be supported by the State while they looked for jobs. The neighbours might be helpful; Mr. Robert Mountford, who lived in Merbury, had already identified Walter, which had saved one of his daughters from carrying out the formality.

"A friend of yours is meeting Sarah at Heathrow. Pam Norton," Carol added.

"Oh, how kind of her," cried Hermione, amazed.

"You get surprises when things like this happen," Carol said. "Unexpected people show support."

She did not add, "And erstwhile friends may turn aside."

25

Detective Inspector Ferrars had viewed the body.

Naked, in a long steel drawer, Walter lay chilled, available for inspection and eventual disposal. Ferrars did not require that he be turned over to expose the fatal wound; Walter's life, not his death, was Ferrars' concern, but he looked at all the photographs and took away a set which had been prepared for him.

The clothes Walter had been wearing when he died were bagged and labelled. His jacket and shirt, both stained with blood and slit by the penetrating knife, would be available as exhibits at Hermione's trial. Ferrars asked that they be checked for human hair other than Walter's or his wife's. Then he went, with officers from Creddington, to the house in Merbury where they found Walter's tweed hat and his raincoat, which they took away. They also removed the shoes Walter had been wearing when he died, and another pair, spotlessly clean and gleaming, which were in his wardrobe. It was like a former soldier to keep his shoes so brightly polished, they thought, unware that this was one of Hermione's tasks. When they were first married, Walter had stood over her like a sergeant with a recruit, teaching her how to achieve that special gloss. Any soil adhering to Walter's shoes, if it was he who had dumped the murdered woman near the A1, would by now have been removed, but there had been a muddy footprint on her blouse, as if she had been trodden on. Forensic experts might make something of this.

They did not find his pornographic magazines. Carol Glossop, going through his papers, was the one who ultimately did, together with the note he'd copied, forging Hermione's handwriting. She understood its purpose. Whether to produce it in court or not was a matter to be decided later; it might confuse the issue, as handwriting experts would have to be called to testify that it was not written by Hermione.

Hermione, weeks later, asked Carol about the magazines, afraid the girls would find them. Carol assured her that she had removed them. Hermione need not be told that they were locked up safely in case they were needed as evidence of Walter's interests.

Examination of the Maestro yielded only a little: there were hairs on the rug in the boot, some of which proved to be Hermione's, and other, longer ones came from the second murder victim. There were also small fibres of a synthetic fabric matching the dead girl's fake fur coat. The rug had probably been used to cover up her body while she was being taken to the spot where she was dumped. Hypostasis staining had indicated that she had been moved after death.

There was other evidence. Ferrars took his photographs with him when he went to see the woman whose description of a violent client had resulted in the artist's impression that resembled Walter.

He had a tattoo on his upper arm. Hermione had had a shock when she first saw it. It had been done in his army days after a night out in Cyprus, and was a replica of his regimental crest. Since then, his regiment had been disbanded and married up with another, but the crest was identifiable and when she saw it, in an enlarged photograph, the woman recognised it straight away. She had drawn a rough sketch of it when she first went to the police and when they showed her illustrations of regimental crests, she had picked it out with no difficulty. She said she had had plenty of time to look at it while she struggled to break free from Walter and, in the end, she had bitten him on the arm.

Army records showed that Walter had served with that regiment. Hard evidence, now, linked him with the London murders, and it looked as if those cases would be neatly solved without the expense and labour of a trial.

Walter, in later years, had regretted his tattoo and it was almost always covered.

Meanwhile Hermione, on remand, knew nothing of this investigation.

The press found the two cases interesting. They could no longer report anything directly connected with Hermione as she had been charged and was remanded, but they picked up the point that an enquiry from the Metropolitan Police had led to local officers calling at the Browns' house. A persistent reporter tracked down the prostitute who had survived Walter's overtures and she lost no time in describing him as a nasty customer. Since he was dead, this did not damage him, as the dead cannot defend themselves from libel and assailing their reputations is not an offence. The woman gave a fruity interview to a paper and was paid a handsome fee. The same reporter went round Merbury trying to prise information about Walter from the local people, but no one would discuss his treatment of Hermione, though her shyness was mentioned.

Jane and Sarah, now living in the house—at first it had been sealed by the police and they had spent two nights at the Nortons', opposite—would not say a word, but the reporter gleaned the information that both had left home as soon as they could.

Hermione only heard of the newspaper reports which linked Walter with the London murders when shown them by other prison inmates. By this time she had been committed for trial; forensic testing and the tying up of evidence in the London case took a while to complete.

She could not believe what she was reading. How could Walter have done those things to those women?

Easily, she realised: he had intended to kill her, and he had wound her long hair round her neck. So there was no mistress. When he came home late, he had been out prowling the streets, looking for prostitutes to abuse and murder.

Other women in the prison told her this would help her case. Walter would be shown, at her trial, to be a hardened strangler; she must plead provocation.

Well, she would. It was in order to save herself that she had picked up the knife. Had she really pushed it into Walter, or simply held it facing him? Again and again she tried to recall those moments, and always she was sure that she had made a movement towards him as he, turned away, was trying to stand up.

In prison with her was a woman whose husband had constantly beaten her; she had crept up on him when he was sleeping and had stabbed him many times. She had been sentenced to life because her crime was premeditated.

"Why didn't you leave him?" Hermione had asked.

"Where could I go?" replied the woman. "And what about the kids?"

What about them now, thought Hermione.

"Why didn't you leave yours?" the woman asked her, and Hermione could not answer.

She still blamed herself for Walter's treatment of her. In prison, where she saw a psychiatrist twice—and later learned she was lucky in that—she began to question this attitude and to see how a similar loss of self-esteem had brought low some of her fellow inmates.

*   *   *

Hermione had lived a lonely, isolated life for years. Because she had no confidence, she was not self-reliant, but she was good at fading inconspicuously into her surroundings and this helped her in her first weeks in prison. To begin with, the dream-like feeling that none of this could really be happening persisted. The shock of being strip-searched, sent to have a shower under supervision, being led off to a cell, prolonged the numbness she had felt since Walter's death. She still could not quite take in what had happened and would suddenly start up into an alert, alarmed state only to realise that one sort of fear was gone for ever, superseded though it was by another.

Her first aim was to get through the days without provoking any trouble, much the same as her objective in her marriage, and it was easier here. She had a cell to herself, and was locked up in it for hours. Being unable to open the door was dreadful, but she reminded herself that no one could burst in on her to harm her and gave thanks for that.

Strangely, Hermione continued to sleep well, as she had done while in the police cell. The prison was very noisy; other women yelled or cried at night, and called to one another through their windows. By day, she found it disturbing and unsettling, but at night, because none of it was directed to-wards her, she could ignore it. In fact she was suffering from total exhaustion and nature mercifully supplied her with the remedy which otherwise the doctor might have ordered.

She began to discover horrifying facts about other prisoners' lives and soon found that showing interest in them deflected their curiosity about her. Some were in for drug offences, others for prostitution and for theft. In several cases, arrest had meant children going into care; there was the risk that the prisoner, once released, might never get them back. Cases existed where such children had been adopted during their mother's sentence. All sorts of tragedies were revealed to Her-

mione in the intervals between her court appearances when her
remand sentence was renewed.

She had persuaded herself, against Carol Glossop's opinion,
that at her committal hearing she would be released; she was
convinced that the lawyers studying the papers would decide
there was no case to answer, but she was wrong. She had
not denied killing Walter, though she pleaded not guilty to
murder. The recorded interview revealed that she had picked
up the knife Walter had dropped when he fell.

"I held it out to stop him getting at me," she had said.

There was only her word for the fact that Walter had threatened her with it, though there were the bruises. They, however, did not prove his intent was murderous, merely brutal.
It was possible that Walter had never held the knife. She could
have taken it from the drawer and seized her chance to stab
him. After she was committed for trial she knew that her stay
in prison would be prolonged.

In her quiet way she had made several friends and had
managed not to attract enemies. Never a rebel, it was easier
for her than for many other inmates to conform to the routine.
Because she had had a hysterectomy, problems other women
had in matters of hygiene did not affect her, but as she gradually became aware of the humiliations they experienced, her
interest turned outwards. She saw women who should have
been in psychiatric hospitals, not in prison, and others who
had committed crimes to raise money for drugs, which, she
soon realised, were to be had inside. She found a girl who could
not read—there were many—and helped her; then another.

At this time, she had a lot of visitors. Jane and Sarah came
twice a week; Pam Norton brought her language tapes and
books so that she could study Russian.

"It's very difficult," she said. "It will be a challenge—
tougher for you than improving your school French."

At first, Hermione decided not to attempt the lessons; then
she began studying the script. Some of the characters were

intriguing; she started to copy them, muttering their sounds to herself, and after a while, as Pam had hoped, resolved at least to master the alphabet. It required immense concentration and for a long time she was not capable of such application; her thoughts would wander to her predicament or she would play over in her mind scenes from her life with Walter, but gradually, for increasingly longer spells, she managed to put the past behind her.

One day, she had an unexpected visitor. Mrs. Fisher's daughter, Wendy Tucker, came to see her.

For a moment Hermione did not recognise her, and when she did, sheer surprise made her blush scarlet. She gaped at her like an astonished child.

Wendy's features moved in what, for her, passed for a smile as Hermione silently waited for the reason for the visit to be given. Then she felt suddenly cold: had something happened to Mrs. Fisher? Perhaps she was dead and had left a note asking that Hermione be told.

"Is Mrs. Fisher—?" she began nervously.

Wendy was not one to give a yard when an inch would do.

"My mother has been ill but is better now," she said. "She told me about your meetings. Of course, it was silly of her to be so secretive but then old people are like children. They enjoy intrigue."

Hermione waited.

"She is very concerned about you," Wendy went on. "Your husband must have followed you, that last day. He came to see her after you left."

"Oh no!" Hermione had realised that Walter must have found out about her visits to Mrs. Fisher but it had not occurred to her that he had been to see the old lady.

"Didn't he tell you?"

Hermione shook her head.

Mrs. Fisher had supposed that an interview about Hermione's activities had caused the fatal confrontation, and when she heard that Hermione would not be allowed bail, she had proposed that they should undertake responsibility for her, if the police would release her into their care, but Wendy had refused to suggest it. It would mean too great a commitment, she had said, and might affect her own work. In vain did Mrs. Fisher mention that Hermione would be company for her and could help about the place.

"We don't know what really happened, that last night," Wendy had said. "From what you say, probably Hermione was provoked beyond all bearing, but nevertheless, she has acted violently. She might do so again."

"She wouldn't be provoked here," said Mrs. Fisher.

"I doubt very much if it would be allowed," said Wendy. "We're not related. She's a new acquaintance. It would not be appropriate."

Mrs. Fisher had not had much confidence in her plan. It would have worked only if Wendy had been determined to make it a success.

"My mother told the police about your husband's visit," Wendy now informed Hermione. "She described his aggressive manner. That may help your case."

"Yes." Hermione nodded. She was shocked to think that Walter had somehow traced her movements and had approached Mrs. Fisher. What else was she to learn about him?

"I've been to see your daughters," Wendy continued. "I've been able to advise Sarah about a place at university. I think she should secure one, somewhere. I expect she's told you."

She hadn't. Their visits had been so fraught, the girls so concerned about her and so intent on reassuring her that all was well at home, that Hermione had had few satisfactory answers to her questions about their plans.

"Then there's this girl, Mandy, and her baby son," said Wendy.

"Oh, she's had it then—it was a boy!" Hermione did show animation now.

Jane had asked if Mandy and the baby could move in with her and Sarah, and Hermione had agreed instantly.

"Yes—eight pounds and noisy," Wendy said. "She's still in hospital but she is going to Merbury with the baby in a few days' time. I'm taking her over. I think it's a good idea," she allowed. "It will benefit all the young people. A baby is a statement of renewal."

"Are people shunning them? They won't tell me," said Hermione. "Will anybody talk to them?"

"Indeed yes." Wendy knew that tabloid newspapers had tried to sign them up for their stories, but so far they had resisted exploiting their situation for financial gain. There was no point in telling Hermione about that. "A Mrs. Norton who lives opposite has been helpful," she said.

Wendy herself had determined to supervise the three young women and the infant, and had been quite put out to discover that Pam Norton had cast herself in the same role.

"I didn't come to see you sooner because I didn't want to unsettle you before the hearing," said Wendy, who had dreaded this visit. She still felt uncomfortable about her part in causing the deception of the secret visits, not that they had anything to do with the death of Walter Brown. Never one in the past to walk away from trouble, Wendy had wanted to, this time. "How are you managing?" Her mother would want to know.

"All right," said Hermione.

"The time will pass," said Wendy. "I shall come again."

"Thank you," said Hermione.

Both of them parted with relief, Wendy with her duty done, Hermione still shocked. Walter, in his anger, might have harmed Mrs. Fisher.

26

The weeks went by, sometimes slowly, sometimes fast. The rest of her life could be like this, Hermione realised: she could be confined for ever, or at best be released on parole after nine or ten years.

There were worse fates. She was better here than living with her husband but she missed the comfort of her home, the things she took for granted such as constant hot water, baths when she wished, and most of all, privacy. When Walter was out of the house, she had had that.

On one of Carol Glossop's visits, at a meeting with the barrister who would defend Hermione—not a name, but a young woman planning to become one—they discussed a plea of manslaughter, which would mean a lighter sentence if she were convicted. It would have been the safe course: the prosecution would have accepted it as a tidy ending and an avoidance of uproar if she were sentenced to life, as would be mandatory with a murder verdict.

"It wasn't premeditated. That's the thing," Carol had told Hermione. "You didn't snatch the knife from the drawer intending to kill him, did you?"

"No. He took it out," said Hermione.

She understood, now, what was at stake, and she was determined to maintain her plea of innocence. The two lawyers thought she had a slim chance; much would depend on the jury and what they made of the story they would hear in court.

If he chose, the judge could direct them towards a verdict of manslaughter. Carol had deliberately selected a woman counsel who could be trusted not to patronise her client nor to overlook any tiny points which might be helpful, though it was Carol's job to unearth those.

Wendy Tucker had approached her, saying that she knew matters helpful to the defence were not always disclosed by the police, and had Carol known about Walter Brown's visit to her mother, Mrs. Fisher, a friend of Hermione's?

Carol, ploughing through the papers, had not yet come on this report.

She went to see Mrs. Fisher, who, lest she be struck down and prevented from appearing in court herself, swore an affidavit attesting to what she knew about the state of Hermione's marriage, the black eye and bruises, and her need to earn money.

One day, Nigel Wilson came to see Hermione. He said he was writing a feature about women in prison, the rigours they had to undergo, the physical indignities and the stresses and strains.

Hermione was astonished to see him and her heart gave a leap in her chest. Colour flooded her cheeks.

"You don't look too bad at all," he said.

"I'm not," she answered.

Women prisoners did not have to wear uniform and she was dressed in a red sweater and a grey flannel skirt. Her daughters had brought her the sweater for Christmas, which they had spent with the Nortons. They had brought her a track suit, too, for practical use, and some pyjamas in much the same style as the track suit.

"Mandy's advice," said Jane. "She's afraid you'll have trouble at night."

When Hermione realised the implication of this, she burst out laughing.

"I'm banged up at night. I've still got a cell to myself," she said, adding quickly, "but that could change. We take nothing for granted here. Thanks."

Her laughter surprised them. They had seldom heard it at home.

"You're being very positive, Mum," said Jane, who was always on the verge of tears at their meetings. Her feelings were partly shame that she and Sarah had deserted their mother and left her so vulnerable, partly pity, and partly fear of the future if things went badly at the trial.

The car had been returned when the police had finished with it, and this made their visits easier. Both Jane and Mandy had licences, and they had determined that Sarah must be taught to drive by a proper instructor and pass her test as soon as possible. Jane had learned during her months with her first lover, Felix.

On their visits, Hermione always wanted to know how they were managing: what about money?

They said that Carol had been wonderful. She had warned them, before the committal proceedings, that Hermione's chance of getting bail was not great; they would be considered too young to take responsibility for her, even though Jane had abandoned her plans to move in with Steve and was living in the house with Sarah. Walter had made no will, it seemed, and had had no dealings with any solicitor since the house was bought except over a boundary dispute soon after the move to Merbury. However, Carol had obtained a copy of Hermione's father's will and could now prove that the original house and contents had been hers. Hermione would have a sound claim to what remained, and if she were convicted of murder, it would be a nice legal point as to whether the method of Walter's death disqualified her from repossessing what was hers. In any case, the two girls would be the ultimate heirs, and because there were some investments, Carol had told them to send her all the household bills—the gas, electricity and telephone. She would make an arrangement with the bank. Meanwhile, if they could earn some money for other expenses, they should try to do so.

"In other words, you're safe in the house but there's no money coming in," said Hermione, and they nodded.

It seemed that Walter had carried no insurance policy. Would she get a widow's pension from the state? If you were in prison, no doubt it was held back to pay for your imprisonment, she thought, and could not bring herself to ask.

When they left her and went home, the girls were always wretched. The prison horrified them; what if she were there for years? Waiting through the weeks and months before the trial was a fearful strain.

Neither knew that Walter had told Hermione he meant to kill her, only that, according to her, he had threatened her with a knife which he had dropped and she had snatched up, and somehow, as a consequence, had stabbed him.

"Do you believe that's really what happened?" Jane had asked her sister.

"Of course I do! Don't you?" Sarah was indignant.

"There's only her word. The police may say she did it deliberately—that she made up her story of him going for her," said Jane.

"Well, if they do, that will only be their word," said Sarah.

"If she'd set out to kill him, she'd have stabbed him more than once," said Mandy. "That's what people do, and the women wait for their husbands to be asleep, so as to surprise them."

"Like Delilah," said Jane, who throughout her life had regularly attended church and Sunday School.

"Who was she?" asked Mandy, who thought Jane must be referring to someone now in gaol. After this allusion had been explained to her, and Sarah had pointed out that Samson had lost his hair, not his life, she said, "Hermione didn't go after him into the lobby. If she'd been meaning to kill him, she'd have done that. Made sure."

"She didn't call for help, either," said Jane. "She didn't ring for an ambulance. She went to bed."

"Not right away," said Sarah. "She sat here for ages, she told me. Shock, I suppose."

The three girls were sitting in the kitchen while they talked. At first Jane and Sarah were reluctant to be in the room where the final scene of their father's life had been played out, but they quickly recognised that this must be overcome. They had scrubbed the whole area with soap and disinfectant, and had then painted the walls and ceiling with several coats of brilliant white paint. They had thrown away the vinyl flooring and scrubbed the tiles beneath until they had worn away the bristles of the new scrubbing brush bought for the purpose.

A stout, elderly woman, very ugly, had called while they were working on this purification rite. She had declared her name to be Mrs. Tucker and had said that her mother was a friend of Hermione's; she wished to make sure that they were managing alone, and had money enough for their daily needs. When she saw what they were doing, she gave them fifty pounds, which she said they could repay later when things were sorted out. They were not to go short on paint, she said, and perhaps they could gradually do the rest of the house to give their mother a fresh start when she was released.

"You think she will be?" the girls asked her.

"We must keep faith that justice will be done," said Wendy. One day, Hermione would come out of prison, even if it were not for years; meanwhile, painting the house was therapeutic for the daughters. "I'll call again," she had said, and kept her word.

The girls found her rather a weird old bat, like an old-fashioned headmistress, but the voice of authority was a comfort to them, and Mrs. Tucker seemed informed about the law.

She and Mandy, who also had knowledge lacked by the sisters, agreed that petitions could be organised if an unfavourable verdict were to be returned.

Mandy applied to the Wilsons for the cleaning post left vacant by Hermione, and was engaged. She drove to Downs Farm in the Maestro, taking Jasper with her. Nigel found her rather slapdash and noisy after Hermione's self-effacing efficiency, but she was capable enough, and her presence enabled him to keep in touch with the progress of the case. He was making notes for a book about it, to publish if things went badly for Hermione.

"Goodness, we're so lucky," Sarah said.

The girls were in the sitting-room, where they had been having supper while watching television. Mandy took this procedure for granted, but the two sisters marvelled at their freedom in this house over which their father had ruled as a tyrant. A fire burnt in the grate and baby Jasper was asleep upstairs. Mandy had washed her hair and it hung in damp ringlets round her head. She was still plump after the birth and Sarah had taken to calling her the Earth Mother.

"Why do you say that? I don't think we're lucky at all," said Jane.

"We are. We won't lose our home, Carol is dealing with the essential bills and we can hang on here even if Mum is cooped up for years," said Sarah. "We're young and we can cope. People are helping us a lot. What if we lived in a tower block with no job and no one to back us up? We could be out on the streets."

"Mm," said Jane, who had not seen their situation like this. She was still smarting from the ending of her brief affair with Steve, for though she had told him she would move in with him as soon as she knew what was happening to her mother, that had daily become increasingly impossible because she felt bound to Sarah and the house; Steve had not understood these other claims and he had dropped her. She saw now that she had used first Felix, her original lover, and then Steve as excuses to avoid standing alone, as Mandy and Sarah had done. Mandy had challenged her, telling her that if she wasn't careful she would end up a victim like her mother.

"If we get out of this—if Mum does, I mean," said Sarah, "we must do something about other poor women who've got no back-up."

"You can do it anyway," said Mandy. "The longer your mum's inside, the more you'll learn about the system."

"What can we do?" asked Jane.

"Well, I'm going to go in for law," said Sarah, who had had time to think and who could see how Carol was working to help their mother. She and Mandy understood, in a way Jane seemed unable to accept, that Hermione might be in prison for a very long time. "I'd like to defend people like Mum, who get themselves cornered," Sarah added. She understood that although Hermione's defence would plead provocation and self-defence, nevertheless Walter had been stabbed in the back, not in a struggle for the knife. Hermione had had no slashes or cuts on her arms or wrists, as could be expected in a tussle.

To Jane, her sister's plans sounded daunting. All she wanted, though she would not admit it to the other two, was to get married. She wanted to live in a neat little house with a neat reliable husband and a baby, soon to be followed by another. She had decided to enrol for a catering course. It would be good training for domesticity, and could lead, meanwhile, to work in a hotel where she might meet a conventional man seeking an unambitious girl, she thought wistfully. Wakeful in bed at night, she was fearful of the future. What if she were to be truly alone? At the moment the three of them were helping one another, but that would not last. Sarah, who seemed to Jane to be as brave as a lion, would be off pursuing her legal goal. Mandy would move on one day. What would she do then? She hated even being alone in the house, but this she did not confess.

Unknown to the girls, Pam Norton and Helen Mountford now had a shared arrangement to keep an eye on them, each taking days in turn to call or telephone so that one was always responsible. Helen was prompted by her sense of duty, Pam because she was convinced that if she had not mentioned Hermione's Tuesday outings to Walter, he would not have followed her on that last day. She told herself that sooner or later he would have discovered what Hermione was doing and that the outcome could have been even more tragic, but that did not assuage her guilt.

None of them knew the story of the final night in any detail. Pam, however, had seen Walter's return, that Tuesday, before Hermione came back from her mysterious outing. She had told the police about it, and how untypical it was; Walter often kept very late hours, she said.

The enquiries made in the village by the Metropolitan Police baffled everyone. People who travelled up and down to London on the train, like Walter, were questioned about his movements and several regular commuters had noticed him getting off at Stappenford. No one had discovered why he did this, for Valerie Palmer had kept silent, even when she realised who Walter was and where he lived.

27

The tabloid newspaper which had traced the prostitute who had identified Walter Brown had not given up the trail. If they could sign up Hermione, especially if she were convicted of murder, there would be great popular interest, and then they could run a crusade to have her and women like her treated with more understanding. Whilst her case was *sub judice*, Walter's was not. By degrees the reporter uncovered much of the truth, and meanwhile Nigel had researched cases where victimised women had finally turned on their tormentors with varying results and attracting differing degrees of punishment. There were those who had attempted to hire someone to commit the murder for them; those who had acted to a plan because they were not physically strong enough to defeat their violent partner in a struggle; and there was Hermione, who had won her duel because of the dropped knife.

He talked to Jane and Sarah, who were distressed by *The Blaze* reporter's persistent efforts to interview them. Discovering their father's secret life had been more shocking to them even than learning the extent of their mother's plight, which was so much worse than they had realised.

"Hermione would never have killed him except to save

herself," he told the sisters. "I'm sure he knocked her about. That's how she got the black eye I saw. But she could have ended it. She could have taken out an injunction against him."

The girls had not heard about the black eye. They knew their father was an overbearing bully; now they were having to accept that he was violent, even psychopathic.

"Mum wouldn't have known that," Sarah said.

"She would have found out pretty soon," said Nigel. "She was beginning to win her independence. Taking jobs was the start. She was gaining confidence—I saw that, even in so short a time." He wished he had questioned Hermione more closely about her black eye. Perhaps he could have made her tell him the whole story and then he could have advised her about her rights. Instead, he had arranged the baby-sitting with her, and the following day she had seemed extremely tired. He knew now that she had not told Walter about her jobs; perhaps she had concealed the baby-sitting from him, too, although she had used the car.

It was Nigel who told Carol Glossop about Hermione's baby-sitting engagement and that he had learned from Pam Norton that Walter had a village meeting the same night. The next time she went to see Hermione, Carol asked her about it. Hermione found it difficult to tell her what had happened, but eventually she described her night of terror.

Walter's crimes attracted only the briefest of reports in the quality papers, which mentioned that following his death the case regarding the murdered prostitutes was closed. *The Blaze* still hoped to get an interview with Jane and Sarah, or one of them, but when their reporter came to the house, Mandy sent him away with a flow of strong language, though not before a photographer had taken a shot of Jane's startled face at the window. The persistent team went only as far as The Grapes, where, to their astonishment, no one would discuss the case, simply saying that the two girls had been through enough, with more to face when the trial came up, without being hounded now. Despite offers of money, no one would relate even a minor anecdote about either Jane or Sarah.

Mandy told Nigel about this when she went to work, and he did a piece about the exploitation of raw emotion which he managed to have syndicated round a group of provincial papers and rewrote for one of his magazines.

"You've exploited them too," Mandy accused, after reading one of these articles.

"But in a protective manner," he said. "Better me than the rest of the pack. Besides, it could help Hermione. Very few people are going to be unaware, at her trial, that Walter was a murderer. The judge will tell the jury to put it out of their minds, but there will have been a subliminal effect."

"Hermione's awfully quiet," said Mandy.

"Even you might be quiet in Holloway," said Nigel.

"I don't think I would," said Mandy. "I think I'd be in permanent trouble for being rowdy and disruptive." She laughed. "That hideous woman, Mrs. Tucker, goes to see her sometimes. Mind you, she does make me quiet. It's the best way of getting rid of her—to sit silent and submissive. She comes to supervise our moral welfare."

"I'm sure that's very necessary," Nigel said, grinning.

"Of course, she feels guilty because her own mother might have died after Walter went to see her. Mrs. Tucker had turned the old thing into some sort of prisoner so that she had to keep quiet about Hermione's visits. I haven't quite understood how they met at all."

Neither had Nigel.

"So she's making amends?" he said. "Mrs. Tucker, I mean."

"Seems like it. She's all right really—she's paid for paint and stuff for us to do the house up and now she wants us to make new curtains—she's paying for the material. It's to make it all seem different and fresh when Hermione gets out."

Nigel hoped this was not a distant dream. The place might need doing up again before Hermione came home.

Carol and Imogen Greig, the barrister who was to defend Hermione at her trial, discussed her calm controlled state after a visit to their client.

"She's not going to make a good impression on the jury, if she stays so wooden," said the barrister.

"She's still in shock," said Carol. "It may take her years to recover."

Hermione had answered all the questions asked by Carol and Miss Greig, but in monosyllables in a level tone, and she had shown no distress. It was almost as though she were being medically sedated, and Carol made sure that this was not so, but in fact Hermione's strange calm was self-induced; she was preparing for the future. These months were an apprenticeship for the years that she would spend in prison. She had committed murder, taken a life, and must pay the price; it would be foolish to harbour hopes of an acquittal and then have to face the brutal reality of a different result.

She would not discuss her case with other inmates, though many of them were anxious to talk about their own. Some of them she grew to like, even to respect, and for many she felt pity. A few had committed minor crimes simply to be housed and fed; there were groups of old friends who had met while serving earlier sentences and who greeted each other like schoolgirls at reunions. Hermione's life had been miserable and demeaning, but she had not been short of food, nor lacked a roof over her head. Now, the sort of apprehension that she felt was not terror such as she had known with Walter; it was more a resigned dread. She tried not to think about the trial; why nourish an optimism which would be shattered? She had seen that in other women who went off expecting to be freed or merely fined, and who returned to serve a sentence. She found Miss Greig direct and confident, and she knew Carol

Glossop was doing everything she could to leave no helpful fact undetected. Hermione, when on the stand, would answer truthfully the questions she was asked; all else was out of her control.

A few weeks before her trial she was moved from her single cell into a double with a young woman accused of shoplifting and who was agonising over her children, who had been taken into care. The reason for placing them together was lest Loraine should try to harm herself. There was a great wave of sympathy for her; for such a charge, the other inmates and even some of the officers thought she should get bail, but the magistrates considered she would reoffend. The plan that Hermione and Loraine should share was for their mutual benefit, however, for as her trial date approached, Hermione had seemed so withdrawn that it was feared she might take some drastic action to avoid the ordeal.

Settling down with Loraine was an effort, but Hermione was horrified that she had been locked up at public expense and her children sent to strangers when she had stolen food and toys from a large supermarket on, she said, a single occasion. Another inmate told Hermione that Loraine had been in before for similar offences, but even if that were true, Hermione thought it was not appropriate treatment for her. Compared with Loraine's, her own problems seemed few, for Jane and Sarah were marching forward with their lives, both now committed to courses which would equip them for future independence, though Jane seemed to be emotionally adrift.

"She feels incomplete without a boyfriend," Mandy said, on a rare visit. She came occasionally, leaving Jasper in Merbury with the other girls. "I know the feeling, but you can't just make do with anyone."

Hermione agreed. She enjoyed Mandy's visits; Mandy was cheerful and seemed far older than Jane or Sarah. Hermione could tell her things about her life in prison which she would never dream of revealing to her daughters. One of the anxieties

she had about being convicted was that this would mean restricted visiting.

"You'll get used to it, and so will Jane and Sarah," said
Mandy, who knew both girls found putting up a good front
to their mother a great strain. When embarked on college
courses, finding time for the frequent visits they had made so
far would be difficult.

Hermione welcomed Mandy's ability to face up to such a
prospect; no one else seemed to think she could do so herself.
Mandy intended to stay with the sisters until they had settled
to their new routine; then she and Jasper would move to a
destination she had not yet decided on, perhaps abroad, before
she grew too soft at Merbury and found herself unable to make
the break.

"It sounds as if people in the village are being very kind,"
said Hermione.

"They're feeling bad about not realising what a mess you
were in," said Mandy.

"What could they have done about it?" Hermione asked.
"It wasn't anyone else's business."

"There's probably a good few other funny goings-on in some
of those nice houses with roses round the door," said Mandy.

"I should have found a different way to end it," said Hermione.

"How could you? You were scared rigid," said Mandy. "And
anyway, you didn't end it. He did. He brought it on himself."

"He didn't ask to die," said Hermione.

"Nor did those two girls," said Mandy bluntly. "Didn't you
wonder what he was up to when he stayed out late?"

"No. I thought he might have a mistress," Hermione replied. "I'm very ignorant about such things, Mandy. You
know far more about life than I do."

"Did you know that Pam Norton had been married before
and she left her first husband because of the charms of dull
Desmond?" said Mandy.

"No!"

"She has two children. They didn't get on with Desmond, so when they were sixteen they left home. That was before the Nortons came to Merbury," said Mandy. "She misses them."

Hermione stared at her, amazed.

"I'd no idea. How did you find this out?" she asked.

"Oh, she told me one day, when she came to see how Jane and Sarah were faring," said Mandy. "They were out fixing up their futures, and Pam and I had a natter in the garden, admiring Jasper. I think she's his temporary honorary grandmother. One of her sons has a baby, but he lives in Hong Kong so it's not much help to Pam."

"People tell you things, don't they?" said Hermione.

"I'm interested," said Mandy.

"What do Jane and Sarah feel about—about their father's— er—about him?" Hermione asked her. "Do they believe what he did? That it's all true?"

"They've got to, haven't they?" Mandy said. "But they don't know the details—who does?"

Later, she and Nigel discussed this.

"You'd think Hermione would have understood something was going on," said Mandy. "But she's like a child in some ways. She thought he might have a mistress."

"Probably hoped he had and that they'd go off together," said Nigel.

"How could she stay with him, once the girls had gone?"

"She'd lost all her confidence," said Nigel. "He made her regard herself as worthless. That's a dreadful thing to happen to anyone, and it often does in marriages, without ending in murder. The victim—sometimes it's the man—thinks it's all his fault. Destruction of another person, whether by death or by bullying and ridicule, or in any other way, is the ultimate evil."

"Hermione thinks she destroyed Walter and deserves to be punished," said Mandy.

"Oh, what a dangerous idea," said Nigel.

28

Before she was taken to her trial, Hermione had once again been through the humiliating ritual of a strip search; it would be repeated at the start and end of each day's hearing. She wondered how long the case would last: three to four days, Carol had thought, perhaps the whole week, but some of the papers had been seen and agreed in advance. In a week's time, Hermione told herself, she was likely to be in a different prison: by now she had heard tales about them all. The best thing was to have no expectations; then she could not be disappointed, whatever happened.

She was driven to the Crown Court in a prison van with two officers who were pleasant enough, neither wanting to score points off her. They discussed the route through the suburbs into the country and one said that she wanted to retire to Devon and take in lodgers. The other spoke of her son who was having learning difficulties at his primary school. The ordinariness of their conversation was soothing; Hermione listened to it with half an ear while looking through the van windows to the world outside. Everything was green and lush with the full growth of summer: she had missed the spring; it simply hadn't happened in prison.

Jane and Sarah had brought her an outfit she was to wear in

court: a shirt-waister dress in an oatmeal linen-type fabric with a navy cotton jacket. They had said she must not be too smart; elegance could come later, they teased, when she was free. Her hair had grown in prison and she wore it in a style suggested by Loraine, twisted into a smooth knot modelled on the Princess Royal.

"You want to look dependable," she had said, pink with concern for her new friend.

"But I'm not, or I wouldn't be here," said Hermione.

"You are—unlike me. Yours was a one-off," said Loraine. "I tempt easily." She admitted it now. "Anyway, it's the appearance that matters. Let them see you're respectable. The guys do it, you know—dress up in sharp suits with ties when their normal gear is leathers and that. It's a game."

"It's no game to me," said Hermione.

The Crown Court was in a modern building in the centre of the county town. Hermione was taken to a cell until it was time for proceedings to begin, and soon Carol Glossop and Imogen Greig, the barrister, came to see her. Carol brought messages from the girls.

"Some of your friends will be in court," Carol warned. "Don't let it throw you. They're coming to support you, not just from curiosity."

Hermione knew that several would be witnesses and they would not enter the court until they were called. She wondered about Mrs. Fisher. Wendy Tucker had said her mother wanted to testify to Walter's state of mind on the last day, but Wendy thought it would be too much for her and hoped she would not be needed. Hermione had weeks ago decided to leave such decisions to Carol and Miss Greig, whose job it was to make them. She felt dull, uncaring: matters were out of her control, and the next inexorable step in the legal process which would establish Walter's final victory over her had begun.

She had not wanted her daughters to be present, but they had said they couldn't bear to stay away.

"We'll be rooting for you, Mum," said Sarah. "And if the other barrister's beastly to you, we'll send out bad vibes against him."

Nigel had been to see them the previous evening to warn them about the British legal system, which would expose their mother to a gladiatorial battle between the opposing lawyers, each seeking to prove their case, neither charged directly with establishing exactly what had happened.

"Things are a bit different in Scotland," he said. "And France. One has the Procurator Fiscal directing investigations, the other a *juge d'instruction*. Mind you, these officials are fallible human beings and can err in their direction of investigations, but it seems a better way of going about things than ours. We may see changes here in the next few years, but that won't help your mother."

"Carol says Miss Greig is very good," said Jane anxiously.

"So she is," said Nigel, who also knew that the prosecuting counsel already had a formidable reputation for reducing witnesses to tatters.

When she was led into the dock, Hermione recognised no one at first because she felt giddy and bemused, disoriented as she had been in the first weeks after her arrest. Only later as the prosecuting counsel made his opening speech did she begin to look round, but she did not survey the rows of faces behind the lawyers. The court was not large; there was not space for many spectators and some people present were reporters. She wondered if Nigel was there but could not see him. She turned her attention to the jury. There were seven men and five women. The more women the better, she'd been told, because they were likely to be sympathetic. Two of the women and three of the men looked very young. One woman, much her own age, was very smart in something green, and with bright brassy hair; another had grey hair and wore spectacles; one was black. The men varied in age and in what they wore; most were in suits but one had an open-necked shirt on, with the sleeves rolled up; another wore a black tee-shirt. What did dress signify? Walter had always been well turned out, yet beneath his clothes lurked a mind diseased. She had begun to think that now; he must have been sick to harbour so much hate.

She paid little attention to what prosecuting counsel was saying. He had a lean, lined face and his wig made him look like a thin sheep, she thought, almost smiling at this notion. He was telling the court that witnesses would testify to the discovery by police of Walter Brown's dead body in the locked rear lobby of his house in Merbury, that evidence would be adduced that he had died of a stab wound in the back—"the back," he repeated, for emphasis—which had caused massive internal bleeding, that the accused had summoned no aid for her dying husband and, indeed, had gone to bed.

As he went on talking, Hermione felt as if he were describing some play he had seen on television. There was talk of the knife. There was no mention of Walter's attack on her, but he was not on trial.

She cast a glance at her own team. Carol Glossop's head was bent as she wrote something down. Miss Greig seemed to find the coat of arms behind the judge's seat of interest.

Witnesses were called.

Detective Sergeant Bagley testified that he had rung the bell at the Browns' house at eleven o'clock on the morning of Wednesday, November 20th, and had had difficulty in arousing Mrs. Brown, who had been asleep, so she said. He had found the deceased in the locked rear lobby beyond the kitchen. The knife alleged to be the murder weapon was on the draining-board, washed. There were some bloodstains on the floor.

"Were there signs of a struggle?" asked counsel.

"No."

"What was the accused's manner?"

"Calm," said Bagley, after a moment's thought.

"Did she show distress?"

"No."

By question and answer the events of the morning were revealed and then it was Miss Greig's turn with the witness.

"Why did you call at the Browns' house that morning?" she asked.

"To ask Mr. Brown some questions."

"Not because you knew what had happened? That he was dead? No neighbour had telephoned reporting trouble?"

"No."

"What did you want to question him about?"

"His whereabouts on certain days in the preceding weeks," said Bagley.

"Why?"

"On behalf of colleagues in the Metropolitan Police."

"They were concerned with an investigation?"

"Yes."

"What about?"

Here prosecuting counsel protested that this was not relevant but the judge ordered Miss Greig to continue.

"The murders of two women on the dates in question," said Bagley.

There was a rustle round the court, and Hermione found that her heart had begun to thump unevenly beneath her neutral-coloured dress. Blood pounded in her ears. She took some deep breaths.

"Was it a characteristic of those cases that the victims both had long hair and it was wound round their necks after they had been manually strangled?"

"Yes."

Miss Greig shuffled her papers and resumed.

"You rang the bell and after a while Mrs. Brown opened the door?"

"Yes."

"You asked for Mr. Brown?"

"Yes."

"What did Mrs. Brown say?"

Bagley consulted his notebook.

"She said, 'I expect he's gone to work. Unless he's still out there,' and she pointed to the kitchen."

"So you went to the kitchen and found the deceased?"

"Yes."

"Mr. Bagley, you said Mrs. Brown's manner was calm," Miss Greig reminded him.

"Yes."

"Could it have been that her manner was not calm but was due to shock?"

"It's possible," he said.

"She'd just woken up, and she said her husband must have gone to work?"

"Yes. Unless he was still—and she pointed," Bagley repeated.

"She could have maintained that he was at work—reasonable enough at that hour. You had no warrant to search the house?"

"No."

"To get to the body you had to walk to the kitchen and into the lobby beyond?"

The jury had been given plans of the house and now they dutifully scrutinised them to see the lie of the land. While they did so, Bagley agreed that the body was in the lobby.

"There is a door to that lobby from the kitchen?"

"Yes."

"Was it closed?"

"Yes."

"Was it locked?"

"Yes."

"You found Walter Brown dead. Did you tell Mrs. Brown he was dead?"

"Yes."

"What did she say?"

Bagley read from his notes.

"She said she thought he was just unconscious."

And I was afraid he'd come back and get at me, Hermione remembered. That was why she had locked the door. For a moment she longed to get to her feet and shout that out to everyone.

The court was silent as Miss Greig took Bagley carefully through what had followed, covering Hermione's arrest and his search of the house. She also got him to tell the court that Walter's car had been examined by the Metropolitan Police and they had found evidence in it to link him with the crimes about which Bagley had originally come to see him. Without calling witnesses, it had been agreed that the court should learn that hairs from Hermione's head had been found on a rug in the car, as well as hairs from the women whose deaths the London police were investigating. Carrot traces had been found on the sole of one of Walter's shoes and the significance of this would be apparent later.

At this point the court rose for lunch, and afterwards the pathologist gave his evidence about the wound which had caused Walter's death; he agreed that the knife now displayed in court could have caused it. It had penetrated between two ribs, piercing the heart. Prosecuting counsel asked questions which established that the dead man had been stabbed in the back.

To Hermione, it sounded as though she had planned the whole thing; in the jury's eyes, she must be condemned already. It seemed hardly worth her while to step into the witness box herself when Miss Greig opened the defence.

She repeated the oath in a low voice and held on to the edge of the box. She looked very pale. Watching, Jane and Sarah were holding hands. Hermione did not look at them; her gaze was on Miss Greig, small and suddenly curiously commanding as she stood ready to begin her questions. As they went into court, Carol Glossop had told the sisters that Hermione would be her own best witness, but she had not warned them about the content of her evidence.

Miss Greig's first questions established the history of the house at Merbury and how it had been bought indirectly as a result of Hermione's inheritance. She told the court that there were papers to prove it, and as prosecuting counsel rose to submit that none of this was relevant, Miss Greig said that it was necessary to establish the nature of the relationship between husband and wife at the outset of the marriage.

"Mrs. Brown, your hair is long enough to pin up today. When was it last cut?" she asked next.

Hermione knew exactly. It was when Jeremy had done it, after he saw her bruises.

"Two weeks before—before that night," she said.

"So it has not been cut since your arrest?"

"No."

"Had you always worn it short?"

"No. I cut it myself about—about—some time ago. About a year," she said.

"Why?"

Hermione stared at her.

"You've grown it again now. You must have had a reason for wanting it short," said Miss Greig, speaking harshly.

Why was she so cross? Whose side was she on, wondered Hermione.

"Walter had—had—" she swallowed.

"Come on, Mrs. Brown. We're waiting," said Miss Greig, in the tone of an impatient teacher.

Hermione's eyes smarted. She blinked.

"He wound it round my throat," she said. Her voice was barely audible.

"So why did you cut it?" Miss Greig was relentless.

"So that he couldn't—couldn't do that again," said Hermione, her voice stronger now. She felt suddenly angry. Only she, among all those present, knew how terrified of Walter she had been. How could they understand such fear? Hermione had wanted to spare her daughters this detailed knowledge of their father, but dread of him had driven them both away from home; they would only be hearing confirmation of what they already knew. Anyway, their father was a murderer; beside that knowledge, what did this amount to?

Miss Greig could not now remind the court of Detective Sergeant Bagley's evidence that the dead women, about whose murders he had called to see Walter, had had their long hair tied round their necks. She would remember to do this in her final speech and would hope that the judge would refer to it in his summing-up. She moved on to the date when Hermione had baby-sat for the Wilsons.

"Where was your husband that night?" she asked.

"At a village meeting," said Hermione.

"Did he know you were going out?"

"No."

"Why didn't you tell him?"

"Because he would have been angry. He would have stopped me from going."

"How did you get to the Wilsons' house?"

"Normally I cycled, but that night I took the car. Walter always walked to village meetings."

"Who did you think would come home first?"

"Walter. I knew I'd be much later," said Hermione. "I thought he'd be asleep and wouldn't hear me."

"What about when you went to bed?"

"We weren't sleeping in the same room," said Hermione. She gripped the edge of the box again. Now, as far as she was concerned, there were only herself and Miss Greig in court, and she must make this other woman understand the reasons for her actions. "I was stupid," she said. "I thought he wouldn't know. I locked the door of my room so that he would think I was in bed when he came home."

"And were you?"

"No." Hermione snapped the answer. Hadn't Miss Greig been listening to what she'd already said?

"So what happened when you did come home?"

"I couldn't get into the house."

"Had you no key?"

"It was no good trying the front door. Walter always bolted it and put up the chain at night. I took the back door key."

"And you used it?"

"I thought I could get in that way. It was my duty to lock and bolt the back doors—the lobby door and the kitchen one. Walter must have checked up on me that night and when he found they were only locked, not bolted, he bolted them."

"So you couldn't get into the house?"

"No."

"What did you do?"

"I spent the night in the car, in the garage."

"Was it cold?"

"It was freezing, but there was a rug in the boot. I put that round me."

She'd volunteered the information without Miss Greig having to prise it out of her: would the jury remember about the prostitute's hairs being found on the rug, along with Hermione's? Miss Greig decided to remind them later.

"Why didn't you knock on the door and ask your husband to let you in?" she asked.

"I was afraid of what he would do to me, if I did," said Hermione. "And he knew I was out there."

"How do you know that?"

"I ran the engine for a little while, to warm up the car. His room was at the front and I didn't think he'd hear. He was a heavy sleeper. I'd left the garage doors open a bit, to let the fumes out."

"Yes. Go on, Mrs. Brown."

Everyone in the court was silent, hanging on her words. Prosecuting counsel wondered where all this was leading.

"He came out to the garage. I saw something in the mirror and just had time to lock all the car doors, and I turned the engine off. He shut the garage doors. He locked me in."

"Why did you lock the car doors?"

"So that he couldn't get at me."

"I see," said Miss Greig. "How long were you there?"

"All night."

"And in the morning?"

"He undid the door. He'd expect his breakfast," said Hermione.

"So you went in and cooked it?"

"Yes."

Miss Greig had got what she needed from Hermione. She moved on to questions about her regular visits to Creddington and her two jobs, eliciting the information that Walter knew nothing about them. Then she came to the night of Walter's death.

"What happened when you got home from Creddington that Tuesday?" she asked.

"Walter was already there. He'd been late so often—I never imagined he'd get home first. He was waiting in the kitchen in the dark."

"What happened then?"

"He hit me," said Hermione. "I fell down, and then he—he kicked me."

"What happened next?"

"He told me to cook his supper," said Hermione. She was calm now, holding the box edge still, but speaking steadily, almost as if she were in a trance.

"And did you?"

"Yes. It was half prepared already. I did that, because I

never knew when he'd be in and he always wanted it at once," she said.

"And then?"

"Then we went into the dining-room, but I couldn't eat a thing," she said. "Walter put some food on my plate and told me to eat it."

She had not told the court about the knife. Miss Greig must get her to mention it, without leading her.

"And did you eat it?" she asked.

"No, I couldn't—I tried to get away but he picked up the knife and told me to sit down and eat."

"Which knife was this, Mrs. Brown?" asked Miss Greig.

"It was one he'd taken from the kitchen drawer earlier. He had it in his hand all the time I was cooking the meal—he followed me about the kitchen with it," said Hermione. Her face was white and tense as she re-lived the scene. "He prodded me with it," she added.

"What next? Did you eat your dinner?"

"No. He suddenly seemed to change his mind about it," answered Hermione. "He told me to add the food from my plate to what was on his, and put that plate in the oven."

"His portion of the meal?" Miss Greig wanted everything to be quite clear.

"Yes."

"With yours added to it?"

"Yes."

"What about your plate?"

"It was to be left in the dining-room." Where Detective Sergeant Bagley had found it the next morning.

"Why did he want this done?" Miss Greig asked. "Did he say?"

"Yes. He meant to eat it all afterwards."

"After what?"

"After he'd killed me. He said that was what he was going to do. In the garage, with the car, like it had nearly happened already. He said that. He said he would tell the police I'd been acting strangely and they'd think it was suicide. But first—" and her voice shook.

"First?"

"First—first he said he meant to—" Her voice faded.

"Yes? Speak up, Mrs. Brown," ordered Miss Greig.

Her curt tone got through to Hermione, who stood up straight and faced the court.

"He said he meant to have his rights," she said. "That's what he called it."

"Called what?" Miss Greig was going to have no misunderstanding; the younger members of the jury might not have heard this description of the sexual act.

"Intercourse. Sex," said Hermione, her voice fading again.

Miss Greig was still severe.

"What then?"

"He came towards me with the knife. I had my back to the stove," said Hermione. "I couldn't dodge away, but I tried to kick him. I caught him on the leg and he stepped back and slipped. Afterwards I found some bits of carrot that had fallen off his plate. He must have slipped on that. I wiped it up afterwards."

"So he slipped?"

"Yes. And dropped the knife. I picked it up." She looked across at the judge. "He was getting to his feet. I held it out in front of me and shut my eyes and pushed it forward."

As Hermione said this, the tears that she had been holding back spilled over, to Miss Greig's concealed delight, for her manner earlier had been so controlled that the jury might have thought her cold and unfeeling.

A murmur broke out in the court room and there was a call for silence.

"Did you intend to kill your husband?" Miss Greig asked, in a firm voice.

"No. I only meant to keep him away from me," said Hermione, in a wail.

When she was calm again, prosecuting counsel had his chance.

He asked Hermione why she had not summoned help for Walter or called the police, and why she had locked the lobby door.

"He'd walked there. I still held the knife—I didn't think he was badly hurt," she said. "I was afraid he'd come after me again."

"You went to bed."

"Not for a long time. I sat there until the smell from the oven reminded me that there was food in there, drying up," she said. "Then I turned off the oven and went upstairs. I lay on the bed—I didn't undress."

"I suggest that you deliberately took the knife from the drawer, waited for your chance to use it and when your husband's back was turned, you stabbed him," said prosecuting counsel.

"No!" said Hermione.

"You waited until he had gone out to the lobby—perhaps to fetch something—then surprised him," counsel pursued.

"No!" said Hermione again.

"I put it to you that you and your husband quarrelled over your visit to Creddington and that you waited for your opportunity to kill him."

"No!" cried Hermione. "I didn't mean to kill him. I only meant to save myself." She looked across the court straight at the tall, thin man. "You weren't there," she said. "I was."

Counsel let her go then, and the court adjourned until the following day.

In the morning, Mrs. Fisher was the first witness called by Miss Greig.

The old lady walked steadily to the box and refused to sit. She testified that she and Hermione were friends and that

Hermione visited her every Tuesday on her way to Orchard House. She described her anxiety about Hermione, who was keeping secret from her husband the fact that she was working. Mrs. Fisher was allowed to speak fairly freely, prompted by questions from Miss Greig, and she said that one week Hermione had not come at her usual time so Mrs. Fisher had waylaid her outside Orchard House, and had seen that she had a badly bruised face—a black eye, in fact—which at first she had said was due to an accident but finally admitted was caused by her husband hitting her. Then Mrs. Fisher described Walter's visit on the day that he died. His manner had been rude and aggressive, and he would not believe that Hermione was not in the house. She had let him in, wanting to detain him, for fear he would meet Hermione on her way to the bus from Orchard House. She related how he had searched every room and in response to a question, agreed that she had later collapsed.

Then Jeremy was called. Miss Greig would not overlook anything that could help to build up a true picture of Walter in the minds of the jury, and he said that he had seen Hermione's black eye. No mention was made of her haircut.

Nigel Wilson came next, and he confirmed the bruising. Then Miss Greig asked him about a night when Hermione had baby-sat for him and his wife. The date was established.

"Did you fetch her?" asked Miss Greig.

"No," said Nigel. "She came by car—a Maestro."

"What time did she leave?"

"Just before midnight," said Nigel. "We felt badly about being later than we'd expected—it was bitterly cold. I cleared frost off the windscreen for her before she went home."

"And how long would the journey take her?"

"Not more than ten minutes, even in the dark," said Nigel. "It was a fine night, but very cold, as I said."

The prosecution had no questions for any of these witnesses

and queried the need for so much testimony about these events, but accepted that the defence rested on proof of Walter's hostile behaviour towards his wife.

After Nigel's evidence, Pam Norton and Robert Mountford both testified to Walter's presence at the meeting they had attended on the baby-sitting night, and confirmed the time it broke up. Both agreed that they had noticed Hermione's bruised face. Then Miss Greig called Detective Inspector Windsor, who said that he had cooperated with the Metropolitan Police when they wanted to question Walter about two murders. Detective Sergeant Bagley had gone to the Browns' house on that matter, and had found the body.

"Although you were not involved with the London investigation, is it correct that your colleagues there would have charged Walter Brown with those murders?" asked Miss Greig.

"Yes," said Windsor.

"And those cases are now closed?"

"Yes."

Detective Inspector Windsor was followed by the doctor who had examined Hermione after her arrest. Photographs were shown to him and he agreed that they were of the accused and showed severe bruising to her ribs. The injuries were very recent. The photographs were shown to the jury, two of whom gasped in dismay.

In his closing speech, prosecuting counsel made the point that the accused had admitted killing her husband. He added that there was only her word that she had spent a cold night shut in the garage—her hairs on the car rug could have got there at any time—and that there were other alternatives to escaping from a bad marriage than murder. There was no doubt in his mind that she had committed that most heinous crime, he said, stabbing her husband in the back, nor should there be in the minds of the jury.

Miss Greig, in her turn, pointed out that Walter, had he lived, would have been charged with committing two murders, that he had treated his wife with violence which had been confirmed by witnesses and by photographs, and that she had been subjected to constant brutal treatment. She mentioned that when he had visited Mrs. Fisher his manner was so aggressive that she had collapsed after he left. It was to Mrs. Fisher that Hermione had revealed the true cause of the black eye which, not wishing to broadcast her troubles, she had passed off as due to an accident. Finally she reminded the jury of the dreadful last night and that certain past murderers had eaten heartily after despatching their victims. Perhaps this was why Walter Brown had planned to eat Hermione's meal as well as his own, but by leaving her plate in the dining-room, meant it to look as though she had eaten too.

"Of course," said Miss Greig drily, "if that had been his intention, he had overlooked the fact that if Mrs. Brown had died as an apparent suicide, there would have been a post-mortem and her stomach contents would have revealed no recent meal, so that in any case he would not have got away with the murder he had planned. He, however, had that intent. Hermione Brown had not; she acted in self-defence and should be acquitted."

As she sat down, Miss Greig wondered if she should have introduced the evidence of the note Carol Glossop had found among Walter's papers; it indicated that he had been copying Hermione's handwriting and might have intended to forge a suicide letter. She had decided there was enough evidence without this; if she lost the case now, that decision would go on to haunt her.

When she had finished her speech, the court adjourned for the judge to sum up the next day, and Hermione returned once more to her prison cell.

29

Jane and Sarah were subdued that night. The strange dignity and leisurely drama of the court proceedings had affected them deeply. Was it possible that, in spite of what had been revealed, their mother could be sent to prison for life? All at once the fact that this was probable was born in on them: in court she had admitted killing their father.

She had looked so alone and defenceless standing in the box. Yesterday she had not looked at them, but today she had seen them and had smiled fleetingly, then looked away, glancing at them again only just before she was led out when the court adjourned. Now she was back in her cell. What was she thinking? How was she feeling?

Nigel had driven them home. He had taken them to the court in the morning.

"We can manage," Jane had said.

"I know, but the press will be out. I can get you past them," he said, and had done so.

"You'll be all right?" he asked, parting from them.

"Yes. Mandy's got food and stuff," said Sarah. Mandy had not come to court because of Jasper, but she had wanted to hear, both evenings, what had happened. She thought it was good for the sisters to spill it all out; then the subject was banned and they had played card games until it was time for bed. Mandy had taught them all sorts of games from Cheat to Canasta.

"If the worst happens," said Nigel, "don't give up hope. There'll be an appeal and we'll organise petitions and all that. We'll do everything we can to get her out."

"She didn't plan it," said Sarah. "That's a big point in her favour."

"Yes," agreed Nigel. He advised them to leave their phone off the hook. "If it's not kindly neighbours, it'll be some journalist," he said. "See you tomorrow."

Mandy had cooked spaghetti that night. Oddly enough, they were hungry; they had not eaten much at lunch-time.

"I did something while you were out," Mandy told them. "You may not be very pleased."

"Why?"

"I took a liberty. You may think I went too far."

"What did you do?"

"I packed up all your dad's clothes and took them to a place that gives stuff to down-and-outs," said Mandy. "Tramps and winos and such. Not Oxfam or Help the Aged."

Jane and Sarah looked at one another and then at Mandy.

"I thought, when Hermione comes back tomorrow, or the next day—however long it takes the jury to make up their minds—she won't want to find anything here that's going to remind her of him."

"There'll be us," said Jane, and burst into tears.

"Come on, Jane, think positive," said Mandy, giving Jane a rough hug. "Look at all the people in history married to absolute sods who've had great kids and loved them."

"I can't understand why they ever got together," said Sarah. "They were allergic to each other."

"You could put it like that," agreed Mandy. "Your mum wouldn't have been such a doormat if she'd married someone who thought a lot of her and gave her a buzz. As far as I can make out, he was always putting her down, and you two, as well. That breaks you, in the end."

"Miss Greig was very snappy with her when she was in the box," said Sarah. "Mum looked quite upset."

"Maybe it was intentional. Maybe she was doing her door-mat act and Miss Greig needed to spark her off," said Mandy. "You'll want to watch that with her, when she's home. Don't let her slide back into thinking she's no one."

"You did the right thing about the clothes," said Jane. "I'd thought of it, but I didn't have the nerve." And she hadn't wanted to touch anything that was his: even opening the wardrobe when painting the room, and seeing his things inside, had made her feel sick.

Mandy was relieved that her action had gone down so well. She'd been quite prepared for a row about it and had decided that at least it would divert them from imagining how their mother was spending the evening.

It was a long night for Hermione. She kept going over in her mind the questions she had been asked the day before and the replies she had given. Should she have said something else? At no time could she think of a different answer that would still have been truthful. What sort of impression had she made on the jury? They must think her a silly, weak woman who could not manage her life. Or would they believe that clever barrister who had suggested she had planned the whole thing?

She couldn't have planned Walter's kicks and her bruised ribs, or the black eye.

Much would depend on the judge. This one was known as a tough man, given to handing out heavy sentences. He might think she was wicked and devious. He might hate all women— some of her fellow inmates thought there were plenty like that.

Next morning the court seemed a familiar place when she returned there, still in her oatmeal dress and her navy jacket.

It had been overcast when they left the prison, and rain threatened. Was that a bad omen?

Today the judge had his hour. It took him no longer than that to sum up. He was a portly man, looking faintly comic in his robes when he entered the court, but as soon as he sat, he achieved dignity. Hermione found the formalised procedure both reassuring and daunting; centuries of tradition lay behind the ceremony, yet was it not ridiculous that grown men and women adopted those odd little wigs—a special but no larger model for the judge? What did this do for them except make them hot? Wouldn't the same results be achieved if they simply wore sober suits and gowns, as in America?

She spent some time musing along these lines and belatedly began listening to what the judge was saying.

He reminded the jury that it was the prosecution's duty to prove that the accused was guilty beyond all reasonable doubt, not for the defence to prove innocence. He pointed out that this was a murder charge but that they could, if they so decided, convict the accused of manslaughter, which he then defined. He told them that they must put out of their minds their knowledge that the victim would have been charged with murder, except in so far as it indicated that he may have had a hostile attitude towards women in general. He said that there was no witness to the events of the fatal night and the only account came from the accused herself, but that the bruises on her body supported her story. She had not, however, sustained a cut from the knife, which could happen during a struggle. He reminded them that she had made no attempt to summon aid for her husband.

At last he dismissed them to their deliberations.

At first people hung about outside the court. Would the jury take long to decide? Carol went to see Hermione, who sat white and silent waiting for the verdict.

"In the Bible it says 'Blessed are the meek,' " Hermione said. "It's bad advice. Meekness can be the same as cowardice. I should have found a way out of this that didn't end in death."

"You'd begun to do that," said Carol. "You'd started to get your act together—working, going out. A few more weeks and you'd have seen a solicitor—me, maybe—and found a way to escape. Walter preempted you by his own actions."

"If you go out in a car and you run someone over, but it wasn't your fault because they stepped into the road in front of you, giving you no time to stop, that makes you guilty of manslaughter," said Hermione.

"It means you may face a charge of manslaughter. It doesn't mean you're guilty of it," said Carol.

"You still killed someone," said Hermione. "I deserve to be punished."

"You've been punished," said Carol. "You've had seven months in prison on remand, after a sentence of more than twenty years with a man who did his best to destroy you. If you can't accept that, you'll never be able to put this behind you."

"You sound a bit like Miss Greig," said Hermione. "She was quite hostile to me."

"You had to get firing on all cylinders," said Carol. "Your spirit is a fragile flame that needs a bit of fanning." She could hardly bear the tension of waiting for the verdict. Juries were unpredictable and this one could decide quixotically that Hermione was innocent of any offence. The judge had not directed otherwise; he had left it to them.

Wendy Tucker and her mother had gone home when the jury went out, Wendy to return to work and her mother to eat the cold lunch, left ready.

When she had finished it, Mrs. Fisher rang up for a taxi and had herself driven back to the court, where she found Jane and Sarah with Carol Glossop and Nigel Wilson.

"They're taking so long," said Jane. "Is that good or bad?"

"It could be either," said Carol.

It could mean disagreement. It could mean a careful discussion of every feature of the case they had heard. It could mean anything you chose to read into it. It could mean a hung jury and a retrial.

In the jury room, points of law were the problem. Five of the jurors wanted to pronounce Hermione innocent of any crime, but the fact remained that she had pushed the knife into her husband—into his back. He had not fallen on it in a struggle, and she had admitted her action.

"What did you expect her to do? Get herself killed by handing it back to the man?" demanded one of the women.

"She could have run from the room—gone to a neighbour for help," said a man.

"She was pinned against the stove. She'd have to get past him to escape—anyway, he was getting up again already. There was no time," said Hermione's champion. "Remember, she'd already been hit and kicked, and those bruised ribs must have hurt like hell."

"Her mistake was to say she'd done it. She could have said he'd slipped against the knife," said a man.

"She said she had told the truth. I believe her," said the black woman. "She was very frightened. She wouldn't be thinking clearly. It would all have been reflex actions."

No one wanted a murder verdict. In the end it came down to a decision between manslaughter and an acquittal.

"That woman can't be sent back to prison," said a bald man, a taxi-driver.

"That's not the point," he was reminded. "It's the judge who decides on the sentence."

"He can't set her free unless we acquit," said the man in the tee-shirt, a green one today.

It took them a long time to agree, but that was their verdict.

*   *   *

Hermione's acquittal was featured in most of the newspapers, and in one of them a piece by Nigel gave details about Walter's journeys to London, mentioning his connection with the murdered prostitutes. There were pictures of him and Hermione.

George Palmer read it over breakfast.

"I see that poor woman's got off," he said. "What brutes some men are." He had followed each day's reports of the case, interested because it was so local. "It seems the husband travelled up to London every day from Freston."

"Yes," said Valerie. "I know he did. I saw him on the train."

"What? You mean you recognised him?"

"I thought it was him in those photofit things in the papers when the police were trying to trace him," said Valerie. She felt almost proud of being able to say this now, when there was no longer any need for silence because Walter Brown, a man whom it was dangerous to know, was dead.

"You never mentioned it to me."

"I didn't want to worry you," said Valerie. What would George have thought if he had known that the man had followed her from the train?

"But you told the police?"

"No."

"Why not?"

"I thought someone else would—someone who travelled with him regularly," said Valerie.

"But one of the features of the case was that no one did," said George. Nigel, in his article, had stated that several regular travellers, noticing the resemblance, had thought it mere coincidence.

"Well, that's not my fault, is it?" Valerie asked.

George did not answer her then. Her attitude astonished him and he needed time to think about it.

Later, over lunch, he returned to the subject.

"Valerie, did you really recognise Walter Brown? Did you see him more than once on the train?" he demanded.

"Oh yes," she said, but she misinterpreted his interest. She decided, however, not to tell him about the episode with the insulting yobs, when she had not particularly noticed Walter Brown but he had taken heed of her, because tonight she would be returning alone from another concert while George played his flute at a local charity gala.

"Why? What made you notice him?" he pressed her.

"He spoke to me," said Valerie.

George was remembering the evidence about his victim's long hair.

"He might have murdered you," he said.

"He went after prostitutes," said Valerie. "I'm not that sort of woman."

"Neither was his wife. He wound her hair around her neck," said George.

"He was in church when I sang the Vaughan Williams," said Valerie.

"You saw him in the congregation? Why was he there? He didn't live in Stappenford," said George.

"Perhaps he was fond of music," said Valerie. But he had followed her that evening, just as he had followed her from the train. She knew that now. She had been at risk. "He wasn't wanted by the police then," she added.

"But when he was, you never said a word."

"No."

"You didn't feel you had a duty?"

"No. I told you, George, I was sure someone else would," said Valerie impatiently.

"But they didn't, and Walter Brown is dead," said George.

"Well, he's no great loss, is he?" said Valerie. "The world's better off without him, I should say."

"But if you'd told the police, they could have arrested him, and his wife would have been spared her terrible experience when he attacked her, and all these months in prison. It's only thanks to the good sense of the jury that she was acquitted of a very serious crime," said George.

"Well, she was acquitted," said Valerie. "Why all the fuss?"

"You don't see it, do you?" said George bleakly. "You don't see that you had a duty."

"I've a duty to you, to keep things peaceful here and not let you be worried," said Valerie, and she moved to kiss his balding head as he sat at the table.

He looked at her in silence. Then he said, "I'm sad that you kept quiet."

"George! What's so important about all this?"

"That man might have killed other women in the interval between the appeal in the paper and his own death. He did try to kill his wife. You could have talked it over with me. I'd have gone with you to the police." He was looking at her as if she was a stranger. "I feel let down," he said. "Disappointed." He stood up and moved over to the door. "We won't speak of it again," he added, and left the room. Later he had gone out, saying he needed some fresh air, and he had not returned when it was time for Valerie to catch her train.

She thought about leaving him a note, but what should she say in it? He was upset because he sensed that she had been in some danger; that was it. It was lucky she hadn't told him about Walter Brown sitting in his car outside their house; it had been a mistake to mention his presence in church.

Her journey home that night was uneventful; the new turbo trains had been introduced some months ago and it was possible to move between coaches if one wished, but she had no need. By the time she reached Stappenford, it was dark and raining slightly. She wanted to get home quickly, to tell George she was sorry if she had upset him. They had never before had a disagreement and she knew that this one was because of his concern for her. She had banished Hermione from her mind.

She hurried up the hill away from the station. Several cars were parked at the top of the road and near one were two figures bent over the driver's door, apparently unlocking it. As she passed they stood up and looked away, one of them whistling.

Something was wrong here. They were two youths in jeans and denim jackets, lounging now beside the Ford. She and George had no car, but Valerie knew it was a Ford because it was like one owned by a fellow teacher who sometimes gave her lifts. Valerie walked on, glancing back at the youths, to see them getting into the car.

It was odd. They must be stealing it, or why, if it was legitimately theirs, had they turned away as she went by?

George would say she should report them, but how? There was a telephone box at the station, but she was not going back there. As this thought formed, a police car came cruising towards her. She could signal the driver to stop, report what she had seen and leave the rest to him. But she wanted to get home; she wanted to make sure that George had got over his strange mood.

The police car went past. It was too late. In any case the youths had probably driven off by now.

They had. As she turned into her road they roared up behind her, swerving close to her, recognising her as the woman who had stared at them earlier and delayed their theft by precious minutes.

They sped out of sight and did a skidding turn at the end of the road, preparing to return and scare her properly.

George Palmer had spent an unhappy day worrying about his tiff with Valerie—for that was all it was, he assured himself. Her indifference to Hermione Brown's fate had dismayed him. If she had gone to the police, they might not have intercepted Walter Brown on the train, but the chances were that if they had questioned other commuters, someone would have confirmed her suspicions. At least she would not have shirked her civic responsibility.

He must not let this come between them. He had said he would not refer to the matter again and he would abide by that resolve. He must welcome her home with his usual warmth. He was back well before she was due and began watching the clock. He should have met her at the station, he thought; that would have demonstrated his forgiveness. It was too late now, unless her train was delayed or she had missed the one she had expected to catch, but he would go to meet her as she walked back.

It was drizzling, a fine misty warm rain, as he put on his waterproof and went down the drive and out of the gate.

The two youths in the stolen Ford had already shot past Valerie for the second time and swerved round again to chase her, zigzagging along the road. Few cars were parked there at this time of night for all the houses had either garages or parking space. The young driver skimmed close to Valerie once more, almost brushing her coat as he mounted the pavement beside her, then veered back over the road again, where he lost control on the wet surface and the car slewed into an unplanned skid.

George stood no chance. He was struck outside his own front gate as the car crashed to a halt against the fence, its engine hissing with steam from the burst radiator. Apart from that there was silence, until the screams began, and they were Valerie's.